Also By J.A. Baker

Undercurrent

# Praise for Undercurrent

'I struggle to believe that this is actually a debut novelist, the story is written with such assurity and fluidity that it has the feel of a more seasoned writer.' **Sarah Kenny - The Great Bristish Book Off**

'An extremely gripping read that was bound in mystery and atmosphere.' **Alexina Golding - Bookstormer**

'From the haunting throwbacks to the past, to the tense and suffocating atmosphere in the present, this harrowing tale sweeps easily and effortlessly from start to finish...' **Linda Green - Books Of All Kinds**

'This is a super book with only a small cast of characters that gets smaller the more you read. Fantastic!' **Susan Hampson - Books From Dusk Till Dawn**

'In terms of the writing, Baker has a gift, a wonderful gift and I am so pleased that she has put pen to paper and delivered such a bloody impressive debut.' **Emma Mitchell - Emma The Little Book Worm**

'This is an enjoyable debut with a fabulous prologue that really creates a desire to invest yourself fully in the plot as it unfolds.' **Joanne Robertson - My Chestnut Reading Tree**

"If you want to keep a secret, you must also hide it from yourself."
— **George Orwell, 1984**

For Rosemary, the sister who nearly was. I hope you found your way home.

# BEFORE

Huge pulsating waves of pain exploding in my head. I drag my eyelids apart, try to focus properly, look around; work out where I am. Darkness everywhere. Nothing to see. No shadows, not even a vague outline of anything recognisable. Just complete blackness. Am I awake? Am I *dead*? I wait; my breath uneven, irregular. Pockets of hot air fall back on my face, shrouding me in a sticky, warm mist. I continue to stare, my eyes sore and gritty. Still nothing. No focus or adjustment to my surroundings. Zero. I cough and splutter as my body gradually rouses itself. My chest is tight and I feel like I'm suffocating. It's quiet. So very, very quiet. I lie still, listening for something - anything at all; any familiar sound to stem my rising fear - the chirrup of birdsong, the north-easterly wind roaring across the fields or rushing through the trees, the distant murmur of people. But there's no sound to be heard from anywhere. Just a lingering silence. My thoughts begin to clear, the fog inside my head lifts as I slowly come round. I have no idea where I am. I'm not in bed. No blankets or sheets covering me. And I am freezing; so very, very cold - my extremities like ice. I grope around, my fingers hitting something concrete-like above. I trail them over the surface - firm, craggy, wet; dripping with condensation. I continue moving them in an arc down to the ground. Narrow. It's all very narrow. Too much so. And the smell - an odour of petrichor. The earthy scent of rain and damp. I shift and wince as something jagged and sharp digs into my back. It's a hard surface, like rock. *Rock?* I frown. Pain whistles through my skull as I blink and shuffle about. Why am I on the ground? I move about some more and attempt to sit up only to find the space is too confined to do anything.

I hit my head and am forced back down. More pain. Like shards of glass tearing at my skin. What the hell is this - some kind of *joke*? I try to control my breathing. It begins to escalate into heavy, uncontrollable gasps for air as reality hits and panic sets in. God almighty. Surely not? I begin to scramble about, a jumble of panicky, uncoordinated limbs grappling for purchase, coming up against an immovable surface. My head pounds. Blood surges through my ears making me nauseous. Solidity surrounds me. This is my worst nightmare. Why can't I move? *Where the fuck am I?* A slow, sickening dawning washes over me. I'm dead. I must be. It's all too much for my brain to take in. Things like this only happen to people in books or movies. But not to me; please don't let this be happening to me. I can't bring myself to think about it, but as I try to sit up once more and stretch my arms out, the enormity of what is happening to me forces its way into my mind like white hot shrapnel. Jesus Christ, this is real. This is actually happening to me. I can't move. I am trapped. My vision blurs and flames lick at my aching brain as the words balloon in my mind. I've been buried alive.

Where was I last? A memory pierces my thoughts, jolting me out of my groggy, soporific state. Raised voices; an argument. A really bad argument. Hitting, scratching, shrieking. A sudden, sharp pain. Then nothing. I pant hard, trying to recall who the argument was with or what it was about. Who in God's name do I know that would do this to me? I lead a normal life. Or at least I think I do. Everything is so muddled and dark. Fragments of thoughts and memories floating about, disjointed and shadowy, flitting in and out of my consciousness. Like a really bad dream. Or my worst nightmare.

I bring my hands up and try to feel for something behind me. They meet with a cold draught. I gradually begin to move my legs, gaining momentum till I am thrashing them about as much as I can. Same again. Great wedges of icy air that bite at my clammy, exposed skin. My feet are starting to go numb. I swallow hard, trying to control my racing heartbeat. Not in a box then - or god forbid, a coffin - more like some sort of tunnel. Hope mingles with horror as the awfulness of it all begins to dawn on me. Even if I can shuffle and propel myself along, which way do I go? What if I end up deeper in this godforsaken place? Dread and terror begins to overwhelm me. If I do nothing, I will die here. Wherever *here* is. Am I underground? Fear muddies my thinking. A cave perhaps? Pain claws at my temples as blood pulses through my veins, growling in my ears. I take a deep breath and try to remain calm. I need to get out - and quickly. With as much effort as I can, I use my elbows and pelvis to push myself forwards, my heels snagging on pieces of sharp ground with every tiny infinitesimal movement. It takes an age to move the smallest distance but I keep telling myself that it's better than doing nothing. Better than lying here waiting for the air to run out and death to take me. My throat closes up at the thought and I begin to gag. Before I have a chance to stop it, I retch - my body convulsing violently, my stomach heaving and cramping. Tears streaming, I turn my head to one side and let it escape, a slick of warm vomit trailing over my cheek, sticking in my hair, pooling under my head. My brain throbs and I'm consumed by an almighty thirst. *How the fuck did this happen?* More to the point - who did this to me? Have I been kidnapped? *Raped?* I swallow hard and squeeze my eyes closed, forcing it all away, the pain and the horror, then open them again. I have to do this. I need to get out of here. A sudden rush of anger bursts into my brain, infusing me with enough energy to continue forcing myself forwards. Got to keep going, ignore the thirst and the pain and the fear. Just keep going. I don't want to die - I *refuse* to die. Not here in this horrific place. I begin to sob, first softly then uncontrollably as hysteria finally takes hold. Dear God I don't think I can stand it. Please don't let me die.

# NOW

## Peggy

S pray crashes against the rocks three hundred feet below her, the sound muffled and muted by the recently fitted window in the tiny kitchen. Peggy stares out, trance like, her eyes drawn to the horizon - an indistinct, blurry line shrouded in mist. She watches the sea, sees how it bounces and sways. This is her spot, the place she stands and stares out most days to admire its vastness and power. The blackness of the water always gets to her, gnaws away at her innermost fears highlighting her insignificance when compared to the forces of nature. She imagines the sheer weight of it, dark and oppressive, forcing her down, compressing her skull, her body helpless against the relentless drag of the tide. She turns away and quashes the very thought of it. She has no idea why she allows herself to think such morbid thoughts. Chamber Cottage is after all, a dream home; their dream home. A place of tranquillity and beauty with outstanding views according to all the brochures they saw prior to buying it, so it must be, mustn't it? Built in the early 19<sup>th</sup> century with constant damp problems and a leaking roof, Chamber Cottage also has its many disadvantages, and if the local rumours are to be believed, a whole host of secrets. Peggy wanted to laugh out loud when she heard that one. What house doesn't have secrets? Especially a two-hundred-year-old one. But Alec fell for it; all the gossip and supposition, the purported tales of smuggling and corruption that took place right here in their kitchen. He also swears blind he's seen something, *someone*. Shadows, flickering movements, nothing he can quite put his finger on. For a sensible, level headed man he often comes out with some nonsense. Peggy is convinced the lady at the estate agents did too good a job of selling them the idea of an old coastguard's cottage with a dark history. 'A house with a chequered past' were her words. Peggy puffs out her cheeks and grabs a handful of damp kitchen roll, dragging it across the worktop as she attempts to eradicate every last crumb and sticky particle from last night's supper. Alec should know better but thoroughly enjoys a bit of drama, a stupid story he can regale people with. He probably even tells his pupils this stuff. She can imagine him, keeping them amused with his stories of ghosts and smugglers come to take back their hidden goods, the kids' eyes wide, fascinated by it all. Peggy often thinks he missed his vocation in life and should have been an entertainer of some sort, not a teacher. Of course, he would argue that they're both the same thing.

She stops mid wipe and looks out again at the gathering storm heading in from the west. It may blow over, it may not. The weather that hovers over the North Sea is nothing if not unpredictable. It's a daily guessing game, working out what sort of conditions they can expect to have thrown their way. She tugs at the blinds as if trying to keep the elements at bay, then shivers and finishes cleaning up. Lathering her hands in moisturiser, she sits down at the table in their more amply sized dining room and switches her computer on. At least working from home has its benefits during the gloomy, wintry seasons; no having to set out in the dark each and every morning to battle against the horrendous howling gales that pummel the front of their cottage. No having to drive off, freezing and windswept in a never-ending stream of traffic to get to a job you most likely hate. Plenty of people do. But not Peggy. This is her office, the place where she does all her thinking. Her fortress. A prison of her own making.

A chill filters down through the open fireplace. The hairs on her arms stand to attention in protest at the cold. She considers lighting a fire but knows only too well that one blast of wind will fill the house with the dusty stench of ash, an acrid odour that will cling to her clothes and all the soft furnishings, resulting in a long and arduous bout of cleaning to eliminate it. She pulls her cardigan tighter around her body and drags the chair closer to the table telling herself that the sense she has of not being alone in this house is all in the mind. A figment of her imagination. She's an author. Dark thoughts are her bread and butter; her mind is constantly focused on death and fear. Why wouldn't she feel uneasy from time to time, when she spends all day, every day, writing about murder and gore? She shrugs the sensation off, thinking about how she laughs at Alec and his talk of lurking shadows while here she is, convinced someone is watching her. She has to stop this. It is childish nonsense. She has work to do. Updating her website is her first job, stopping only to get another cardigan before finally relenting and turning up the heating thermostat. Damn this freezing cottage and its determined attempts to bankrupt them.

By mid-day she has completed her blog and written a good, solid chapter of her next book, pleased with its twists and turns and flowing style, and is ready for coffee. Behind her the growl and occasional hiss of their ancient boiler kicks in. She stops and listens to it, silently pleading with a greater deity for it to see them through the winter. April. That's when it can finally breathe its last. April; when it will be warmer and they'll have money saved up to replace it. By then her third book will have been published and Alec's new salary from his recent promotion will have had a few months to gather in the bank. That's the plan anyway. Peggy drapes a hand over her eye and drags it through her hair. She takes a deep breath and snaps her laptop closed. Experience tells her that even the best laid plans have a tendency to go awry.

The chair scrapes across the flagstone floor as she pushes it back and stands up. The rush of the sea far below her gains impetus. The storm is almost upon them. She can feel it in her bones. A glance at the barometer hanging on the wall over the sink says it all - a sharp plummet since last night; the dial indicating a severe weather change is about to take hold. She shuffles off into the kitchen and flings the fridge door open. A row of bare shelves stare back at her. Their weekly grocery shop is long overdue. She should have done it by now but couldn't quite muster up the strength, and online shopping is beyond her. The last time she had a go at it, the metric weights had her completely flummoxed and she ended up with enough bananas to start her own plantation, so she now does it in person despite hating every minute of it. Shopping is an ordeal. For Peggy, leaving the house is an ordeal. There are days when she looks in the mirror and sees an average looking young woman staring back at her; if she keeps the lights dimmed, strategically angles the blinds and narrows her eyes that is. Then other days ... well, those other days see her holed up in her cottage, too low to go out and face the world with all its pitfalls and reminders of what a truly awful place it can often be. But not today. She reaches up to her face and carefully traces the lines of her scars. They may fade over time but the memory of how they got there will never leave her. Sometimes she visualises them as stretching over her entire face, growing and morphing until they are so vivid and so shocking, she has no features left worth speaking of - just a mass of angry red welts. Today however, her mind is in a better place; not so fragile, ready to desert her at the slightest provocation. A staring shop assistant, whispers from insensitive people, the pointing fingers of innocent children. They all mount up, gather in the shady corners of her mind until she can no longer take it and her brain shatters into a million, tiny pieces. That won't happen on today's outing. She is feeling stronger, more resilient. Today she will do her level best to put the past behind her. Exactly where it belongs.

*** 

It's back again. Peggy stands, empty shopping bags tucked under her arm, key held tight between her fingers, feeling her chest tighten a fraction. She cleaned it yesterday. And the day before. How can it have appeared once more? This is complete madness. She reaches down and places her fingers on the stain that is covering the back step. Dry to the touch. Shoving the car keys in her coat pocket, she flings the door open again and storms back into the kitchen, suddenly furious. This is utterly ridiculous. How many applications of bleach is it going to take for this thing to disappear? Grabbing the bottle, Peggy heads back out, twisting the cap off with more force than is necessary, then stands at the back door and watches as a stream of the viscous, clear liquid covers the brown mark and spreads out slowly over the old, stone step. She shakes her head despairingly. If this doesn't clear it, nothing will. Leaning in, Peggy snatches at the brush hanging next to the door and begins to scrub in a vicious circular motion, a creamy lather quickly forming, turning the entire step into a rectangular, white slab of foam. Her back and arms ache as she continues to drag the brush back and forth, round and round, refusing to give up until sweat coats her face despite the icy wind that has picked up and is swirling round the cottage. Standing up with an exhausted grunt, she heads back inside and comes back with a jug of hot water. She rinses away the foam, careful to aim the water so it doesn't spill over inside the cottage. She doesn't imagine that two-hundred-year-old flagstone flooring will take kindly to half a bottle of bleach being thrown on it. She continues to swill the step; jugful after jugful of hot water, watching as it rinses everything away. Then standing stock still, hands on hips, she surveys the newly cleaned step. The mark has gone. For now. Windows, masonry, even the paintwork on her car - they all struggle against the elements up here, the wild winds and salt air eating away at them day after day, an army of invisible mouths slowly nibbling into metal and bricks unrelentingly, yet a small stain refuses to vanish. She pointed it out to Alec a few days back. He dismissed her remarks, reckoned it was scarcely visible, said it was all in her mind. He always knows exactly what to say; chooses each word with excruciating precision. To her it stuck out like a sore thumb. A vivid mark like a blemish on her soul. She isn't even sure why she mentioned it. It's not as if they don't have other things to focus on. He shrugged it off. Said it wasn't important. Anyway, cleaning this place isn't his job. It's hers. Peggy is the one who does it all, the sweeping, wiping, washing, ironing. Some days it seems like a never-ending chore. Some days she can hardly bring herself to get out of bed, never mind clean up. She gives the step one last quick glance before locking up and getting into the car. There are times lately when life seems so bloody difficult. She has to make sure today isn't one of those days.

Her battered old Clio kicks up gravel as she puts it into reverse, does a three point turn on the tiny postage stamp size drive next to the house and sets off into town.

# Alec

He grabs the invitation and shoves it deep inside his jacket pocket, already thinking of a stream of plausible excuses as to why they can't go. *We were on our way when Peggy took ill; we've got another function on that evening - what are the odds? We'd love to come but Pegs has a writing deadline that week and usually works through the night to get it finished.* He knows them all off by heart. And he's new here. It gives him the chance to work his way through the old, apologetic explanations he trotted out at his previous school before he has to think up new ones. In the end the staff there stopped inviting him, and who could blame them? Peggy and Alec's continued absences were an insult to the efforts of those involved. Nobody wants to be continually ignored or rebuffed. It shouldn't have happened. He shouldn't have allowed it to happen. He should have been firmer with her, coaxed her, told her everything would be all right. But after a while it becomes wearing, having to prop someone up all the time, to constantly pander to their needs. So, he stopped. But this time around he really needs to stick to his guns, to up his game socially. He has to make a good impression at this place. He's the deputy head for God's sake and has a duty to mingle with his team, be friendly, approachable. The last thing he wants is to come across as superior and aloof. This is a tough school - he needs them on his side. Alec pulls the piece of paper back out of his pocket and reads it again. A get-together to welcome new staff members at a local bar. Dear Lord, how awful would it look if he didn't turn up? His own welcome party and he can't even be bothered showing his face. He pictures it in his head, an empty space in the pub, people whispering about him not being there, conspicuous by his absence, then closes his eyes and visualises Peggy's expression when he mentions the invite. She will go pale and gingerly stroke her right eye and he will feel guilty for asking her and watch her as she shuffles off, huddled in her own blanket of misery.

The door creaks and Alec looks up to see a slim, nervous-looking woman standing in front of him. Good looking, nice hair. He places the paper down on his desk and gives her his best welcoming smile, hoping she doesn't spot the crack in his veneer. He has to make a good impression here. This is his chance to shine, an opportunity to make a difference. She steps forward and hands him a sheath of papers.

'The Year 5 targets you asked for?'

'Ah yes, of course …' Alec murmurs as an unexpected redness creeps its way up his neck.

'Ellen,' she whispers nervously and tugs at her skirt to straighten out a crease that has gathered around her midriff.

'Ellen …' Alec repeats her name, enjoying the feel of it as it rolls off his tongue. 'Ellen,' he says once more, 'thanks for these, I'll get them back to you first thing in the morning.'

She nods and stands for a while seemingly unsure what to say or do next, her eyes taking in the pictures and framed certificates hanging in the room before landing on the recently placed family photographs on his desk. One of him and Peggy, arms tucked tight round each other's waists, another of Peggy on her own, a side profile of her taken in a restaurant on their honeymoon, when she wasn't looking - her good side - the only side she wants people to see. A long time ago. Or at least that's how it feels. An era when they were happy. A time when passion was their overriding emotion. Back in the days when Peggy smiled.

'Anyway, better be off,' she says quietly, 'Rory was on the point of kicking off as I left. Don't want to leave poor Jeanette on her own for too long. We've had a right morning of it over there.'

'You can always send him over to me.' Alec pulls at his collar. It feels unseasonably hot in his office. Perspiration begins to gather round his neck as he unfastens his top button and loosens his tie.

Ellen raises her eyebrows in mock astonishment and makes a light whistling sound, 'You sure about that? The last deputy head who said that ended up getting spat at,' she says, her mouth pursed, 'by Rory's brother, funnily enough.'

Alec nods and straightens up the papers in front of him, 'Well, why don't we give it a go? See how he gets on. Tell him I need someone to help set up the P.E. equipment but he can only do it if he finishes his work first.'

Ellen runs her tongue over her teeth with a small flick and gives him an appreciative nod. Alec is well aware of how much it rankles staff when naughty pupils get the best jobs and all the attention. It's all about balance when it comes to dealing with children and behavioural issues. There are no easy answers. And he should know. The vision of his father's fist landing with a crack on his cheekbone splits into his thoughts. He feels the warmth of the blood as it runs down his face and brings his hand up, faintly surprised to find it dry. Another memory jolts him. Yet another beating he received when he pushed his fists into another child's face shortly afterwards, full of misdirected hurt and anger, imagining it was his father's belly. Alec runs his fingertips over his knuckles, recalling the feel of soft skin against bone, the screams of the other boy, the bubbling fury he felt all those years ago. The fury he still feels now.

He gives a small shiver and smiles, his face a frozen grimace as he watches her bustle out of his office, her pert bottom remaining rigid with every step. He keeps his eyes firmly focused on her panty line - a sharp, neat triangle through the fabric of her skirt. Alec feels a small buzz of excitement. He wonders if she'll be at the welcoming evening and then quickly chastises himself. He shouldn't even be entertaining the idea. She is a colleague, one he barely even knows, come to that, and he has to stop this. He's acting like a bloody teenager. He's got Peggy. She is his wife and she needs him. Things haven't been great for them lately but then, find him a perfect marriage and he will find you a pair of liars.

Rory was quite the angel when in the presence of a six-foot-four-inch male who holds a position of authority. They spent the next hour hauling basketball stands out of the P.E. cupboard and sorting out table tennis nets which had become tangled into small tight knots.

'Thanks Rory. Couldn't have done it without you, lad. A job well done.'

The ragged-looking boy beams at him and skitters off over the playground. Alec sighs as he watches him as he makes his way back towards class, the boy's demeanour changing visibly the closer he gets to the door - head down, shoulders hunched. Poor kid. All he wants to do is play football and roll about in a bit of dirt and instead he's shut up in a classroom all day, trying to digest how best to use fronted adverbials, modal verbs, and relative clauses, and attempting to work out what the difference is between an active and a passive voice. What has the world come to when a person is defined by the number of adjectives they use in a piece of writing? What on earth happened to learning the times tables and a bit of physical exercise for youngsters? Alec turns and heads back into his office. There are times when he questions the very essence of why he ever became a teacher.

He spends the rest of the afternoon sifting through the papers with a fine toothcomb and analysing the data, his eyes heavy with exhaustion. By the time he switches his office light out and tugs on his coat he already has this welcome party problem worked out in his head. It flitted in and out of his thoughts all afternoon, demanding his attention. Somehow, he will persuade Peggy they should go, mither her, remind her of his duties, do whatever it takes. And if his powers of persuasion aren't enough, then he will go on his own. He wouldn't usually do such a thing, but this is his life as well. God knows he has helped Peggy through enough tough times. He deserves her support for a change. Enough is enough.

It's late when he finally leaves school. Vera, their site manager is standing impatiently, keys in hand as he closes his door and heads out into the darkness, the sound of jangling metal telling him she has had enough of waiting around. When he first took the position here at Park Tree Primary he promised himself there would be no more late nights, no more hanging around doing last minute jobs, but time continually seems to get the better of him and he is always the final one to leave.

His footsteps crunch over the small patch of gravel outside the office as he hurries into the car park, head down against the bracing autumnal wind. He stops suddenly, a shadow ahead catching his attention. Alec tries to stem the uneasy sensation he has that somebody is watching him. He's had it before, the eerie feeling that he isn't alone. He thinks of Peggy and her caustic laughter when he told her he thought he had seen something or *someone* at their cottage. He shakes his head and continues on, head dipped against the growing breeze. She's right of course. He reads too much into things. And why on earth would anybody want to watch him? He's a regular thirty-something man leading an average life in the north-east of England, not a bloody film star. He continues to stare into the darkness, his fingers twitching nervously as he narrows his eyes and scans the area.

Small spots of rain hit the back of his neck. Alec looks up and squints. He needs to make a move before it escalates into a downpour. Visibility can get pretty bad on the coast road in the rain. Plunging his hand into his pocket he rummages around for his keys. *Come on man.* He lets out a deep throaty growl of frustration, bone tired after a ten-hour day. He just wants to get home now. He locates them and curls his fingers around the serrated edge of the cold metal and stops to stare around, tiny splashes hitting his eyelashes, misting his vision. *There's nobody here. Stop over-thinking everything.*

His briefcase lands with a smack on the leather seat and he climbs in, suddenly grateful to be getting away from the office. It's been a long one and he needs a hot bath to rest his aching back.

The engine roars into life, the headlights spreading an off-white beam of light around the small, enclosed space, a tiny glow in the surrounding darkness. His eyes are drawn once more to a flicker in the shadows next to the bushes. He dismisses it. Just his imagination in overdrive, a trick of the light. Who would want to hang around here after dark? It's starting to rain and blowing a hoolie out there. Probably a fox on the prowl, watching, waiting, ready to raid the bins once the place is empty. He slips the car into reverse and stares in the rear-view mirror as he manoeuvres his way out of a corner space. That's when he sees it. A figure standing next to the fence; a blur of a silhouette in the shadows, framed in the moonlight. This time there's no mistaking it. Alec looks away and tries to ignore the troubled sensation he feels down in the pit of his stomach. A pulse thrums in his neck, hammering out a steady, dull beat as it works its way up through his ears and into his head. When he looks back, it's still there. An outline in the darkness, grey and shadowy and deeply unsettling. And it's staring straight over at him.

*'We shouldn't be together. This isn't right.'*
   *'Why?'*
*'You know why. We have to stop this.'*
*A long, drawn out sigh - dramatic and contrived.*
*'I'm married. This has to stop.'*
*'I can't stop. I need you.'*
*Stillness, heavy and sour, punctured by the sound of distant weeping.*
*Another sigh, softer, sincere.*
*'Don't cry. I can't bear it when you cry.'*
*Movement, footsteps, a barely audible breath, hot and passionate. The sound of linen crushed under the weight of bodies tumbling together in the darkness, falling into each other. The molten heat of skin meeting skin. Murmurs in the darkness, an intensity so deep it hurts.*
*Minutes passing, hours perhaps. Time loses all meaning.*
*'I have to go now.'*
*A heavy stillness, loaded with simmering anger and resentment.*
*'You always have to go. Is it too much to ask that you stay for a while longer? Do I mean so little to you?'*

*'Don't. Please don't. You know I have to. I can't stay, you know that.'*

*Another air of protracted silence. Breath ragged and harsh, building in strength and power. Rhythmic. Powerful. Threatening.*

*'I don't know anything anymore. You're always running away. Always running. It's all you ever do. The only thing you're good at. Go on then. GET OUT.'*

*'Why are you acting like this? You should know better. You of all people ...'*

*'Do NOT use that line on me.'*

*'It's true. You know it's true.'*

*'I said get out!'*

*'Okay, as you wish.'*

*The rustle of clothing and the soft echoes of remorse as the door clicks closed. The thump of footsteps fading. Moving further and further away. Then emptiness. Nothing but a cavernous void; silent and bottomless.*

*'I'm sorry. I didn't mean it. Please don't leave me. I need you ...'*

# Peggy

Peggy unloads the car and drops the bags at the back step, her eyes drawn to the grey stone. No mark. She lets out a small breath, hot and slightly sour, pushing it out through pursed lips and unlocks the door. The door swings open as she picks up the bags and staggers into the kitchen, hands red from the exertion. It was an easy journey. Easier than she anticipated. None of the usual shit that accompanies her whenever she leaves the house. No awkward silences or long, hard stares at her face from perfect strangers. No people scurrying past pretending to shift their gaze elsewhere; in a shop window, at a passing car, anywhere but at the patchwork quilt that is her face.

She drops the bags onto the kitchen floor and puts everything away, then makes herself a sandwich, knowing she should eat. It's been hours since breakfast, her stomach just hasn't realised it. That's the pattern lately - eat because it's time, not when she's ready. She places a thin slice of cheese between two pieces of wholemeal bread and feels her stomach flip as the smell hits her. Staring at it as if it were poison, Peggy picks it up and throws it into the bin. So much waste. Instead she makes a cup of tea as she waits for her laptop to whirr into life. A series of emails pop up, most of them spam that have somehow slipped through her junk filter. Seems to happen more and more these days, as if the entire system is struggling to cope. She deletes them and stares at the screen. Two remain - one from an agent she had dealings with last year and one from a sender whose name she doesn't recognise. Hand hovering over the mouse, Peggy decides to open the one from the mystery person, braced for another bad review. It happens sometimes; people feel the need to vent their spleen when a book isn't to their liking. An iron fist clutches at her stomach, squeezing hard as she reads through it and then quickly hits the delete button. That's something she wasn't prepared for. Silly really, her mother creating a new email address thinking Peggy won't spot it. She's quietly pleased Alec isn't here peering over her shoulder as she opened it. He would have harangued her into replying, told her what's done is done and she should forgive and forget. That's never going to happen. Not while she has breath left in her body. Alec has no idea what goes on in her head when it comes to matters concerning her mother. She opens the other email and scans it; a sycophantic missive about a possible representation from an agent who only last year turned her down. She bins that as well and lets out an angry cackle. Funny how once your books start to be successful, people come flocking. Fans, agents. Psychotic parents.

A noise somewhere behind her catches her attention. She stops what she is doing and waits. It's there again - a dull, scratching sound. She turns around, stands up and heads over to the window. Peggy would love to convince herself that it's a branch scraping the roof tiles were it not for the fact that the nearest tree is almost a hundred feet away. The wind has strengthened but it's a mere whisper compared to what they are used to hearing here, perched high up on the cliff top. She listens to the rocks being lashed by the sea below; angry, wet claws tearing at the very ground beneath her feet. A different sound altogether but again, a familiar one. She peers out. The impending storm seems to have passed them by, headed off northward, its grey, bulging mass now a threat to the unsuspecting folk of Norway. A few drops of rain hit the window. Just a short shower. Not the downpour they were expecting. Peggy leans forward and watches the sea still bashing the coastline furiously, then up at the cobalt sky above. How quickly the weather changes, altering its trajectory, proving forecasters wrong time and time again. She feels a tug of mild relief. They will have enough inclement weather to deal with soon enough. The winters up here are fierce and unforgiving.

She shuffles back over to where the grating sound is emanating from and stands motionless, her body heightened to every movement and breath of wind, her skin prickling as the noise gets louder, becoming amplified under her feet. It's down there somewhere, moving around the floor, each noise accentuated in the emptiness of the room. She kneels down, her ear to the floor, and listens once more.

Sitting up as if burnt, her skin crawls with dismay and disgust. *Mice.* Shit, shit, shit. Bloody mice in their basement. Steel arms wrap themselves around her innards. Small rodents fill her with complete and utter dread. She thinks of the cellar floor covered with their scaly feet and long, swishing tails and feels a juddering pulse take hold in her neck. Ringing pest control is out of the question. How would she handle a perfect stranger walking about under their house? Somebody has to do it. It can't be her. Definitely not her. And getting them in will cost money, something they currently don't have a great deal of. Friends laugh at their financial woes whenever the subject crops up. *'But he's a teacher and you're an author!'* they cry in unison.

*'You must be rolling in it!'*

*'You live in a listed property. Only people with money can afford to do that ...'*

If only they knew the debt Peggy had gotten into whilst waiting for her books to sell. And everyone knows about teachers' wages. As for living in a listed property - Chamber Cottage-beautiful though it is, is a money pit. Their latest expenditure - double glazing - was a necessity to keep the raging elements at bay. Right now, the one thing they don't have is any expendable income.

By the time Alec arrives home, she has convinced herself that the mice have multiplied a hundredfold. She can visualise them scurrying around under the floorboards, gnawing at wires, getting up through a crack in the brickwork and crawling over her body as she sleeps. She slaps her palm over her mouth to stop herself from gagging.

'I'll do it,' he says nonchalantly, 'It's no big deal. I'll get some traps first thing in the morning. Good job it's the weekend, eh? Or you'd have your furry little friends running around under your feet for a bit longer than you'd like.'

Peggy wants to scream out loud at him; at his lackadaisical attitude, at the fact they don't even have enough cash in the bank to call somebody in to see off an infestation of mice. They are down there, darting and bustling about, living off God knows what, running amok beneath her feet, spreading their germs around like poison and he is making a joke of it. She should have gone down there herself but the thought of entering that place ... that dank, musty, old hole; somewhere that sets her nerves jangling. She would rather it was sealed off permanently. Forget it even exists. She closes her eyes, shivers dramatically, and turns away.

'I hate the very idea of them being so near to me. Won't they go away if we just ignore them? Surely they'll just die off eventually?' Her stomach is in knots. Nausea rises as she stares at him.

Alec sighs. His voice is a low croak as he speaks, a murmur of reassurance, 'Like I said, Pegs, it's nothing to get all het up about. Just one of the joys of living in an old cottage. They get in through the air bricks - and before you ask - no they can't be closed up. Not unless you want damp coming up through the floor. It'll be sorted by tomorrow afternoon. I'll go out first thing and get armed to the teeth with traps and chocolate.' He smiles, revealing a row of perfectly white teeth, a gift from the care system, the only decent thing it afforded him, 'Little buggers can't resist the stuff apparently. Now can we just relax and enjoy the weekend?'

His tone suggests that the matter is closed. Peggy stares at his face. A line of anxiety sits between his eyebrows. He looks tired, worn out. More than that - exhausted. Pushing the matter any further is pointless. She looks away, blinking back tears. Stupid bloody mice. Once they are dead, then the cellar can be closed up for good and forgotten about once and for all. She will seal the trapdoor and throw away the key.

'I got some shopping in today,' she whispers, her eyes downcast, already knowing what he will say. An overreaction will ensue. He doesn't disappoint. Alec's face changes and he grabs her hand, strong and powerful, and then gives her a firm hug. Peggy stands stiffly, waiting, knowing what comes next.

'Great stuff, Pegs. Keep it up. You'll be pleasantly surprised at how easy it is once you get into a routine.'

She screams inwardly, knowing he would make something of it. Blow it out of all proportion. This is what he does. Piling on the pressure for Peggy to conform to normality is one of his least endearing traits.

'So anyway, now you're deciding to venture out a bit more, I was wondering if you fancied this?' He leans over and produces an envelope from his jacket pocket, his manner jocular and childlike. The sight of it makes her stomach plummet. God, he is so utterly predictable.

'It's a welcoming party - well not a party really,' he interjects rapidly as he susses the look on Peggy's face, 'more of an informal get-together to say hello to the rest of the staff and their families ...'

The words hang heavily in the air. She should have known this was coming really, been more prepared for it. She feels his eyes on her, watching and waiting for some kind of response. Well, for once, she will surprise him. She needs to get out more; of course she does. She realises that. She can't go on forever, shut up in this place. And as much as she fears the outside world, sometimes these four walls are not always enough. In fact, just lately, she has feared them even more. Today she felt confident - no, not confident, that's too over optimistic a word, but not as panicky, not as - whatever the word is that eludes her, the point is she felt better about facing the outside world. Feeling slightly unsteady, Peggy slumps into a nearby chair and stares down at her feet. She needs to choose her words carefully; remember to not touch her face. He hates it when she does that. It riles him up, makes him convinced she's looking for sympathy. She isn't. Why would she want anybody's sympathy? Behind her the scratching continues.

Alec doesn't seem to hear it but Peggy can. It circles around her head, growing louder and louder, taunting her, reminding her. She has to go with him. She really, really needs to do this. Alec is scrutinising her every move, she can sense it; every twitch, every breath that exits her trembling body is under observation. She has to say yes, get out of here, get away from this place. The last few weeks have been hell. Her hand begins to travel up to her right eye. She stops it, seeing Alec growing more and more infuriated. She doesn't want it to be this way - the slightest everyday chore an uphill climb. She wants to be normal, be like everyone else. But she's been like this for so long now, she can no longer remember what normal feels like.

Tears prick at her eyes and everything sways as she strives to find the right words. She has to speak soon, before his temper gets the better of him. She is in no fit state for one of his rages. Having to put up with one of his thunderous moods right now would very probably be the undoing of her; send her crashing down into a place she would rather not visit. Images flood her mind, meshing and overlapping, stabbing at her innermost fears; her mother's email, an army of mice down beneath her feet feeding on God knows what, an ever-growing stain that has haunted her for weeks now. Run of the mill events that others are able to deal with she simply cannot handle. It's the ordinary stuff that sends her into an almighty meltdown. But she did manage today. She actually did it. If she coped today then she can cope with tomorrow and whatever it may bring. And if she can keep on coping, building on it day by day, then everything will be just fine. Making a conscious effort to keep her hands pinned tightly in her lap, Peggy looks up at Alec and speaks.

# Alec

He drags his fingers across the stubble on his chin and sighs. Jesus fucking Christ. Why does she make everything so bloody hard? Is it her sole aim in life to balls up every social event that they're invited to? She's going to refuse. He can just tell. That's how well he knows her. Like the back of his hand. Standing with his feet slightly apart, Alec furls his hands into tight, hard fists, his nails digging into his palms as he clenches and unclenches his fingers. All he is asking for is a little bit of support in his new job. The job that pays for their car; the job that helps pay for their lovely little cottage with views many would give their pension for. What will it take for his wife to start acting normally? He wants to holler at her, tell her to leave her face alone and fucking grow up. But he doesn't. Instead he takes a few deep breaths - in out, in out. His temples throb and burn with unspent rage.

'Where is it?' she asks, her voice tight and husky.

He stops and stares, blinking rapidly. He's misheard her, he must have, 'Where is it?' He repeats her words. This a new one. No refusals, no tears, no rubbing at her scars. This is progress.

'Yes. Where is it? I might go with you.' She is calm, her eyes glassy, unreadable. 'If you want me to, that is?'

A small buzz takes hold in his head as it hits him. His breath catches in his chest, a bubble of expectation, 'Really? You'll come with me?' He stares hard, unable to take it in. This is a new sensation. It takes a few seconds for her words to fully register.

'I just said so, didn't I?' Peggy stares up at him and smiles, 'I ventured out today. Nobody stared, nobody said anything. Nobody gave me a second glance, Alec.'

He gets down on his haunches, takes her face in his hands, suddenly overcome with gratitude, 'That's because there's nothing to see, sweetheart.'

She starts to speak but is stopped. Alec holds his hand up and stares hard at her face, 'I know you think these stand out like a sore thumb,' he says, gently tracing the mesh of her scars, 'but they really don't. You have lovely skin and a winning smile. That's all you need.'

A short silence as she gives him a half grin and shrugs nonchalantly, 'I'm no stunner, never have been. Even before this,' she points to her face and then lets her hand drop onto her lap, 'so you don't have to butter me up. I'm all too aware of my standing in the beauty stakes.'

Alec exhales and pats her hand then stands back up, 'It's Wednesday next week. Won't be a late one as we've all got work the next day. It's at a pub in Lythe. I'll drive.'

\*\*\*

They eat their evening meal in near silence, Alec too tired to converse. It may be a Friday but he has a stack of paperwork to get through. He either does it this evening or has it waiting in store for him sometime over the weekend, which is even less appealing. He watches Peggy as she pushes her food around the plate before declaring she wasn't really hungry anyway. Her mind is elsewhere - her book, the cottage, the invitation. Her mind is always elsewhere. There is always something to worry about, something to keep her from him. He thinks of Ellen standing in front of his desk today, her fine golden hair glinting in the late afternoon sun and the trail of perfume she left in her wake, then eyes his wife as she gathers up the dishes and hobbles off towards the sink. At only thirty-five she has the gait of somebody much older, shuffling around, shoulders hunched, head permanently tipped forward. He suppresses his anger. Her many miscarriages have taken it out of her but without a doubt, the main reason for her current state is the scars. She has always been self-conscious to a degree, but lately the whole thing seems to have gotten out of hand. When she was younger she wore make-up, did her best to disguise them, threw her head back when she laughed. But these days she rarely even smiles, and as for make-up and attempts at looking glamorous - well, only yesterday she was still in her pyjamas when he got home from work. There was a time, not long ago, when she started getting out, going into town more. Her therapy seemed to be working. And for a while she was happy. But then it stopped abruptly and since then it's been a downward spiral. Alec shakes his head despondently. There are times when he could swear she actually *enjoys* being miserable and mildly disfigured.

'I'll come with you in the morning.' Peggy is at the sink staring out at the barely visible line where the black sky meets the dark, shimmering sea. He watches her as she focuses on the small flecks of silver, moving and swaying with the ebb and flow of the tide. Such perfect rhythm and beauty.

'Where am I going?' Alec picks up his case, grabs a manila folder and slowly flicks through a wad of papers that are tucked inside.

'To the hardware shop in town for mouse traps. Remember?'

He rolls his eyes and grabs a pen from his jacket pocket, 'Ah yes. Mouse traps. How could I forget?'

Sitting down at the table, he finds himself secretly hoping Peggy will have a bath or watch TV or do anything rather than write. He's not sure he can hack having her so close at the minute. He needs a bit of space from her woes. It's good she's getting out and coming to the pub but he knows her well enough to realise this may well be short lived. What she rarely realises is the fact that he too has a whole heap of worries roaming around in his head. If anyone knew the things that flit in and out of his brain throughout the day ... he swallows hard and stops himself. That route is not an attractive one. He shifts his thoughts elsewhere. There is work to be done. He needs to stay focused, not allow himself to get bogged down with memories he would sooner forget. He stares hard at the papers set out before him and quickly becomes immersed, scribbling away, scanning data, doing everything he can to keep the darkness at bay. Because once it descends, there's no telling what will happen.

# Peggy

She is determined to accompany him. She needs to. It was an unsettled night; one of many. She woke on the hour, every hour; lying as still as the grave, listening to the ominous roar of the thrashing waves outside, and now she is exhausted but armed with a steely resolve to do this, to go with Alec into town. The recent email from her mother kept her from sleep, gave her more than enough reason to lie awake into the early hours wondering what it would be like to be somebody else, somebody beautiful. Somebody worthy. She likes to think she has that aspect of her life sorted, that she handles it pretty well, but truth be told, contact from her mother still makes her nervous, stops her from functioning as she usually would, which isn't good at the best of times. It rakes it all up again in her head, thoughts of that period in her life. That day. Looking in the mirror is bad enough. A shadow of the person she used to be stares back at her. Any sort of contact makes her head swim. And when the content of her mother's email wasn't lodged in her mind, her book was there; how to add to the intricacies of characters' intentions and how best to plug the gaping holes in the long and convoluted plot. As a result, she feels like death warmed up, but no amount of exhaustion is going to weaken her will. She strokes her face, feeling the web of lines underneath her fingers, thinking how little they have faded over the years. Just like the ones she wears inside her head - vivid, harsh, ugly.

'I need to get straight back. Got some figures to work out.' Alec slips his arms into the sleeves of his jacket and grabs his keys out of the fruit bowl by the window.

'I thought you finished everything last night?' Peggy feels a frisson of annoyance run through her. He was there till well after midnight, flicking through papers, tapping away on his laptop. How much work is he expected to do every weekend? Besides which, he constantly complains about her not leaving the house and when she finally relents, he wants to come back home as soon as possible - what is all that about? She quashes her anger, eager to spend some time with him, this virtual stranger she calls her husband. She glances in the mirror - always shocked at the reflection that stares back at her - and sees a person in disguise, a splash of blusher, a slick of lipstick. A bright, shiny face - full of colour, devoid of emotion. A mask of insecurities. She purses her lips and applies more lipstick then sneaks another quick glance. The image that stares back tells her everything she needs to know. She is passable. No goddess, but then as Alec so casually reminded her yesterday with his backhanded compliment, she has a winning smile. What more can she possibly need? The confidence to live her life as it should be lived perhaps? Because as it is, living in fear of living is no life at all.

'Still got some bits of paperwork that need sorting. I'd rather do it sooner than later. Don't want it preying on my mind all weekend.'

Peggy suppresses a sigh. A lump forms in her throat, hard as rock, immovable, solid. She wants to enjoy their time together, make a go of it. She hoped that this morning could be the start of something better. Things haven't been great between them for some time and she has to take some blame for that. Her inability to move on from the past has hindered things. And over the past few months she has convinced herself that it's their working hours that have been the main contributor to their marital decline. But deep down she knows that's not entirely true. Because of course there was Sheryl. A dark, heavy mood descends at the thought of her. Sheryl with her contagious laugher, effervescent demeanour and porcelain skin. Oh God, that gorgeous, blemish free skin. She was so utterly fresh looking and perfect she practically sparkled.

'Right, you ready?' Alec has the chrome ring looped over his forefinger and is swinging the hefty set of keys impatiently. 'The sooner we get there, the sooner we get back.'

\*\*\*

The town is almost empty despite shops being overstocked with early Halloween items strategically placed to entice children in with protesting parents in tow. An array of gaudy coloured masks and brightly coloured capes line the shelves, a sea of orange and green plastic, as Peggy and Alec collect their items and head back outside.

Peggy turns to head over the road and take a short cut up through the side street, a tiny, winding lane away from it all. Fewer people, less hassle. A place in which to hide. She watches as Alec stops suddenly and his eyes darken, 'Can we take a different route?'

She turns and looks around. And then she sees it. The door, that place. Of course. She had forgotten. How could she forget about that? Too late now. The memories are back, bubbling, resurfacing, gasping for air.

'Sorry,' she mutters and swiftly turns around, back the way they came, cutting through the crowds, their eager, darting bodies slicing past them, through them. A desperate need to quickly disappear and slip silently into the shadows.

They reach the car and Peggy manages a weak smile that isn't reciprocated. *Shit.*

She watches him as he swings the steering wheel around with more force than is necessary. Always quick to anger. Nothing has altered, nothing has changed. *It was all a complete waste of time.* She stares at the side of his face as he concentrates, his eyes focused straight ahead while he waits for the lights to change, and wonders what he is thinking, whether or not he is slowly falling out of love with her. She wouldn't blame him. She's hardly an attractive option at the minute - dowdy, miserable, distracted. She needs to move on. God, how she hates that phrase. Such a trite and insincere way of telling the damaged and the vulnerable to just get over it.

'Think I'll do some writing up in the spare room if that's okay with you?' Peggy says as they pull up outside the cottage, the car grinding to a halt with a crunch, spewing gravel far and wide, a metaphor for their damaged lives.

'Suits me. Once I finish setting these out I'll get my work done as well.'

Peggy feels a flush creep up over her neck. Alec's moods are notoriously mercurial. Always have been. And she is part of the problem. She has to pull herself together and get things back on track, forget all that's gone before. It's the only way; leave the past behind and erase all thoughts of Sheryl and her mother. Focus on the future, focus on her marriage. The words roll around her head with ease, shiny and alluring. A life full of promise; a life filled with hope.

# Audrey

The atmosphere in the house is oppressive and heavy. Dust motes swirl lazily in the thin shafts of late afternoon sunlight that filter in through the blinds. Audrey inhales deeply and scowls. She can smell the musty odour of stale air. It lingers in her nostrils, clings to the cushions and worms its way into the fibres of her clothes, refusing to budge. God, she hates living here. The entire house smells like an old care home. She takes a long swig of scotch, her first of the week and savours the sensation as it trickles down her throat, warm and peaty. She's started rationing herself. That's the problem with living on your own - the temptation to do whatever you want, whenever you want, is too great. Nobody around to sigh loudly or raise their eyes in consternation when you go for your third glass. Or your fourth. If somebody had told her twenty years ago that this is how her life would pan out she would have told them to stop being so bloody ridiculous. Twenty years back when she was happily married with two teenage daughters and living in a large house in the suburbs. She has to stop herself from turning around and surveying the tiny room she is currently sitting in. Perhaps not tiny for many but compared to her previous home, it is positively miniscule. A shoebox. She is used to space and the freedom to move around without jamming your leg against a sofa that is squashed into a tight corner or banging into a cabinet she should really have discarded when she moved here but hung onto for sentimental reasons. There are days when it feels as if the walls are closing in on her, ready to swallow her up, crush her into a tiny compressed being, a husk of her former self. The other house was her home. This is just a place where she exists day after day.

Given half a chance, she would go back in time, change it all; alter the past, improve the future. That was when she last felt happy, all those years ago. And although the girls would often drive her half insane with their constant bickering and moaning, she doesn't mind admitting that she hankers after those times. The times when she laughed more. The times when she felt loved. She misses her daughters and she misses Peter. God how she misses him. If she shuts her eyes tight and keeps completely rigid, she can transport herself back there; to the past. It plays in her head like a movie reel. She watches it over and over, smoothing out the kinks, rubbing out the mistakes. She can almost hear the shrieks of her teenage daughters and their feet thundering up above her as they tear around their bedrooms, and then the familiar slam of the door as Peter's voice filters through, announcing he is home. She takes a deep, shuddering breath, tips her head back and drains the glass before the tears escape. She stares down at the bottom of the empty tumbler wondering if it's too early to have another. Audrey shrugs, leans over and pours herself a long slug of amber liquid. Who makes the rules anyway? A welcome haze begins to descend as the drink oozes its way down her throat, acrid and smoky, blurring out all thoughts of what went before. Who needs money and a big house and who needs to be surrounded by people all the time anyway? All they ever do is let you down and leave you in the lurch. When was the last time she heard from either of her children? She thinks of Beatrice and imagines her eldest daughter running barefoot across the sand like some Hollywood movie star, staring up at her beach-front home, her white linen clothes blowing gently in the warm, Californian breeze. Of course, the reality is probably not half as romantic as that. But then how would she know? She rarely hears from her. All she knows is that Beatrice is currently living with some American man that she met on the internet and now works as a teacher in a school somewhere, thousands of miles away. She knows hardly anything about her. A virtual stranger. So, she makes things up in her head instead - imagines her daughter's face, smiling, tanned, living a life of luxury on the other side of the Atlantic. And then there's Peggy. Peggy who she thought would stick with her, and who ended up deserting her when things got tough - long before they got tough actually. Peggy just upped and left, never to return. She sometimes wonders if children are put upon this earth to constantly upset and disappoint you. She taps at the crystal glass, a dull thunk against her fingertips. Well, now Peggy needs her mother's help and Audrey will do all she can to get in touch with her. Despite all the arguments and differences, despite all the acrimony and the tears, Audrey would still walk over hot coals to help her children. Except Peggy doesn't know she needs help. She is blissfully ignorant of what's going on right under her nose.

Audrey stares at her laptop, willing her inbox to ping into life. It remains stubbornly empty. Finding her daughter's email address was a cinch. Her books now line the shelves of most of the shops in town. She's an acclaimed author; an established writer for heaven's sake. Who would have thought it? Quiet little Peggy - famous at long last. Audrey runs her hand over the keyboard. A collection of plastic letters that could change her future; the sheer complexities and power of a qwerty keyboard. She's not particularly au fait with using computers so the whole thing is proving so damn difficult. John has given her his email address to use. He has no idea why she wanted it; just handed it over without question. He's a good man, a really good guy and he has helped her through some tricky times. Just lately though he has asked for more from her, but at this point in her life, she simply cannot give it, or at any point if she's being honest. He's a kind man, a loyal man. But he's not her man and nor will he ever be.

Peggy didn't reply to Audrey's previous email, probably because the address contained her full name, so she now hopes that a bit of anonymity might help her case, get her the reply she so desperately wants. It's the waiting around for a reply that's so hard, the not knowing if the bloody thing has even been received or read. And she really does need to get in touch with her. Not just because Peggy is her daughter and she misses her. That goes without saying.

It's because she needs to speak to her to warn her. Peggy deserves to know about what has gone on, about what could happen again. She is acutely aware that her daughter hates her, despises the very ground she walks on actually. That's a fact she can neither dispute nor alter. Most children do hate their parents at one time or another don't they? That's just how it is. But their rift goes back so far it pains her to think of it. In fact, it's gone on for so long now, she has, in a perverse sort of way, gotten used to it. She certainly doesn't take any pleasure from it but, in her own odd way, has a resigned acceptance to it all. Of course, it changed her life completely and nothing is the same now and probably never will be. But it doesn't have to stay like that indefinitely, does it? She can make amends - do the right thing. Try to put it all right and make everything better. She often wonders if she should have just left things alone all those years ago; let them get on with it. They've managed so far on their own - Peggy has even become a prominent author for goodness sake. But now it's all starting to fall apart. Just as Audrey predicted it would. She just knew if she stuck it out long enough, waited around, kept a close eye on how their lives progressed, then sooner or later the truth would emerge and his true colours would show through. Audrey drains her glass with a self-satisfied air. She just knew it. She was right all along.

She continues to stare at the screen, her patience waning until she eventually gives up and snaps her laptop shut. She knows where they live. If Peggy continues to ignore her, she will leave Audrey with no option other than to confront her daughter with the ugly truth. She may not wish to hear it but it simply cannot be denied. Not this time. She has evidence, lots of it. This time Audrey will prove to her daughter that her old mother isn't such a dreadful harridan after all and that perhaps she should have taken heed of her words all those years ago.

Audrey leans back and drains another scotch as she re-opens her computer and stares at the black screen. She can wait. The one thing Audrey does currently have is plenty of time. Whether or not her daughter does however, is another matter entirely.

# Alec

He can see her from where he is standing, looking lost, desperately trying to make conversation with Colin Birkstall, a curmudgeon of a man who is married to Eva, the Year One teacher. Eva, the tiny, mousy slip of a thing who is counting down the days till her retirement. Alec stares at Peggy. She is looking really nice tonight. Her hair is twirled up and held in place with some kind of glittery clip and she is wearing a figure-hugging dress he's pretty sure he hasn't seen before. She's lost weight - a lot of it, more than he realised - and is wearing a pair of black suede stiletto sandals and she looks better than nice, she looks pretty damn amazing, albeit a little on the thin side. This is the old Peggy, the Peggy he fell in love with, the Peggy he would like to sleep with without the need for a baby at the end of it. The Peggy he would like back. She stares over and manages a weak smile. He waits to see if she trails her fingers over her eye and blinks nervously at him, but before she has a chance do anything Colin takes her arm and leads her off to another group on the opposite side of the room until she is no more than a blur in his peripheral vision; his wife - the ghost in the corner.

'You made it then?' Ellen appears in front of him, her blonde hair shimmering under the spotlights as she cocks her head to one side and smiles.

'Hello! Yes, we're here. Me and Peg—'

'Come on,' she cuts in, 'you must come over here and listen to Anthony telling everyone about his days as a student at Durham Uni. He is an absolute hoot. Did you know he once spent three days in a row drinking and riding on buses around the city asking strangers what colour underwear they were wearing?'

Despite not warming to Anthony since starting in his position, Alec follows Ellen, noticing how slim her ankles are in her grey velvet slingbacks. They become immersed in the large group, exchanging anecdotes about their student days and all the while Alec is acutely aware of the distance between his arm and the curve of Ellen's hipbone. Is he imagining it or is she deliberately moving closer to him? At one point, she leans forward for her drink and Alec catches a glimpse of her small, yet beautifully formed cleavage, cupped into place by a curve of white lace. The perfect body. He rapidly diverts his gaze, wary of being labelled a lecherous, old man by the throng of watching eyes. Her perfume wafts its way towards him, both musky and sweet at the same time. He pictures her naked body sprawled underneath his and then stops himself. *Stupid, stupid, stupid.* He thinks of Peggy on the other side of room, stuck with that old fart Colin, and is wracked with guilt. He has to stay focused, keep his eyes away from Ellen's breasts and hourglass figure. If only she didn't smell so damn good.

Time dissolves as they talk about past colleagues and future plans. He listens as Ellen declares to everyone that her days as a teaching assistant are numbered. She plans to go back to university, get her PGCE and go into teaching. Better pay, better union she declares testily. *And no time for a life*, Alec wants to say but remains tight lipped. He thinks of the void her move from Park Tree Primary will leave and wonders if he should speak with her about whether or not she's making the right move, quelling the voice that is telling him his talk is fuelled more by his attraction to her than his professional concerns about her future. He gazes down at her wedding finger. Bare.

'There you are.'

Alec turns to see Peggy standing behind him, a sheen of perspiration covering her face from the immense heat of the lights overhead. Her eye twitches as she attempts to wedge herself in between Ellen and Alec. Alec feels himself flush as she glares at him and worms her way in. Is it really that obvious?

'I was beginning to think you'd gone home without me.' Her voice is quiet, chirpy even, but Alec can spot the obvious undertone as Peggy sweeps her eyes over Ellen's slim frame and listens to her chirruping laughter. Like the delicate chime of crystal on ice. He turns to see Peggy move her gaze from his face to Ellen and then slowly and deliberately, back to his. She holds it there, her pupils like jet black pinpricks, scrutinising his expression so closely he starts to feel like bacteria under a microscope.

'I'm ready whenever you are,' she says and he quickly suppresses an eye roll, knowing exactly what that phrase means.

Alec looks around to see people beginning to filter away and file out of the door, bidding their goodbyes, saying what a shame they couldn't have planned this for a Friday. He can sense Peggy's disapproval, is aware of her brewing mood. He refuses to cave in, he will not succumb to her suspicions, her need to create a scene and cause a fight.

The atmosphere in the car is solid, Peggy's face set like stone. Alec leans forward to turn the radio on. The dulcet tones of Phil Collins' voice fills the air for a brief period before Peggy grasps at the button and switches it off again. Alec's knuckles are white as he clasps the steering wheel. *Here it comes, Alec, she was watching your every move.*

'She was very pretty, wasn't she? Expensive looking outfit, too.'

He can feel the full force of her stare as he rounds the bend out of the car park and onto the A174 that leads back to the coast. He remains silent. What is it she wants him to say anyway? That he still loves her despite the fact she turns her back on him night after night? That he still finds her attractive even though most days she is still in her pyjamas by lunchtime and hasn't even brushed her teeth? That she is, and always will be, the only woman for him even though they haven't had sex for over a year? Because all of it is true. He has no idea what it is she wants from him - to beg? Because he can do that. God knows there have been times when he's felt like it and he is pretty certain she knows it, but it doesn't ever soften her resolve. She is made of solid stone. Peggy won't budge an inch when it comes to their sex life. Intimacy seems to revolt her. He is beginning to think it's actually *him* she finds repulsive. And if that's the case then what the hell are they doing together?

'Alec? Did you hear what I just said?'

His voice is reedy as he tries to disguise his anger, 'Yes, Pegs, I heard you. We've had a good night. Let's just keep it that way, shall we?'

He hits the accelerator hard as they speed along the narrow road that cuts through the vast swathes of North Yorkshire countryside, the route ahead pitch-black, the headlights of the car just a small beam of light in the crushing darkness. From the corner of his eye he sees Peggy begin to slink down into her seat. She hates this, the demon that comes to life in him when he gets behind the wheel, loathes it in fact. *Good.* He presses his foot down, enjoying the sense of speed and the faint smell of burning rubber filtering in through the vents, then glances her way, gaining a small amount of satisfaction from seeing her squirm. He knew she would somehow find a way of ruining a perfectly good evening. He's glad she's scared and miserable. That's his life most days now - not knowing what he's coming home to, what kind of mood she's going to be in. Whether or not she has had a good day writing or whether she is going to be stuck in the depths of despair, huddled under a quilt, the sink piled high with unwashed dishes. Her desperation for a baby once ruled their lives but the focus has now shifted to her scars. And if it wasn't the scars there'd be something else. Because there is always something else. They no longer have a sex life because Peggy has given up trying to get pregnant. It's as simple as that. Doctors found no reason for the miscarriages. Physically she is absolutely fine. Her mental state however, is another matter.

'Alec! Slow down for God's sake! What are you trying to do - kill us both?'

He glances at the speedo and slowly brings his foot up off the pedal. Almost a ton. Jesus. He hadn't meant to go that fast, not on this road; an accident blackspot. He stays silent, not knowing what to say. His thoughts are so fucking muddled lately he's not even sure he could put any of it into words anyway.

They're almost home when it happens. The force of the connection knocks Peggy sideways. Her head smacks against the window with a sickening crack. She lets out a high-pitched shriek and Alec finds himself releasing a deep, throaty growl of pain as he is flung forward, his neck grinding and clicking viciously with the strength of the impact.

'Fuck! What the hell was that?' Ignoring the burning pain in his upper spine and Peggy's quiet whimpers, Alec, fumbles with his seatbelt and is up and out of the car before she has chance to say or do anything. The cold is an assault on his body as he stumbles outside, his feet crunching on loose fragments of tarmac. In the distance, he can see the dim light of their cottage, the warm, welcoming haze of home. So close by yet still so far away. He slams the door shut and starts to make his way round to the front of the car but is stopped when a voice behind him pierces the night air and turns his blood to ice, 'Murderer! How could you? You've killed him! YOU'VE KILLED HIM!'

Alec feels a sharp pain in his head as he turns to see a small shadow hunched over in the darkness, a crooked bony finger outstretched towards him.

'Murderer!'

It takes him just a few seconds to shake off his fear and shock. His voice projects across the countryside as he bellows at the tiny figure standing watching him, 'What the hell …? Who are you calling a fucking murderer?'

His heart thumps wildly as he continues round to the front of the car, his legs liquid at the thought of what he might find there. Alec's breath catches in his chest as he lays his eyes on a small bundle tucked under the front end of his Qashqai. Considering the strength of the impact there seems to be very little damage but with only the car headlights for illumination it's too difficult to inspect it properly. A sickening, dragging sensation pulls at his guts as he bends down and stares at the amorphous shape lodged under his front wheel.

'Christ, what is it?' Peggy's voice is shrill, about to break as she tentatively steps out of the car and scurries round to the front end, clinging onto the bonnet to steady herself.

Alec thinks of her head hitting the glass and flinches, 'Are you okay? You might need to stay in the car.' It was quite a crack. She shouldn't be out in the cold.

He rubs at his neck and lets out a long moan as he feels a dull ache set in at the top of his spine.

'I'm fine,' she murmurs, her eyes glued to the black mound on the floor. She stares up at the tiny frame standing on the craggy, moss covered tract of land next to the road and then back to the unmoving shape.

A voice fractures the still air, 'Maude! What are you doing? Stay there and don't move!'

A tall, lumbering silhouette bounds towards them from a distant farmhouse which is almost eclipsed by a copse of trees and high privets. Alec and Peggy stand transfixed by the surreal situation unfolding before them.

The silhouette reaches the edge of the car. Alec can see it's a young lad in his early twenties and he is clearly distressed. Panting for breath he stops to rest his hands on his thighs before draping his arm around the tiny shoulders of the hunched figure who has started to cry. Alec rolls his eyes and does his best to curb his anger. *Never mind your tears! What about my fucking car?*

'I'm really sorry. She managed to slip out while my back was turned. Really sorry,' gasps the young lad as he starts to guide her back to the house.

'Hey!' Alec calls after him, 'What about this?' He points to the black object on the road and raises his hands up as if to emphasise his point.

'Yeah sorry. That's just probably Bobbin. Nothing to worry about.'

'Bobbin?' Alec shouts, his voice echoing across the wilderness. *Who or what the fuck is Bobbin?*

'It's Maude's cat. Sorry I'll come and get it.'

Alec feels his insides tighten another notch and watches out of the corner of his eye as Peggy slumps slightly against the front of the vehicle. They both wait silently, eyes wide as the lad leans down and says something to the woman, and then strides over to the front bumper bar. He kneels down and attempts to haul a black sack out from under the front of Alec's Nissan.

'It's jammed. Sorry, can you reverse? I'll be able to lift it out if you move your car back a bit.'

'A cat?' Peggy squeaks, her voice laced with anguish. Alec looks at her. He fears she might bubble up and burst; her cries and wails proving to be his final tipping point after a disastrous journey home.

The young man smiles and Alec suddenly wants to punch him square in the face.

'Sorry,' he says humbly, sensing Alec's unabated fury, 'I should explain. Aunt Maude has Alzheimer's and I'm here looking after her tonight while her daughter is out working. Bobbin is her comforter - her toy cat.'

Alec groans then shakes his head in disbelief as he jumps in the car. The wheels screech as he revs the engine and the car jumps back slightly, releasing the object. He is back out in an instant, his impatience and fury palpable in the cold, evening air.

The young man reaches down and lifts the bag up off the road. Shoving his hand into the bottom of the sack the lad pulls out an old, tattered cuddy toy, decayed from years of use. He holds it out under the beam of the headlights for them to see. A ragged, filthy streak of fur.

'And what else is in there?' Alec growls, his temper augmenting by the second. That bang was caused by something much bigger than a bloody kid's toy.

'I'm really sorry,' the young man stutters, 'but I need to get Maude back home. She's only wearing her nightgown and in her condition—'

The sound of plastic being torn apart fills the night air as Alec grabs the bag from him and rips it open, staggering back as half a dozen bricks and a handful of large rocks scatter noisily at his feet missing his toes by a fraction.

'What the fuck?...' he cries as he stares down at the pile of rubble sitting on the road.

'Look, as I said, I'm really sorry. I have no idea how she got out or where she got this lot from. If you give me your name and number my cousin will pay for any damage and—'

'Too bloody right she will, pal!' Alec feels Peggy's light touch on his arm. He picks up on her subliminal message to rein his temper in. Bollocks to that. The silly old bitch nearly caused a major accident. She could have written his car off. He will *not* rein his temper in.

The lad taps at his breast pocket, slips his long, slim fingers inside and produces a stubby pencil and an old receipt. He hands it over to Alec who quickly scribbles down their details and points over to their cottage in the distance, 'That's our place over—'

The shrill voice cuts into his words, forcing the hairs on the back of his neck to stand on end as the old lady begins to shriek again, 'I saw you! I SAW YOU!'

He and Peggy stare at one another, dread twisting at his insides as the old lady continues to point at them. Her voice is like a physical attack as they watch wide-eyed in the darkness, 'You hit her! Shouting, lots of shouting and then you hit her. I saw you! It was you - I saw you...!'

'Come on, Maude, you've done enough damage for one night. You're scaring these poor people. Let's get you inside.' The young man turns and speaks to Peggy and Alec, 'I'm so sorry. It's the Alzheimer's, you see. She does this sometimes, gets really upset and aggressive. It's just part of her condition. That's why she was able to put that lot into the bag and carry them all the way down here,' he says, pointing at the bricks and stones.

'And throw them into the middle of the bloody road!' Alec barks. A vein bulges on his temple, a crooked road of anger snaking out of his skull.

'Yes, as I said, I'm really sorry about that,' the lad replies, 'it's just that she has these fits of rage and inhuman strength. I know it doesn't look possible but sometimes she can be so strong and determined. And once she gets an idea in her head, there's no stopping her. It's really difficult for Brenda caring for her all the time and sometimes ...' his voice trails off and Alec wants to laugh out loud at the absurdity of it. Shouldn't *he* be the one here who is upset? Not this slip of a kid who seems to be fishing for sympathy.

He shakes his head in disbelief as Peggy steps forward and places her hand on the young man's arm, 'Don't worry about it. Just get your aunt back inside out of the cold and we can sort it out.'

He wants to holler at her, to tell her not to side with the enemy, to distance herself from an old woman who is screaming out to the whole of North Yorkshire that he beats his wife up, but instead stands incredulous, his attention focused on how much the damage will cost to fix. With such a high excess, it might not even be worth going through the insurance. Stupid fucking, screeching old woman with her even thicker idiot of a nephew. What kind of fool would let a demented old woman escape into the darkness onto a road right near the sea for God's sake? Perhaps madness runs in their family. Perhaps he even did it on purpose.

The pair of them head back over to the farmhouse, the tiny woman muttering under her breath with the lad soothing her and coaxing her along. Alec sighs and stares at the floor. He knows he should accompany them, *he knows that*. It's the right thing to do, to help the lad get her safely inside. She's an old lady, a tiny frail thing, but his temper is still too raw to think about anything but his car and the huge dent this whole unnecessary scenario will leave in his bank balance. Maybe tomorrow evening when he gets in from work he'll call in to see if they're all okay, talk rationally, be pleasant. Then he thinks about the old woman's accusations levelled at him and feels a tic take hold in his jaw. Or maybe not.

'Come on,' he says to Peggy through gritted teeth, 'Let's get back home. I'm fucking freezing.'

# Peggy

She wakes with the old lady's words rattling around in her head and drags herself up and into the shower before Alec even stirs. She's seen the dilapidated farmhouse in the distance before, but has always presumed it was empty. It's usually shrouded in darkness. She wonders if the old lady lives there alone or whether or not her daughter lives there with her. Such a sad existence. For both of them. Peggy tips her head back under the hot water and tries to block it out of her mind. She doesn't have room for anybody else's problems. She has enough of her own to deal with. Today she wants to stay focused, finish a few more chapters, tidy the cottage, and do her best to drag herself out of the mire she has found herself in over the past few months. It's not right, the way she has let things lapse, let her life spiral out of control. Especially her marriage. She is losing Alec. She can sense it - the rift - and it's growing wider by the day. She needs to stop it, nip it in the bud. What she actually needs to do is sharpen up her act. Alec is an attractive man. She can't risk losing him. Not now. Not after everything they have been through. Earlier in the year they almost lost one another but hung on by their fingertips. She did her utmost to sort it out, she really did, and look how that particular event turned out. An inferno starts up in her head, billowing flames attacking her brain, hot, fiery, persistent. She simply cannot go through anything like that again, so she will do whatever it takes to make sure her marriage remains intact. She has done it in the past and will do it again. Last night she had an air of confidence, she felt content, even happy. Until she saw Alec chatting to that other lady. Tall, willowy, blonde. Nothing like her. More like Sheryl. An intense load presses down on her at the thought of Sheryl. Peggy baulks and scrubs at her skin until it stings then steps out of the shower, her arms and legs red raw from the force of the exfoliating sponge that she has dragged across her body. She wraps her dressing gown around herself and stares into the mirror. The area around her eye is swollen and pulpy. Extreme heat always aggravates it, makes it seem especially raw. Like a re-opened wound. Lurking, waiting, always ready to remind her of who she is and what she's been through. She dabs at it carefully, her fingers slowly tracing the tangle of scars. It's an ever-visible reminder of how your life can suddenly be irrevocably altered, the rug pulled from under your feet at any given moment, and there's not a damn thing you can do about it.

Alec staggers through the door, naked and bleary eyed just as she wraps a towel round her head.

'You're up early,' he says, eyeing her up and down, taking in her washed hair and pink skin. 'Everything okay?'

'Everything is absolutely fine. Just thought it was time I started getting into a routine.'

Alec raises his eyebrows and nods as he stands in front of the toilet and empties his bladder, the splashing sound echoing around the bathroom as his urine hits the porcelain. Peggy stares at the amber stream and turns away as he catches her gaze, her cheeks hot with mild embarrassment.

'Good idea. Maybe you can venture into town a bit more often as well.'

Peggy is prepared for his comment. 'Getting out more' is Alec's answer to all of her problems. A catch all solution to her current predicament.

'Perhaps,' she mumbles as she sidles past him into the bedroom and shuts the door with a sharp click.

***

Peggy is dressed and making breakfast by the time Alec comes downstairs. He snatches up a slice of toast, crams it into his mouth and manages a sip of juice before he grabs his briefcase and picks up his coat... Always in a hurry.

'No time for coffee?' Peggy holds the percolator up and gives it a slight shake to entice him back.

Alec stops and looks at his watch. He sighs and shakes his head, 'Sorry, no can do. Got a meeting first thing.' He starts towards the door and stops, 'I'll be late back. I'm going to call in to the garage, get them to have a look at the front of the car. With any luck, they should be able to tap it out and T-cut it. If not ... well our bank account will be fucked for the next couple of months.'

Peggy nods, silently praying the costs will be minimal. Even if the woman in the farmhouse pays up, the whole palaver will just rile Alec and she will be left to deal with the aftermath. What she wants right now is to be able to smooth things over and get their lives back on track. The memory of Alec's hand wandering over her body last night burns bright in her mind. A glowing reminder of yet another rejection. She did her best, she really did try to go through with it but eventually feigned exhaustion and listened as he sighed heavily and rolled over away from her, silently seething before falling into a deep sleep. He has no idea why she is so averse to sex lately. He thinks it's because of the miscarriages, which in a way it is. The difference is, Alec thinks she won't make love to him because there's no point if there is no baby at the end of it but that's not it at all. She is terrified of falling pregnant again. Because falling pregnant is the easy bit. It's keeping a baby inside her that is so hard to do, and the thought of losing another one - it's almost too much to bear. It fills her with such a gnawing feeling of inadequacy. It only happens to other women, this falling pregnant business, giving birth and bringing up children. Everyone except her. Women everywhere with huge, swollen bellies, pushing buggies, chatting with their posse of yummy mummies, having three or four children; taking it all for granted. She can't bear to look at them, to be around them or even speak to them. They have no idea how fortunate they are. Not a bloody clue. They expect everything to fall into their tiny, perfectly formed little laps. And in most cases, it usually does. They have it all these women - looks, fabulous symmetrical faces, perfect little families. Everything Peggy doesn't have. What Peggy has is scars. Long, vicious lines etched deep into her face. So why would anybody as popular and handsome as Alec be interested in her? He once said in the heat of an argument after yet another rebuff, that he was convinced she was repulsed by him. If only he knew. It's actually the other way around.

Two cups of coffee later and her manuscript is almost complete; plot holes plugged, language sharpened. Peggy leans back and closes her eyes, aglow with a warm feeling of self-satisfaction. For the first time in a long while, she has a sense of regaining control. She shivers, feeling suddenly chilled, and turns to look behind her. She also has a sense, once again, of not being alone. What is it with this house? Something clicks in her brain; an uninvited thought. She brushes it aside, pushes it away to a shadowy corner. Standing up abruptly, she shakes the feeling away that somebody is close by. Absolute nonsense. It has to be. There is no such thing as ghosts. She doesn't believe in them. Never has. They belong in films and books; the only place for such rubbish. Once you are dead, you are dead. She stops and listens. There is nothing. Just a wall of silence, which is good isn't it? No more scratching or scurrying. No more faint noises that threaten to send her into a complete meltdown. The mice appear to have gone - run straight into the traps at the prospect of a chunk of chocolate. Quite sad, really. She visualises their tiny broken bodies scattered about the cold concrete floor beneath her feet, their coal black eyes, staring and lifeless in the darkest recesses of the basement. At least they're gone now. One less thing to worry about, thinks Peggy, as she shivers and stands up to turn the thermostat up as far as it will go. Bugger the cost. This cottage is bloody freezing. She needs to be warm.

# Audrey

All the papers are laid out on the floor and Audrey is kneeling over them, hands flat on the rug as her eyes roam over them all once again. This is the thing with being retired - it gives you time to think, to get things sorted in your head. When she worked as a nurse, her life was a complete blur of fitting in housework, shopping, and cooking around her working day, as well as attending a constant stream of dentists and doctors' appointments for the girls. The chores were endless, the time far too limited. But now her mind is clear, her thoughts organised and precise. Too precise. So much so, it's chilling.

She runs her hand over the printed sheets and reads them once again. Not that she needs to. Every word is etched in her brain, tattooed into her every thought. What if she's wrong? What if she's way off beam on this one? She's thought it often enough. It's not as if she has willed this on them though is it? None of this is her doing. Her eyes roam over the collection of papers spread out in front of her, re-reading every single word. She isn't though. She definitely isn't wrong. And she doesn't need this plethora of evidence to prove her point. Her memories alone could have told her what was going to happen. She knew it the first time she laid eyes on him. A small boy sitting at the corner of the street, shoulders hunched, his small fists curled up into tight little balls. A mean, thin line furrowed his brow and he sported a dark yellow bruise underneath one of his eyes. She initially felt sorry for him, sitting there all alone, not a single soul around for him to play with.

'I know you!' he had shouted after her as she unloaded the shopping bags from her car, 'you live in my street!'

'I do,' she had replied, as she slammed the boot shut and locked it, turning to look at the sad little boy who had nobody.

'Wanna see my new friend?' his voice cracked as he giggled and shook his little hands about and stared down at his lap.

Audrey had felt her stomach tighten. She had no idea why at the time, and has spent the last thirty years wishing she had gone with her gut instinct and had the good sense to ignore him and carry her bags indoors. But she didn't. He was a lonely little boy, ignored by his peers, neglected by his parents. She would just be another to add to the long list of people who had turned their backs on him. It would only take a few minutes to humour this sad, little creature and listen to what he had to say. What harm would it do to chat to a young boy who was in need of a friend? If only she had known. If only...

'See, here he is. My new mate,' he had squealed with excitement as Audrey began to stroll towards him, her heels clicking on the pavement, the noise echoing like castanets through the early morning emptiness of the street.

'I don't see him,' Audrey had murmured as she reached the boy and leaned down, squinting against the glare of the low winter sun.

'Cover your eyes,' he had whispered, his voice rising in pitch, squeaking with barely disguised excitement. 'Cover your eyes!'

He stared up at her, his black eye and unwashed face a stark reminder of how lucky she and her children were. Everyone in the area knew about Barry Wilson and his drinking problems. And how handy he was once he had seven or eight pints inside him. Which was most of the time. Social Services were a regular feature in the Wilson household, yet still the boy remained there, subjected to regular beatings day in, day out, week in, week out. Audrey had shrugged the thoughts off and held her hands still over her face as she waited. She had enough problems of her own without taking on somebody else's disasters. If the police and social services and the school didn't see any problem with letting it continue, what could she do? Be kind to the boy perhaps? Which was exactly what she was doing. He was feral, she knew that. Often embroiled in fights with other children and in trouble at school. Perhaps if she showed him a little kindness, taught him how to behave around others, some of it might stick. God knows he needed it.

'You can look now!' His voice was filled with anticipation as Audrey slowly removed her fingers and stared down, her skin turning icy cold at the sight before her. A throb took hold in her neck. Dizziness washed over her.

'Where did you find this?' Her voice was just about capable of being heard, her throat suddenly dry and thick with terror.

'Found it in the bushes,' he had replied nonchalantly unaware of her reaction to his grand unveiling.

She stared hard at the bloodied rock laid beside the bird and tried her best to ignore the sickly sensation that had settled in the pit of her stomach. An iron fist had clutched at her intestines and refused to let go as she watched the small, battered bird begin to twitch and convulse on the pavement.

'Oh, I thought it was dead,' the lad said softly as he stroked its satin feathers which were shiny and sticky with coagulated blood. And before Audrey could utter a word or stop him or do anything at all, he picked up the rock and brought it down onto the bird's small body with a loud crack.

Audrey's feet refused to work properly as she turned away, bile rising up her gullet, burning at her throat. The ground swayed violently as she stopped, fearing she might throw up on the pavement. She finally found herself able to move, her legs wobbling as she rushed home away from the mini-massacre, tears blinding her.

'Where are you going?' he had yelled after her, his voice a dim cry in the distance. 'We need to have a funeral for him! Come back. I was only trying to help him...'

Audrey brushes her hand through her hair and is surprised to see she is trembling. All these years on and that incident still has the capacity to reduce her to near tears. That was the last she saw of him. One beating too many triggered a final visit from Social

Services whereupon the lad was taken into care. Barry Wilson was arrested and imprisoned and the wife fled to the other side of the country to live with her sister. She doesn't remember the Wilson lady ever coming back, although if she had, Audrey doubts their paths would have ever crossed. They were very different people with divergent lives. The mother was a small mousy thing. Brought up on the wrong side of town; the side Audrey was never allowed to visit as a child. The only time the poor woman ever left the house was to go to the corner shop or an occasional visit to the bingo. Audrey wouldn't be seen dead near such places. She would sooner stick hot pins in her eyes than associate with the type of people who frequented the Globe Bingo Hall. It was full of fishwives and hysterical women. Not her kind of place at all. She had her embroidery and language classes to attend. Bingo was for commoners.

Audrey thought she had seen the last of the Wilson family. Or hoped she had. But then it happened. That summer afternoon; the one that still wakes her up nights, the day her fifteen-year-old daughter walked through the door with her new boyfriend on her arm. Even now Audrey's stomach plummets at the memory. The sight of her youngest daughter, all doe eyed and giggly as she stared up into the eyes of the boy Audrey once knew, the twisted child. The killer of small things.

'Mum, Dad, this is Alec,' Peggy had gushed, her words a hurried squeal of excitement.

Audrey had felt her head pound as he held out his hand for her to shake, cool and soft with manicured nails. He clearly didn't have a job that involved manual labour. And he hadn't changed that much, although admittedly he was a real looker and a darn sight healthier and happier than the sad, warped little boy she remembered from all those years back. He still had a shock of dark hair and those piercing blue eyes. She could understand Peggy's attraction to him. Of course she could. Who wouldn't fall for such a man? And had Audrey not known the sort of things he was capable of, she may have overlooked the age difference.

Peggy was only fifteen and he was almost twenty. Far too big a gap for her liking. Practically paedophilic, however one she would have been prepared to tolerate had she not known his past. But she did know and refused to ignore it. She simply couldn't find it within her to put up with that relationship. And of course, if she had overlooked it, the argument wouldn't have happened and perhaps, just perhaps, Audrey would now be in regular contact with her youngest daughter. Then at least she could make sure that Peggy knows what she knows. The darkest secret of all. The secret that once unleashed, will be impossible to put back in the Pandora's box of horrors. The secret that will rip her daughter's life into tiny pieces ...

# Peggy

Her head thumps painfully as she sits bolt upright and looks around. A trickle of saliva runs over her cheek and her throat is like sandpaper. Disorientated, Peggy squints, looks down at her watch and frowns. Two o'clock. She has no idea how long she has slept for. It certainly wasn't planned. Daytime naps aren't usually her thing but an inability to switch off at night has obviously caught up with her. The noise sends a wave of pain screeching up her spine and into her jawbone. It takes a couple of seconds for her brain to register the source of the almighty racket. The door. Someone is knocking at the front door. Scrambling up, Peggy adjusts her clothing and tugs at her hair, pulling it behind her ears with thick, clumsy fingers. She catches sight of herself in the mirror as she pads across the hallway to answer it; her make-up is slightly smeared and her hair frizzy and wild looking. Her skin is lined where she has lain on the cushion and her eye is swollen and red. She looks an absolute disgrace. Even worse than usual after being unceremoniously dragged from a deep, afternoon slumber. Her heart batters around her ribcage as the knocking becomes more insistent, developing into a furious hammering. Her stomach tightens. She isn't expecting anyone. The postman rarely knocks. They're remote enough for him to leave packages tucked down the side of the house without fear of anything getting stolen. It would take some kind of strange opportunist thief to travel up to the top of a cliff in the hope of finding anything worth stealing. The rugged path that leads up to their house is not for the faint hearted. Chamber Cottage was built as a residence for the local coastguard and stands proud on the cliff top, just close enough to the edge to make people wary.

There's only one access path that branches off from the main road and it stops right at their front door. Apart from the farmhouse on the other side of the main road, there are no other houses and the path is uneven and full of potholes. Only delivery men ever call and even that is a rarity. Which is exactly how she likes it. Peggy feels her cheeks burn as the knocking comes again. Loud, deliberate, unrelenting. Why can't they just go away? She isn't in the mood for visitors and as always, looks a complete mess. She runs her fingers through her tangled hair in a bid to freshen up her appearance and comes away with a mass of stray, wiry hairs which she throws to the floor in frustration. Wouldn't it be lovely to be the type of woman who wakes up looking mildly dishevelled but with a slightly smouldering look about her? Whereas Peggy bears the look of somebody who has been dragged through a hedge backwards. Such is her life. She should be used to it by now but every now and then she longs for a face that doesn't look as if a herd of cattle has stampeded over it. Trudging through the hallway, Peggy places her fingers around the chilly metal of the handle and stops, a cold realisation washing over her, waking her up out of her stupor. Of course. It's her. It has to be. She should have been expecting a call from her after last night's carry on out there on the road. Peggy's thudding heart falters and slows to a near normal rate as she opens the door and plasters a smile on her face. She takes in the well-groomed appearance of the woman standing there and stands aside to let her in.

'Hello,' Peggy says breathlessly, tugging at her clothes and flicking hair behind her ears in a bid to flatten it into submission, 'please come in. I thought you might call round today.'

The woman frowns slightly and steps over the threshold before following her into the living room. Peggy watches her carefully. Taller than she is, her visitor has short blonde hair cut into a bob and is wearing tight jeans and a short, brown leather jacket. Peggy guesses that she's in her late twenties or early thirties. Not what she was expecting. Not what she was expecting at all. She had envisaged somebody slightly older, stockier. Someone with an air of resilience who is tough and robust; somebody able to cope with the demands of a demented parent. This woman before her looks more like a librarian or a primary school teacher; gentle, thoughtful, passive.

Peggy offers her a seat and sits opposite, hands interlaced tightly in her lap.

They sit for a few seconds, a sharp silence lodged between them until at last Peggy speaks,

'Sorry; you caught me unawares. I didn't realise the time,' she says as she shuffles about and tugs at stray wisps of hair that have flopped in front of her face, 'anyway, I just want to say that you needn't worry too much about it all. Alec, my husband, is calling in to a garage tonight to see if he can get it sorted. We're hoping it won't cost too much.'

The woman opposite frowns and stares hard at Peggy. She leans forward and wraps her hand around her knees tightly, her knuckles white, circular bones strained against papery skin.

'I'm sorry?'

'The car,' Peggy replies, 'he's taking it into the garage to get the bumper bar assessed. It shouldn't be too much of a job. I'm pretty sure the paintwork was all still intact.'

The woman sits silently, watching Peggy talk, her eyes narrow as she assesses her words, 'Anyway, how's your aunt today? and that young man? Must have been a bit of a shock for them. He looked pretty upset about it all ... Brenda. Sorry, that's your name, isn't it? Your cousin mentioned about how difficult it is for you and I just want to say if you ever need any help at all don't hesitate to call. My gran had dementia. It was terrible to watch. Such a cruel disease.' Peggy stops, aware she is rambling slightly.

The blonde lady shakes her head, her mouth slightly open and a puzzled expression on her face. Her hair swings softly as she moves her head from side to side. A frown has etched itself across her forehead as she starts to speak, a channel of confusion.

'I don't know what you're talking about, I'm afraid,' she says, a slight tremble in her voice, 'I don't know anything about a car or a young boy or dementia. And I'm not Brenda.'

A familiar stirring starts up in Peggy's chest again, clattering its way up her throat. She suddenly feels very silly. And concerned. If this woman isn't the lady from the farmhouse here to discuss the car, then who the hell is she?

'Right,' Peggy murmurs, her calm tone belying the rising inner turmoil she is starting to feel. 'Sorry about that. I was expecting a call from a lady about a minor accident we had last night out on the road back from Lythe.'

The other woman nods in recognition, the line above her eyes deepening as she listens to the garbled explanation. Her lashes flutter slightly as she concentrates; as if the words she wants to say can't quite find their way out.

'No problem,' she replies softly after a few seconds of deep thought, 'I hope you don't mind me calling unannounced but I didn't know what else to do. You see, I'm beginning to feel quite desperate.' She takes a deep breath, her mouth trembling slightly.

Peggy watches as her eyes glass over and a lone tear escapes and runs down her cheek unchecked. A tight band has begun to wrap itself around Peggy's chest as she waits for this forlorn creature in her living room to tell her why she is here.

'It's fine,' Peggy whispers. That's all she can manage right now. She holds her breath, waiting for the story to unfold, 'I just hope I can help you as you seem quite upset.'

She doesn't know what else to say or do or how to placate this stranger sitting here in her living room on a dark autumn afternoon. What else is there to say?

'It's just that I know you and your husband are quite good friends with her and I've spoken to the other friends and they said you might be able to help because they don't seem to know anything …' she stops, her breath coming out in small gasps, 'so I was just wondering if you've heard from her recently?' Another tear rolls down her face and spreads along her jaw in a shimmering wet line.

'Heard from who? Sorry I don't quite follow,' Peggy leans forward and tries to make eye contact with the weeping woman who is now struggling to hold it together. Her eyes glisten with tears as she meets Peggy's gaze.

'My sister. I'm Rachel and I was hoping you might know something. Maybe she told you? She didn't tell me anything.'

Tears now begin to cascade down her cheeks, brisk and unchecked, a river of anxiety. Her face is suddenly a damp, snotty mess. She brings her arm up and rubs at her eyes which are pink and streaked with rivulets of black mascara. Peggy stares at her sodden face then stands up, grabs a tissue from the box on the coffee table and hands it over. Rachel takes it and presses it hard against her eyes before sighing heavily and dragging it over her face in a rough circular motion. She sniffs deeply and lets out a long trembling sigh, her chin quivering with the effort.

'Sorry, it's been such a stressful time lately. I'm just asking all of her friends if they know anything and one of them gave me your address so I hope you don't mind me calling here?'

Peggy feels as if she has been submerged underwater, everything suddenly distorted and muffled. What on earth is this woman expecting from her? She has no idea how to reply or what to do.

'I'm really sorry, Rachel, but I'm still in the dark here. I don't think we even know each other.'

'We don't,' the young woman replies as she shuffles her backside around then stretches out and stuffs the tissue deep into the pocket of her jeans, 'it's my sister that you know. That's who it is I'm looking for. It's Sheryl who knows you and your husband.'

'Sheryl?' Peggy feels the oxygen being sucked out of the room as she speaks. She swallows and tries to control a wave of vomit that threatens to travel up her gullet as she hangs onto the arm of the chair to keep herself steady. *Sheryl ...*

'Yes, Sheryl is my sister and she's gone missing. She has — well ...' Rachel takes a deep, rattling breath and looks around the room before speaking again, 'she's left home. And apart from a text message saying she was leaving to get her head together, it's as if she has just disappeared into thin air.'

It takes all of Peggy's resolve to stay upright, her body threatening to cave in on itself. A line of pain travels up her abdomen and circles around her neck, a wild, throbbing ache that makes her feel quite sick. She has to hold it together in front of this lady. Sheryl is gone. Disappeared she said.

'I - I don't know what to say,' Peggy stammers, her heart crunching madly in her chest.

'You haven't heard from her then?' Rachel says, a glimmer of hope evident in her expression.

'I'm sorry, no, I've not seen her in a while.'

Peggy watches as a veil of sadness and disappointment descends over her face. There's nothing Peggy can say to make any of this better. She wishes she could send a stream of platitudes Rachel's way but finds herself without a voice. She wants to say that perhaps it's better that Sheryl has taken herself off and that she was nothing but a devious troublemaker but remains silent instead, her mind too frazzled to say the right words.

'Okay, well I'm sorry for bothering you. I just hope that - anyway, if you hear from her will you please contact me?'

Rachel hands over a piece of paper with her details on it. Peggy stares at it, wishing she could tell this poor creature something positive.

'Of course I will,' she whispers, her eyes misting over as Sheryl's face looms large in her mind. Gorgeous, vibrant, effervescent Sheryl who would stop at nothing to get exactly what she wanted.

'Thank you.' Rachel leans over and places her hand over Peggy's. Her skin is warm to the touch, unlike Peggy's ice-cold fingers.

'My pleasure,' Peggy replies quietly as she stands up and shows Rachel to the door.

\*\*\*

Peggy watches as Rachel drives off, her car a small speck in the distance, before she closes the door and leans back on it heavily. Should she inform Alec of this visit? Or is it best she keeps it to herself? Either way the fact remains that Sheryl has gone missing.

Left *to get her head together*. Any mention of her will send Alec into a spin. Probably best to leave it. For now, anyway. She's not even sure she could bring herself to have that particular conversation. She rests her head back on the cold glass of the door before slumping down onto the floor in a crumpled heap, her stomach slowly turning to water. She curls up on her side, hands tucked under the side of her head and begins to sob.

# Alec

It's been a bastard of a day. Staff squabbling, children brawling, and now this.

'So, what you gonna do about it then? I want to see some heads roll.' The woman sits with her arms folded, a scowl plastered across her shiny, acne-ridden face. The husband leans forward and bangs his fist on the table causing a stack of papers to fall to the floor. They float past Alec's legs and scatter around his feet, a carpet of confidential documents strewn far and wide. He leaves them there. No way is he going to take a lower vantage point and break eye contact with these two. He doubts either of them is even capable of reading and digesting the contents of the papers anyway. They contain a heap of educational esoteric jargon, littered with acronyms and the latest buzzwords. Not an easy read even for those in the know.

He eyes the pair of them cautiously. He's seen the way they carry on, arguing with other parents, bringing their kids in late with a stream of inane excuses, constantly pushing the boundaries with a refusal to adhere to school policies regarding uniform or attendance, or any bloody thing really. According to the children's teachers, neither pupil has ever completed a scrap of homework and they constantly spend their time bragging about staying up on their Xboxes and PlayStations till the early hours of the morning. And now here they are, the parents who feed their kids coke and chocolate for breakfast, wanting to lodge an official complaint against a newly qualified teacher because one of their offspring watched a 12 certificate film when they haven't signed the consent form. Jesus. Some people just love moaning and making their voices heard even if what they have to say is utter tripe.

'She had no fucking right, subjecting our kid to stuff like that without our consent.' The man turns to look at his wife who is nodding vehemently, her brow now so furrowed Alec feels sure he could shove his whole fist in there and she wouldn't even notice.

'I can see how upset you are but if I can just ask that we steer clear of using foul and abusive language it would be very much appreciated. Now let's see if we can resolve this issue so that everybody feels satisfied with the outcome.' Alec's brain is reciprocating, screaming a stream of obscenities at them while he smiles and remains polite and courteous. All in a day's work.

The man grimaces at Alec's words but knows better than to argue.

'Now, I'm led to believe that the film in question was in keeping with the class topic which is WWII, and it was a film that was made ostensibly for a young adult audience.' Alec leans down and picks up the DVD that he placed under his desk in readiness for their visit. He brandishes it in the air and points to the title, *The Boy in the Striped Pyjamas*. This is the one, yes?'

Both parents lean forward and scan the cover before looking at each other for affirmation.

'Is that the one?' the father says, as his eyes roam over the case for clues, 'Our Troy said it was about a kid that ran around half naked and then ended up getting murdered at the end. Bloody disgraceful if you ask me. Whatever happened to letting kids watch cartoons and stuff eh? *Age appropriate*. Isn't that what you would call it?'

Alec slides the DVD over the desk towards the parents and leans back slightly in his seat, 'Have you seen this film Mr. Boyd?' He watches them silently, savouring the moment.

Boyd's face reddens at Alec's words. His wife snatches up the case and squints as she reads the synopsis on the back. Alec notices her hand is shaking slightly as she nudges her husband and passes it to him, a dark shadow passing over her face. He reluctantly takes it and stares hard at it, turning the cover over and over with his large, dirt-ingrained fingers. He places it down on the desk with a clatter and meets Alec's gaze.

'Right. It's about WWII. But it's still a 12 certificate and our Troy is only eleven,'

'Only turned eleven last week as well!' Mrs Boyd chips in, and they both nod as if this piece of information somehow strengthens their argument, gives credence to their complaint.

'Yes, so his teacher said. Now from what I'm led to believe, she sent at least two consent forms home for you to sign, possibly even three?'

They sit in silence, their simmering anger palpable. Mr Boyd's nostrils flare - dark, pock marked and vaguely unsettling as he waits for Alec to continue.

'And none of those slips came back, which left us with a bit of a problem. Obviously, we wanted Troy to be part of the lesson as this film is very informative and crucial to the piece of writing the pupils were going to complete after watching it.'

Alec watches and notices that Mrs Boyd is starting to look distinctly uncomfortable. Or is it just his imagination? He hopes it's the former. He's about to present his trump card.

'So, in line with school policy and procedure, we got your contact numbers from our records and tried to ring you to get verbal consent.' Alec is convinced the mother has got the gist of where this conversation is heading. He continues, feeling slightly smug. He enjoys the self-satisfied sensation that is giving him a warm glow, 'but unfortunately all the numbers we have for you on file are no longer in use. Can I just ask, have you changed phones lately, Mr and Mrs Boyd?'

He watches a crimson flush creep up both of their faces and waits patiently for a reply, 'because there was another reminder sent home for parents to inform school of any changes to contact details in case of an emergency ...'

The silence in the room threatens to swamp them until eventually Mr Boyd clears his throat and turns to face his wife, 'Right, well look, we can't sit here all afternoon. We need be off don't we, Annie?

I'll give our Troy those numbers to bring in tomorrow morning. We told him he must have got it wrong wi' that film but he went on and on at us saying some of the kids were crying and stuff, didn't he, Annie?'

Mrs Boyd nods emphatically, 'He's a right one for spinning a tale is our Troy. We shoulda known really.'

They smile at Alec and roll their eyes. He nods and stands up then offers his hand to shake. They both take it and leave the office exchanging pleasantries like old friends. He closes the door behind them and slumps into his seat thinking perhaps the Boyd's aren't so bad after all. They were easily bamboozled and that always helps. Troy and his younger sibling may be a bit of a handful but it could be a whole lot worse. No fists to the face or a father who drinks himself into a stupor. At least the Boyd's listen to their children, taking notice of what goes on in their lives. Not like Alec's own father who once beat him with a belt when Alec started to tell him he had come 1st in cross-country. It was a hot afternoon and Alec had danced on air all the way home, itching to tell everyone and anyone who was prepared to listen, that he had won. His dad was sitting on the doorstep basking in the late afternoon sunshine, beer can in hand, when Alec came sailing around the corner. He should have been prepared for some sort of backlash; experience should have taught him that Barry Wilson wasn't the kind of father who took pride in his son's achievements, but the adrenaline was still coursing through his system and he always lived in hope. Bounding up the street, he mistook his father's nod at his appearance as a show of interest in his day. Worst move ever. Alec had walked up to him, brimming with excitement, blurting out the details of his victory.

'1st you say, eh son?' he had mumbled, the can placed at his lips as he eyed his small son up and down.

'1st, dad!' Alec had squeaked, too young and naive to notice the subtle change in his father's temperament, too young and sensitive to realise what was about to happen.

'Showing off now are yer?' his dad had growled, his yellow teeth visible as he tipped his head back and drained the can before tossing it into the street with a clatter. The empty tin rolled around the pavement, tiny spurts of beery foam dripping from the lip before finally lodging in the gutter, rocking back and forth, its metallic echo filling the soft, unnatural silence between them.

Alec had felt himself shut down. The beating didn't last for too long. Not as long as some of the previous ones had. After scanning the street for witnesses, Barry had grabbed his son's arm and dragged him indoors, punching and smacking at anything he could connect with. It did last long enough however, to leave a line of red welts on the young boy's back that stayed hidden from view until they had healed over. Six weeks they took to disappear. Six weeks of slipping into his P.E. shirt at breakneck speed to avoid the glances of suspecting teachers or the probing questions of fellow classmates. Six long, painful, worrying weeks …

Alec wiggles his jaw, a headache beginning to form deep in his temples. He closes his briefcase with a crack and grabs his coat from the back of his chair. No, he thinks, considering what some families go through each and every day, the Boyd family aren't such a bad lot after all.

*'You came back to me.'*

*'I haven't come back to you. I'm here for other reasons. We need to talk.'*

*Fingers drumming on wood, an atmosphere thick with anxiety.*
*'About what?'*

*'You know what.'*

*'I don't know what.'*

*'Yes, you do. Stop being deliberately obtuse.'*

*'I don't want to hear this. You need to turn back around and go. Don't say things that I don't want to hear.'*

*'If I go, I won't be coming back here again. And we must never speak of this. Ever.'*

*'And what if I do?'*

'Do what?'

'Speak of it.'

'Is that a threat?'

'You really think so little of me that I would start issuing threats? Jesus ...'

Anger slowly festering; resentment; fear. Deep rooted fear at the thought of the loss. An unbearable, gaping hole where love should be, where loved used to be.

'It's over. You know it is.'

'Why? Why does it need to be over?'

'Because it does. It should never have started. You know that.'

'So, you're saying it was a mistake? You're saying I was a mistake?'

'That's not what I said. You're twisting my words.'

'Just unpicking the real meaning of them. You're too scared to say it, that's all it is.'

'I'm not too scared to say anything. What I am saying is, this is over. This relationship is finished.'

'So, you walk in here and think you can call all the shots? Who the fuck do you think you are?'

'I'm leaving now. It would be easier if we didn't see each other again.'

'Easier for who? Jesus what a fucking narcissist you are! Not everything is about you, you know!'

'Easier for both of us. Stop this right now. You're being deliberately difficult. I thought you were better than this.'

A shriek of anger, furniture scraping, pushing, falling.

'Stop this!'

Arms flailing in defence. More pushing. Screaming. The rush of heat as a hand connects with a face. A pause, the prevailing mood charged with fear and retribution.

'Don't ever touch me again. EVER.'

'I hope I never see you again. Get the fuck out of my house!'

'Don't worry, I'm leaving. Never to return.'

'Good! Now get out of here before I fucking kill you with my bare hands ...'

*'Kill me? Jesus. Just listen to yourself. You are a complete psychopath. How did I not see that before? And you call yourself a professional? I should report you for this. You're not fit to hold your position.'*

*'GET OUT!'*

*'Oh, don't worry. I'm leaving.'*

*A door slams. Weeping, growing in crescendo. A sudden almighty shriek. Then silence ...*

# Maude

She leans over and rummages in the corner of the sideboard drawer. It's in here somewhere. She's sure of it. It's been a long time since she has written anything but she knows there's one of those things stuffed away; probably tucked right at the back, hidden from view. Or was it in one of the kitchen cupboards? Brenda often hides things from her and lately Maude seems to get so muddled and forgetful. Sometimes it's hard to keep up with all the alterations that go on around here. Only last week the cooker and the fridge changed places. Just like that. One day the oven was on the left and the next it was against the right-hand wall next to the window. She didn't worry too much about it. After all, this isn't her house, is it? As she keeps on reminding Brenda, she's only lived here for a short while. She's just looking after it for a friend. Maude's own house was bombed a few weeks back and she's still waiting to get a new one. Goodness knows when that will happen but then what can she expect? There is a war on after all. She'll just have to be patient.

A handful of books cascade down on her head knocking her against the wall as she pulls at the contents of the shelf in the dresser. Stunned, Maude stops and touches her temple. Red. Her face has red on it. She thinks she knows what it is but can't be entirely certain. She'll just wait here a minute until she stops feeling dizzy and then it might come to her. That's just how it is lately. Everything takes time. Much longer than it used to. Maude closes her eyes for a second and when she opens them it's all different again and she can't quite remember where she is or why she is here. Looking round she decides to sit down. Her head hurts and she doesn't know what is causing it. A pile of newspapers sits on the coffee table next to her seat. On the top of the papers is a thin silver thing. She leans over and picks it up. Narrowing her eyes, she studies it, turning it around and around in her tiny, pale fingers. Words dart in and out of her head, all jumbled and confusing. She takes her time - tries to slow them down until eventually it all becomes clear to her. A pen! That's it. A pen is what she wanted. She stares at the newspapers. All covered in words and pictures, no space to write anything. Maude takes a look around the room, casting her eyes over every surface and shelf. Lots of things - books, more newspapers, items she can't remember the names of. But nothing for her to write on. Why is everything so hard to find in this place? It's that woman, that Brenda. She hides things. Puts them away so Maude can't get to them. She leans back in her chair and wonders where that Brenda lady is. Some days she seems to disappear for hours at a time. At least it feels that way. Where is she right now for instance when Maude needs something to write on?

A scraping sound diverts her attention away from all thoughts of Brenda. Maude turns around to see a young man standing behind her. She lets out a small shriek and pushes herself back into the cushions, her body bending almost double as he approaches her.

'Where's Brenda? I want Brenda!'

'Aunt Maude, it's me.' He holds up his hands but Maude continues to sink back into the fabric of the sofa, her eyes wide with fear.

'It's Andrew. I'm here to keep you company. I was just upstairs for a minute.' He steps forward and lets out a deep breath, 'Maude, what's happened to your head?' Kneeling down on his haunches he takes a tissue from his pocket and dabs at the side of her face.

'Somebody hit me. Or it might have been the bombs. That's probably what it was - I did it when the roof came in. Dust everywhere and bits of bricks and sand falling in on me,' she says, nodding vehemently, her fingers reaching up to the wet patch on her temple.

'Well I'm sure it would be a lot worse if a bomb had hit you. If I'm not in the room, Aunt Maude, you need to remember to stay in your seat. I was only in the bathroom for a minute.' He gently removes the rest of the blood and smoothes her hair down with his long, slender fingers.

'What would you know about it? You weren't here, were you? You were too busy off gallivanting with that Doreen from number forty-three. You need to watch her, she's a right one she is. A proper floozy.'

Andrew smiles and stands up, 'I wasn't with Doreen, Maude. I was here all the time.'

'Where?' She stares up at him with small, dark eyes.

'Here, in your house. I haven't been with Doreen.'

'Who's Doreen?'

Andrew sighs and looks at his watch, 'Brenda'll be back soon.'

'Has she got the thing to write on?' Maude is still watching him. She does that sometimes and it unnerves him, as if she can read his mind. This house doesn't help - an old farmhouse out on its own. No neighbours or streetlights. The only other place in the vicinity is that old cottage near the end of the cliff half a mile or so away. He shudders when he thinks of that incident last night. Jesus, that was close. Maude could have been injured or even worse. He blocks the thought of it out of his mind and rubs at his eyes as he stares outside. If it's isolation you crave, then Aunt Maude's farmhouse is the place to be. He only offered to do this babysitting malarkey to help his cousin out and to shut his mum up. It's all right for her. She's on holiday in Tenerife right now, sunning it up with Ron, his stepdad. The money is good though. He felt guilty initially for taking it but Brenda insisted. Said she was managing to get loads of overtime in at the hospital now he was around to help look after Maude, so it isn't a problem. And it's not for long. Brenda is selling this place and taking Maude to live with her in Whitby. With the money from the farmhouse she can afford to employ a full-time carer to look after her mum while she's out at work. Bit of a shit existence for both of them though, especially Brenda. Maude's mood changes can be horrific. So far, he has only witnessed one and that was bad enough. At only five feet two inches and weighing next to nothing, Maude somehow managed to pick up a solid wood dining chair and throw it across the room missing the window by only a couple of centimetres.

'So, has she?' Maude is scrutinising his face closely. Andrew snaps out of his thoughts and stares at her.

'Has she what, Maude?' His voice is gentle. He doesn't want to frighten her in any way or upset the fine balance that he's managed to create in Brenda's absence. It's draining being this thoughtful all the time, keeping the noise down to stop her tipping over the edge.

'Got some of the white stuff for me to use this on?'

Maude holds up the silver pen she has found and brandishes it in Andrew's face.

'Paper?' he says. 'I can get some for you if that's what you're after. Why do you want paper, Maude?'

She taps the side of her nose and smiles enigmatically, 'That's my secret, young man.' Her white, flyaway hair flops comically from side to side as she shakes her head at him, 'You'll see soon enough, young fella. You'll see soon enough.'

# Peggy

She is all fingers and thumbs as she drags her wellington boots on and shoves her arms into her wax jacket. Dark clouds have filled the vast sky and the temperature has plummeted. Pulling on her gloves, she steps outside, the wind catching her by surprise, leaving her breathless and disorientated.

Peggy trudges down the gravel path that leads to the main road. She is heading down to the beach, desperate to clear her head. Deciding she needs the exercise, she takes the rugged route away from the main road. It consists of a well-trodden furrow that spirals down the steep bank at the far end of the cliff. Tourists coming up to take in the view sometimes attempt it and most are thwarted by the sheer incline. It's a good mile away from Chamber Cottage but well worth the walk. Traffic-free apart from the sudden drop at the other end, it is a twisting, partly gravelled path that funnels into the side of the road, an area known to locals as Devil's Hook, due to its staff shaped curve and proximity to the fast-moving cars below.

Head down against the gathering wind, Peggy sets off, her eyes already streaming from the cold before she has barely begun. Her fingers trace the shape of the torch she keeps in her pocket, an item she uses all year round when out walking - a must in this neck of the woods. Rumour has it that many years back a young girl became lost and disorientated after a lovers' tiff and plummeted to her death over the edge of the cliff. Her boyfriend, in a bid to find and placate her, met with the same fate. After hearing her cries, he had followed the sound and tumbled over just five minutes later. Peggy shivers at the thought. It's not as if it's even a clean drop. More of a rugged curve, making the descent more treacherous. According to local reports, they hit every rock and boulder on the way down. By the time their bodies were discovered on the beach below a few hours later, they were an unrecognisable snarl of bones and blood spread far and wide. Two young people reduced to no more than fodder for the circling gulls and gannets.

Peggy lengthens her stride. The nights are getting shorter and although she doesn't mind being out on her own in the dark, given the choice, she would sooner get back before the sun dips beneath the horizon. Her breath mists up in front of her and she feels her hair begin to take on a life of its own in the damp autumn air. By the time she gets home it will be sticking out at all angles, a huge, wild mess of knots and tangles. She pulls her collar up and dips her head down. It hardly matters. This is the North Sea at its finest - fierce, unpredictable, unspeakably beautiful.

It doesn't take long to reach the bottom. Her trusty wellingtons hold her fast as she stumbles down the last couple of feet onto the side of the tarmac. A lone car hurtles past, almost dragging her along in its slipstream. She hobbles along the edge, hugging the inside of the white line until she eventually reaches the path that leads down to the beach. There are a handful of dog walkers about but in the main, the place is deserted. Peggy feels her soul lighten. This is perfect. Too early in the afternoon for those who are still at work and too cold and drizzly for the less hardy. It's amazing the effect a bit of weather can have on people, sending them scurrying indoors once the temperature dips and the sea takes on its pre-winter swell. Not Peggy though. She loves a good storm. It means she has the place to herself. Just how she likes it. Crowds have never been her thing. Even before her scars, which make her want to curl up and disappear, she always preferred solitude over socialising. Kicking a collection of stones out of her way, she marches onto the sand, enjoying the sinking sensation as she treads amongst the shards of rotting wood and broken shells. In the distance, a line of sodden seaweed clings to the edge of the water while the tide rhythmically pushes its way in. Her walk will be shorter than she anticipated. Should have checked the tide times. A silly and marginally dangerous move for a seasoned beach walker but then her afternoon took on an unexpected twist leaving her feeling slightly off kilter. More than slightly, truth be told. She spent a good hour after Rachel left, trudging around the house, thinking about Sheryl. Why is it everything always seems to come back to bloody Sheryl? Checking her watch, Peggy stares ahead at the swelling shoreline. She should have an hour or so before the water begins to creep its way up the cliff face. Too many folk misjudge the rapidity of the sea and its all-encompassing power. Every few weeks the local lifeboat is called out to the aid of people cut off by the tide. So thoughtless and completely avoidable. Peggy watches it all unfold from her living room window and wonders when people will ever learn. You can't fight the ebb and flow of the deluge of water that crashes into these cliffs. It's the most powerful thing Peggy has ever witnessed and it would take a special kind of stupid to think they could survive it.

Twenty minutes is all it takes to walk the stretch of sand that sits at the foot of the cliff face. Peggy turns and stares up at the speck that is her cottage; a small white building overlooking the vast coastline of the north-east of England. She stops, breathless and ruddy faced, and thinks that no matter how often she walks this route, the sheer enormity of what nature has created never ceases to fill her with awe. She delves in her pocket to retrieve a tissue. Dabbing at her eyes, Peggy ponders over how difficult life must have been hundreds of years ago, living up in Chamber Cottage with no heating or indoor plumbing. The privy at the bottom of their garden is a daily reminder of the struggle families must have gone through. She has often tried to imagine hot footing it to the outside toilet for a pee at two in the morning, in the dead of winter, with no light and a howling gale biting at your face. Doesn't bear thinking about. The place is freezing at the best of times never mind two centuries ago with no heating or hot water to hand. And then of course there were the rogues and beachcombers to deal with. And the smugglers. For years the rumour mill has churned out stories of how a certain smuggler was so successful at his trade, he built a house in a neighbouring village where he stored his contraband. That much is true. The house still stands, a grandiose edifice built from his ill-gotten gains. But how he managed to smuggle them unseen whilst under the watchful gaze of the coastguard is another story. Without any substance to their stories or any evidence to speak of, people claim he built a series of tunnels under the cliffs that are still there, all of them leading to the large white house perched high up on the cliffs in the village beyond. Peggy smiles every time she reads about it. Such ignorance from people who are convinced they know every inch of this place. As if a crudely built tunnel carved under the cliff could reach the two or so miles to the next village. Stupid really, but then it makes for a good story to tell the tourists. And everyone loves a good tale, don't they?

Peggy stares down at the foaming water that is beginning to gather at her feet. Time to head back. The last thing she wants is to become one of the idiots she regularly scorns as they become stranded and cut off by the tide. Picking up her pace, Peggy heads back towards the other end of the sand, invisible fingers of wind pushing at her back, buffeting her along. She still hasn't worked out what to tell Alec, or indeed whether she should say anything at all. The thought of anything to do with Sheryl makes her feel physically sick. For the most part, she has finally managed to block that woman out of her brain. She is a forgotten person in their everyday lives. Or at least that's what she has tried to tell herself. Besides which, Alec sees it as some sort of failure on his part if her name is brought up.

The image of Sheryl's face has implanted itself in her head as she trudges back along the sand. Sheryl's sister did the wrong thing coming to see Peggy this afternoon. If, as she says, Sheryl has gone away to clear her head, then why hasn't she left the whole sorry scenario alone? And according to Rachel, the police have more or less said the very same thing but she is refusing to settle for that - setting up a Facebook page to find her sister even though the police haven't yet officially filed her as missing.

Peggy can recall the first time she met Sheryl. So clear in her mind. It had been through a mutual friend while they were at a function to celebrate the thirtieth birthday of a close friend. Heads had turned as she sashayed her way into the room, her gold sequinned dress shimmering and glinting under the glare of the rotating disco lights. Peggy had wanted to shrink away, disappear into the ether as she watched this glamorous creature captivate the hearts and minds of everyone she came into contact with. Including Alec. He was practically putty in her hands. Other friends failed to see it; Sheryl's outward charms and devious ways. But Peggy saw it. She observed from a distance as she wrapped everyone around her little finger, oozing confidence and so much sex appeal it was actually painful to watch. Sheryl was undeniably gorgeous. The kind of gorgeous that made Peggy want to crawl away and hide her head in shame, disappear under the duvet and claw at her face till it bled. Too self-conscious to be in the same company as somebody so outstandingly beautiful and charming, Peggy began to draw away from parties and functions. What she didn't expect was for Sheryl to try to contact her, to be her friend, to try to cajole her into socialising again. A gust of wind takes her by surprise and Peggy looks up to see the water lapping at a thin stretch of sand in the distance. A sinking sensation settles in her gut. She is going to have to run at an almighty speed before the tide reaches her. How could she have been so stupid? She knows this beach like the back of her hand, constantly scanning the shoreline from her window, watching the waves as they greedily suck at the cliff face, dragging chunks of rock away with each hit. She even listens to the Shipping Forecast for God's sake and knows all about the moderate and rough sea states in 'Dogger, Tyne'. Yet here she is, almost trapped at the foot of the cliffs, just a short distance away from her own home, her mind filled with thoughts of Sheryl. *Shit!*

Picking up her pace, Peggy starts to gallop, her feet sinking into the sand, its forceful suction action slowing her down, pulling her to the floor. She begins to pant hard. It's like wading through treacle. Her legs burn and her breath escapes in short, sharp bursts. What if she doesn't make it? She visualises her demise, the sheer force of the mountainous, foaming waves hauling her out to sea. Then the aftermath when her body is washed up further down the beach. And of course, the press reporting on her - analysing her history, digging into her past. They would love nothing more than to rip apart and publicly dissect her life, a local-born writer with issues and secrets. That's what they do, isn't it? Tear people down and let the public have a feeding frenzy with the remains. Well, that's not going to happen. With a sudden surge of energy, Peggy tears across the dirt-brown sand, her thighs going into spasm, her calves threatening to seize up at any given moment. By the time she reaches the other side, the water is already up to her knees, her wellies filling with freezing water. She feels its grasping, icy claws as it wraps its way around her legs, desperate to pull her back into its murky depths. Not this time. Not any time. Tears blinding her and snot streaming, she trips and falls into the freezing foam, letting out a sharp shriek as an icy wave laps over her back. She looks up, frantic for help; the place is completely devoid of people. All sensible, all at home, battening down the hatches. With one final push, Peggy throws herself out of the water, away from its strengthening grip and is able to half walk, half crawl out of the sea, her wet hair hanging over her face in huge, black, sodden clumps.

Hobbling up to her feet, she staggers onto the path and then slumps down again, ripping the wellies off and emptying them of sea water before plunging her soaking feet back in them, wincing at the sensation. She begins the long walk back up to Chamber Cottage, wet jeans scraping at her skin with each step, chafing her freezing, sore legs.

By the time she arrives, her teeth are chattering violently. The thought of slipping into a hot foamy bath kept her going for most of the way back up, stopped her from giving up.

With trembling, numb fingers that refuse to work as they should, she clumsily slips the key into the lock and steps inside over the pile of post on the mat. Grabbing the wad of envelopes, she heads straight to the bathroom and placing them tightly between her knees, leans over the bath and turns the hot tap on, enjoying the feel of the pulsating heat as the water begins to cascade into the wide porcelain tub. It doesn't take long to fill and Peggy is grateful to writhe her way out of her wet clothes, her skin pink and mottled as she peels them off. She throws her wet jeans into the laundry basket and climbs into the bath, leaning back and closing her eyes, the hot water a welcome sensation against her freezing flesh. It laps over her stomach and breasts as she slides further down, the snow-white bubbles forming a peak at the base of her throat. She lies still, feeling her skin sizzle under the hot water, enjoying the tingling sensation that starts at her feet and works its way up her body. Tears unexpectedly prick the back of her eyes and a lump rises in her throat. How could she have made such a stupid mistake? A schoolboy error on her part. She knows this stretch of the sea, is in tune with its ebb and flow, its propensity for change, its ability to draw you into its vast, clawing depths in a matter of seconds.

She swallows hard and blinks the tears away, remembering the stack of letters next to her in a pile on the floor. Sitting up, Peggy leans down and picks them up - British Gas, Northumbrian Water, Tesco Clubcard points. Nothing too exciting. She stares at the unmarked envelope. No address, no stamp. Possibly another offer for tokens to spend at a local supermarket or an advance notice about roadworks being carried out at the bottom of the cliff. God knows it's needed. The entire stretch is a death-trap and some sort of improvement is long overdue. She rips it open, ready to toss the contents onto the floor, and feels a pulse start up in her neck as she pulls a piece of paper out and stares at it in horror. Sheryl's face jumps out at her from an A4 sheet with the words MISSING typed above it. At the bottom in a distinctively recognisable scrawl that turns Peggy's stomach and makes her want to throw up are the words, *WE NEED TO TALK.*

# Audrey

udrey sits in the car park opposite the beach. It's an empty sprawl of uneven, cracked concrete littered with holes, discarded crisp packets, and battered coke cans that roll around in the prevailing wind. It never ceases to amaze and disgust her how some people don't seem to care. They barge their way through life, discarding items, leaving them for others to clean up. Such thoughtlessness. Such arrogance. She drums her fingers on the steering wheel and stares up at the house on top of the cliff, wondering if she has done the right thing. The timing had to be just right. She didn't want to do it when he was around but she also didn't want to run the risk of Peggy seeing her. She could have done the obvious thing and driven to where he works to make absolutely certain he is where he should be. She has been doing that for some time now, following him. Men like Alec Wilson can't be trusted, you see. They say one thing and do another. And they are everywhere, these philanderers; leading double lives, ruining families. She has spent the last six months or so doing a bit of research, following his every move, and what she found out about him didn't surprise her. Not one little bit. He has been seeing someone else. Of course he has. But then what else did she expect from someone with such a dreadful upbringing? No thought for others. The morals of an alley cat. The idea of keeping track of his movements didn't actually start out as anything sinister. She simply wanted to see her daughter, albeit from a distance. She has tried for so many years now to make contact, to attempt to explain to Peggy how much she misses her family and how lonely she is since the death of Peter, but, of course, she tried it at his funeral and look how that went. Peggy shouting at her to stay away, holding her hand up to her eye, screaming at Alec for him to rescue her from her mother. Her own mother for heaven's sake! As if she would hurt her own daughter. How little Peggy actually knows her own mum. If anything, she has remained loyal over the years, not disclosing what she knows about Alec's past.

Audrey shakes her head sadly thinking of that Sheryl woman and what could have happened to her. She hoped Alec would turn out to be a better man than his father but with this piece of awful news it seems like his past has finally caught up with him. The apple rarely falls far from the tree, does it?

Three men in black wetsuits carrying multi-coloured surfboards stalk past her car and run onto the sand before flinging themselves head first into the frothing waves. *Risk takers* thinks Audrey. The world is full of them, diving into the freezing sea, jumping off buildings, climbing up mountains without any harnesses or safety equipment. She sometimes wonders what the world is coming to with such behaviours. Or maybe she is too old fashioned. She just doesn't see the point of it all. Life is hard enough. Why anybody would want to make things even more difficult for themselves is beyond her. They must have easy and unfulfilled lives, these people, if they feel the need to throw themselves into the face of danger just to prove they exist.

Her gaze follows them as they ride the crest of an inordinately high wave that carries them up in an arc and then down again. The whole spectacle is surreal, the sort of sight you would only expect to see in exotic, far flung places, not here on the north-east coast where the weather is challenging to say the very least. She continues to watch, her eyes flickering along the length of the horizon and over to the foot of the cliffs. That's when she sees her. *Peggy!* She is sure of it. *Peggy! Her Peggy* … She's a fair way off but Audrey can tell that it's definitely her. She would know her own children even if she were blindfolded. Any decent mother would. She feels overwhelmed with affection and wants to laugh out loud. There was no need to creep around the side of the house and plead with the postman to take her letter after all.

Peggy was down here all the time. Audrey feels her heart swell as she observes the young woman in the distance, strolling along the beach. Like a character out of a film. She watches for a short while, her eyes misting over with decades of unshed tears, a lump the size of a large rock stuck firmly in her gullet. This is what she has missed out on for so many years. It should be her living up there with Peggy, not him. He might have pulled the wool over everyone else's eyes but he hasn't fooled her. She has him all worked out, knows what goes through his head; knows what sort of depraved things make him tick. A flicker in her peripheral vision cuts into her thoughts. The crashing wave that the surfers are so keenly riding rises up, spreading along the entire coastline, gaining in momentum and pushing the sea further and further in at such a rapid pace, that within minutes, the remaining expanse of sand is covered with water. Audrey watches in horror as Peggy is dragged down by a smaller wave and falls to her knees with a crash. She grasps at the door handle, twisting it open, and is up and out of the driver's seat in a heartbeat, her stomach clenched in dread at what she is witnessing. And then something happens that catches her unawares. She finds herself caught in a trance-like moment as, in the distance, Peggy looks over her way, her face crumpled with fear in an obvious cry for help. Without thinking, Audrey suddenly darts down behind the car door out of view, her heart thrashing around her chest, too scared to do anything, frightened of being caught spying on her own daughter. It's all over in a matter of seconds, and when she glances up again, Peggy has managed to free herself and is stumbling out of the freezing clutches of the sea, wading out of the water onto the path nearby. Swamped with guilt, Audrey flings herself back into her car, thumps her fists on the steering wheel, leans forward and begins to sob, big fat tears rolling down her face and dripping onto the dashboard leaving a dot to dot of wet splashes. Perhaps Peggy is right and she is a useless mother after all. *Toxic.* That was the word Peggy spat at her at Peter's funeral. On the day she lowered her husband's body into the cold, hard ground, her daughter screamed and hollered at her own mother that she was a toxic waste of space. Audrey sniffs and wipes at her eyes, her jaw lolling as she scrapes around in her handbag for a tissue. Maybe she is right after all. What kind of mother would stand by and watch her daughter almost drown? What sort of mother would *hide*, knowing her child is in danger? Dear God, is this what she has become? A passive bystander, the sort of person who watches helplessly whilst those around her struggle? She thought she was better than that. She considers herself a good citizen, a decent, thoughtful person. And yet look at what she has just done … With trembling fingers Audrey shoves the key into the ignition and turns it. She needs to get away from here; to give herself time to think, to mull over what has just happened. She isn't proud of herself over what has just taken place, but then it has been so long since they have spoken, Audrey isn't even sure what she would say to her own daughter. And how wrong is that? The words should just flow, especially given the length of time they've been apart. They have so much catching up to do, so many years' worth of thoughts to air.

Audrey pushes her foot down on the pedal and looks in her rear-view mirror. Anyway, the whole thing took her by surprise. And Audrey isn't a fan of surprises. She likes to plan, have everything done in an orderly fashion. Once she gets home and has a drink, everything will seem a lot better. And by then, Peggy will have seen the note and know what is going on. Surely then, she won't continue to ignore her own mother? She'll get in touch, they'll talk; Audrey will explain everything. And if Peggy doesn't contact her, then she will return, and when she does, she will make absolutely certain Alec Wilson is made to face up to what he has done. Perhaps then she and her daughter can finally be reunited, picking up with their lives where they left off all those years ago. Audrey wipes at her eyes and pulls on her pale blue leather gloves. Just the thought of it makes her feel better, the very idea that she will finally regain some control, get her life back on track.

She turns out of the car park with one last fleeting look up at her daughter's cottage, a solitary, squat building atop the cliffs. Such a stupid place to live. He will have been behind such a move, keeping himself apart from all the normal people, all the decent, law abiding people. But that won't stop her because she is already planning the next visit in her head. Because there will be one. If Peggy chooses to ignore the letter, then by God she will be back, and when that happens they will all know about it. Next time, there will be no stopping her.

# Alec

He rips open the envelope and stares at the words on the slip of paper, unable to process what he is seeing. Alec clears his throat and tries again, this time reading each word slowly and carefully, trying to digest the contents of the letter. The words blur on the page, and he is gripped by a bout of dizziness as he quickly looks around and wipes his eyes. *No way. No fucking way is this happening!*

A noise behind him causes him to jump. He turns to see Peggy open her laptop and sit down in front of the screen. She catches his eye and smiles. He reciprocates, suddenly overcome with a sensation he can't quite put his finger on. A renewed sense of love and attraction? Perhaps. He has seen a change in his wife just recently; that much is certain. She's been in a routine; up and writing by the time he leaves the house every morning, taking care of herself, taking more care of the house. He doesn't expect her to be a domestic goddess - her writing is a full-time job, but he doesn't mind admitting it's been a relief getting in of an evening to a tidy kitchen and hot cooked meal. After the incident with the car last week, he fully expected a lapse in her behaviour but if anything, it seems to have had the opposite effect. He thinks back to the other day - was it the day after it happened? She came down with a really bad cold, shivery and flu-like. She was in bed when he got in from work and his stomach plummeted. *Here we go*, were his first thoughts. She was turned on her side, her hands clasped tightly around a small object. She obviously hadn't heard him coming in as she jumped a mile high and quickly shoved whatever it was she was holding into her bedside drawer the minute he opened the bedroom door. The object had already been moved by first light the next morning. His curiosity piqued, Alec had taken it upon himself to have a good rummage while Peggy was downstairs making breakfast but all he came across was a tangle of thick winter tights and a handful of old receipts.

'Everything okay?' Peggy has turned and is watching him carefully, scrutinising his face.

Alec screws the letter up and pushes it deep into his breast pocket, 'Fine. Just a letter from the insurance about the car. All sorted.' He immediately regrets his words. He has been caught off guard. Such a bad lie. A terrible one.

'I thought you weren't going to bother? Your mate at the garage said he could knock it back out no problem, didn't he?'

'What? Yeah, just a note acknowledging we're not using them now.' He feels Peggy's hard stare and knows she can see straight through him. He could just tell her, show her the letter but then she would start asking questions and it will just bring it all crashing back into his mind.

'Can I see it?' Her words cut through his thoughts; a knife through hot butter.

'See it?'

'Yes, I'd like to have a look at the letter. If that's okay? I was going to call and see Brenda from the farmhouse and let her know the costs won't be so high after all. She rang yesterday, flustered to death over it all and deeply apologetic for not getting back to us sooner. She was on nights and her cousin forgot to tell her. Too embarrassed at the fact that he lost her mum I think.'

Alec feels a flush creep up his throat as he attempts to think up another feeble lie to cover his tracks. Silly really. Why bother? Head tight with anger, he pulls the piece of crumpled paper back out of his pocket and hands it over to Peggy. What is the point of trying to conceal it? Nothing will be gained by creating more secrecy. May as well just hand it over and be done with it. Then once she's read it he can take it back, tear it into a thousand tiny pieces and throw it into the fire where it belongs.

She straightens it out and Alec watches as Peggy reads and re-reads it, murmuring the words out loud as she scans each line until she reaches the bottom and looks up at him, her eyes dark with apprehension,

'Oh Alec, I don't know what to say! What are you going to do?' She gets up and starts to walk towards him, her arms outstretched. He steps back and shakes his head. No sympathy. No pity. That man took enough from him all those years ago. He won't allow him to control his life any more.

'What am I going to do? Throw the fucker in the fire, that's what I'm going to do!' and he snatches the letter back and begins to tear it into tiny pieces. Peggy watches him, unable to say or do anything.

'How did he find you?'

'Oh, come on, Pegs, in this day and age nobody can hide anywhere. There's the internet, the electoral roll, the school website. It could have been any number of those things that led him to me.' Alec stalks over to the fireplace, throws the tiny strips of paper in and watches, mesmerised, as they flutter into the air and land on the small pile of ashes sitting at the bottom of the grate.

'So, what are you going to do then?'

'Do? I'm not going to do anything. As far as I'm concerned, the old bastard can rot in hell,' Alec shouts, his face turning a deep shade of scarlet as he paces up and down, his heels clicking on the tiled flooring.

Peggy nods at him. He can see she is wise enough to not to push it any further. She heads back to her computer and begins to type, her fingers softly pressing the keys, her gaze fixed firmly on the screen.

'Did you read the bit about him being off the booze?' Alec suddenly roars, the pulse in his neck visible beneath his shirt.

Peggy stops typing and nods, 'And you believe him?'

'Are you fucking kidding me? He will *never* be off the booze. Drinking to him is like breathing to any normal person. He might have fooled his probation officer and the team of social workers he's had dangling on a string for the past thirty odd years but he'll never fool me.' Alec is breathless with rage. He sits down and wiggles his jaw from side to side.

'Why do you think he wants to see you?' Peggy grabs a handful of her thick hair and attempts to tie it up out of her face only for it to spring free and fall back down again.

'No idea and I don't really care. He's probably short of cash. Well he can piss right off. He's getting nothing from me. Nothing!'

Alec drags his hair back and pulls at his collar, a habit he seems to have acquired of late and one he would rather stop. He hates outward displays of weakness and a nervous twitch is definitely a sign that he is struggling to control the mass of dark thoughts roaming loose in his head. That's the stranglehold his father still has over him. Even after all these years; turning him into a nervous fucking wreck just by writing a letter. There are times when Barry Wilson's face jumps into his mind unbidden - Alec can be lying in the bath or walking through town or sitting in a meeting or doing any fucking thing at all, any menial task - and he has to quell the urge to punch someone. Doesn't matter who. Sometimes he just craves the sensation of being able to take all of his frustrations out on somebody else's face, preferably a person who has waltzed through life with no fucking idea of what an awful struggle his own has been. After being saved from the blows of his father, his childhood was spent being passed from one foster family to another. All were adequate - not loving or nurturing. Not the sort of environment you would want to spend any length of time in. Just tolerable; providing him with a bed to sleep in, clothes to wear and food to eat. It was Mr Biddell, his English teacher and form tutor who saved him, stepping in and inspiring him; showing him how to make something of himself. Mr Biddell taught him how to think and manage his emotions - fed his thirst for knowledge by supplying him with an endless supply of literature - *To Kill a Mockingbird*, *Of Mice and Men*, *The Great Gatsby*. He devoured them all. Without him, Alec could have very possibly taken the same route as his father. Because, on those occasions when Alec has harboured thoughts of smashing somebody's face in, he has wondered if he has inherited the gene; the Wilson propensity for violence. And the thought of it terrifies him; the idea that he has a rogue gene whistling around his system, driving him on, fuelling his anger, making him do things he really, really doesn't want to do. But of course, he always manages to drag himself out of it, to talk himself round, to convince himself that he's quite a good guy after all. He has a decent job, a nice house. Despite everything, he has managed to pull himself up by his bootstraps and make something of his life. There is no way he is about to let his father back into it and watch him ruin everything Alec has worked so bloody hard to achieve. No way will he let Barry Wilson march in and try to take it from him. Not a fucking chance.

Alec stares down at the paper mingled in with the ashes in the bottom of the unlit fireplace. He will do whatever is required to stop that from happening. Whatever it takes to keep that man out of his life, he will do it.

# Peggy

Her skin is like ice as he stalks up and down the room, pacing like a Gestapo officer, head dipped, arms clasped behind his back. She hates it when he gets like this; full of pent up anger, a bubbling volcano, eruption imminent. It makes her edgy, perhaps even a little scared. Bloody Barry Wilson. What the hell does he want anyway? To put right his many wrongs? As if he could *ever* do that. Alec would have to be reborn and live the first twelve years of his life all over again for that to happen. Peggy chews at the insides of her mouth until she feels a sharp pain and tastes the metallic flow of blood as it oozes through her mouth like warm oil. First her mother with her leaflets and posters and empty accusations and now this. Why is there always something? Every time things get back on an even keel, their world tilts precariously on its axis, knocking them off balance and there is yet another situation for them to deal with. Why can't life just leave them both be? Let them get on in their own unobtrusive, little way?

Leaning back in her chair, Peggy inhales and then stops quickly. That dreadful smell again. Such an awful stench. A horrible, creeping sensation twists round in her belly. Alec hasn't noticed it but then her sense of smell is so much keener than his. It started a while back and has grown stronger by the day. Bloody Chamber Cottage and its multitude of problems. At least the stain has stayed away. Thank heavens for small mercies. Sometimes she feels as if she is actually losing her mind, as if this cottage, this place she calls home, is trying to drive her insane.

'Think I might head up to the hills for a walk if that's okay? Need to get away from here for a bit.' Alec has stopped pacing and is standing staring out of the window at the frothing sea outside. 'Do you fancy coming or are you busy?' He nods towards her computer then turns back to the water, his breath misting up the glass.

Peggy thinks about Alec's dark mood the last time they visited the moors together and how impossible it was to keep pace with his gigantic strides. It wasn't a stroll or a gentle amble. More of a regimented march as if there was somebody chasing him. Which to be fair, there usually is. Not a visible entity as such but a niggling army of demons perched on his shoulder constantly throwing him bait to see if he will bite. Alec's countryside walks are anything but leisurely.

'I was thinking of High Cliff Nab or maybe parking the car at Clay Bank Top and taking it from there?'

Peggy smiles, knows what his ploy is. He's doing his best to put her off. That suits her. She is behind with her work. She needs to write and Alec needs to take his frustrations out on the ground beneath his feet, force his anger out into the open countryside where it can be released into the wild.

'I'm okay here. You get yourself up there and blow off a few cobwebs.'

He nods and plunges his hands into his pockets, 'Think I'll make myself a flask and take a couple of sandwiches.'

'Why don't you go and get yourself changed? I'll do it.' Peggy stands and makes her way into the kitchen, catching the look on Alec's face as she passes.

'Wanting rid of me?' he says, his eyes dark, full of contempt. It doesn't take much to set him off, to unsettle him and bring his fury to the fore.

She feels her face flush and grits her teeth, 'Just thought I would slow you down, that's all. You really want me to come along?' Peggy turns and smiles at him, gives him her best humble look, the one where she dips her eyes slightly and lowers her shoulders. She is humility personified.

He shakes his head and stares down at his feet sullenly, 'No, no. You're right. I need a good walk. Get it out of my system. Sorry, just feeling pissed off.'

'Go and get yourself sorted. I'll make you up a flask and a few snacks,' Peggy says and reaches down to pull a small black bag out of the kitchen cupboard, shaking the dust off as she unzips it, 'Coffee and ham sandwiches do you?'

***

For someone who was desperate to get out of the house and clear his head, Alec took forever to do it - shuffling around the place, swapping walking boots, changing coats, hunting for maps that he decided at the last minute he didn't need anyway. It seemed to go on for an eternity. But now he's gone, Peggy leans back against the door and surveys the debris he has left behind. Stuff everywhere - old handkerchiefs, empty crisp packets he pulled out of his backpack, laces, frayed and snapped in half, all manner of useless items - they all lay strewn across the living room floor. She sets about gathering it all up, sifting the rubbish out and binning it and then salvaging things such as socks and an old bandana, an item he wore once and discarded with a fair amount of scorn claiming it made him look like a complete prick.

It doesn't take too long to clear the decks. She gives the place a quick vacuum and puts everything away before tackling her next job.

A band of worry wraps itself around her head as she shuffles into the kitchen and snaps on a pair of rubber gloves. The odour coming up from under the floor is starting to become unbearable. She has to do something about it. The thought of going down there fills her with complete dread. She knows what this is. She knows only too well.

Peggy gets down on her haunches and tugs at the oblong raffia mat that sits in the centre of the kitchen floor. Pulling it to one side, she rolls it up into a long rectangular tube and stuffs it down the side of the fridge freezer. The handle on the hatch to the cellar glints menacingly and Peggy feels her heart begin to thump arrhythmically as she leans down and lifts the heavy trapdoor up. A waft of something so indescribably horrendous hits her in the face causing her to wretch. Gagging, Peggy reels backwards leaving the door to slam back down with a loud crash. *Jesus Christ*. She had no idea it would be so pungent once unleashed. Her arm is spread over her face as she scrambles up and drags a cloth out of the kitchen drawer. Tying it round her face, she takes a few deep breaths then reaches down and begins to pull at the hatch again. The makeshift scarf is no barrier against the almighty stink that immediately springs up from below, but it's better than nothing. Gasping and swallowing hard, Peggy turns and descends backwards down the metal ladder and into the darkness beneath. Her hands flail around for the light switch. She hits it with an uncoordinated slap and suddenly the basement is lit up like a football stadium, a carpet of yellow light spread over the grey concrete under her feet.

She glances around, sickness gripping her. The floor is littered with the rotting carcasses of dozens of dead mice, their tiny, black bodies slowly becoming desiccated with the passing of time. They stare up at her accusingly, their eyes glazed, their bodies stiff. The stench of death chokes her. Such a distinct and unforgettable odour. She can never erase from her memory the smell of rotting rodents from her time working in a grotty pub in Newcastle. No matter how often they got the pest control guy in, the little blighters kept coming back. She was once serving on a busy Saturday night and had felt one crawl up over her foot. She had shrieked as she looked down to see it scamper across the floor into a hole in the corner of the rotten skirting board. In complete turmoil, she had panicked and accidentally thrown a full pint over a waiting customer who roared in her face that she was 'a fucking useless bitch who deserved to be slapped about.' Peggy finished her shift that night, hung up her apron and left, never to return.

Breathing through her mouth only, she grabs a bag from one of the metal units against the wall and looks around for a dustpan and brush. Propped up against the far wall is a tatty old hand brush, its bristles bent and twisted with age. Trying to stop the vomit rising, Peggy picks it up and sets to, sweeping up the mass of dead mice, desperately doing her best to not count them all as the bodies continue to mount up. Some are still in the traps; other have struggled free but died after escaping, their injured limbs twisted and broken and sticking out at horribly peculiar and unnatural angles. Using a large spade, Peggy gathers them up and shovels them into the bag. They hit the bottom with a sickening thud, sending her stomach lurching down to her boots. Without looking inside, she quickly ties the bag up and then deciding one layer isn't enough to stop the smell escaping and foraging foxes digging it open again, she grabs another bag and puts it inside. The odour is still there, foul and cloying in its intensity. Choking and spluttering, Peggy starts to make her way back to the steps. Her right hand reaches out and she clasps her fingers around the bottom rung, its cold, hard sensation a shock on her burning skin. That's when she hears it - a sinister scraping sound. A deep, grating echo that chills her to the bone. Too loud to be mice again. It's something else. Something bigger. She carefully places the bag on the floor and slowly edges towards the noise. It seems to be coming from behind an old chest of drawers that is placed against the rough surface of the wall. Peggy feels her throat begin to close up. She creeps forward, her breathing irregular and ragged, then stops and listens, her ears attuned to the raging rhythm of her own heartbeat as it pumps through her veins with frightening ferocity. She brings her hands up to her forehead and presses her palms into her eye sockets to alleviate the pain that is beginning to burn at her brain. Is it possible for a person to collapse from fear? Because she feels that at this point in time, her body could easily rupture from the strain, her blood squirting out like a jet wash, spraying the bare brick walls of the cellar a deep shade of crimson. Swaying slightly, Peggy removes her hands from her sockets and finds herself staring into a pair of dark, prying eyes. Her head begins to pulse and vibrate as she watches a huge, grey rat make its way towards her from under the old cabinet, quickly followed by another one of similar size and shape, their bodies casting long shadows across the dusty floor.

Unable to catch her breath properly, she lets out a short guttural grunt and starts to back up the ladder then remembers the bag of dead mice at her feet. Quickly snatching them up, Peggy slots her feet onto the first rung and hauls herself up, her hands shaking uncontrollably. She leans down and before she has chance to flick the light switch off, feels her gaze drawn to them as the two large creatures turn and head back under the arched legs of the furniture and disappear out of sight.

The black sack swings from side to side, weighted with the bodies of well over a dozen dead mice - probably more - as Peggy slips and stumbles her way back up out of the basement. She half falls onto the top rung and flings herself through the opening, landing with a thump onto the narrow kitchen floor. The thought of a pair of scavenging, disease ridden rats in hot pursuit, forces her up off her knees. She grabs at the hatch and swings it closed with a huge, desperate crash. The pots on the small nearby dresser wobble and rattle in protest, one of them falling off and rolling round the floor, coming to a standstill at her feet.

Peggy rips off the material draped over the lower half of her face and feels her stomach go into an involuntary spasm as she is hit with another blast of the death stench. Two bags suddenly seem a weak barrier against such an overpowering smell. Picking it up, she flings the back door open, marches outside and dumps it in the wheelie bin, then thinking better of it, retrieves it and goes back inside where she double bags it again before striding back outside and finally disposing of it. A gust of wind whips up, swirling around her feet and forcing her back against the gritty, whitewashed wall of the cottage. Peggy secures and closes the door of the small wooden shed that houses their collection of bins. She stops next to it to catch her breath and let her racing heart slow down then narrows her eyes against the glare of the sky and stares out over the horizon wondering where Alec got to in the end, which route he decided to take. Peggy shivers as her body cools itself, the breeze welcome, as it caresses her burning flesh. Wherever he is, she hopes he is wrapped up warm. The easterly wind is raw at this time of year. Shielding her eyes from the glare of the low, watery sun, Peggy watches the line of tankers that are stacked up out at sea, waiting to enter the dock and unload their cargo. She thinks about the fishing boats that still set sail regardless of weather and riptides and the myriad other reasons that would stop most people from even entertaining any idea of going. Not the fishermen on the north-eastern coast. Come hell or high water they always set sail. It's in their blood her father would say when she once questioned why her cousin Frank used to still go fishing even after losing his best friend overboard in the height of a winter storm. Peggy blinks. The thought of her father is still enough to bring a lump to her throat. Fifty-nine is no age to die; no age at all.

Peggy scurries back inside, the breeze building into something more powerful. She wrinkles her nose and closes her eyes against the smell. It's everywhere. She flings windows open to rid the house of the stench of decay. A gust of wind whips the torn shreds of paper up out of the grate. They flutter about, swirling around her like blossom. Peggy sighs and reaches down to gather them back up. Why on earth would Alec's dad suddenly want to contact him after all these years? Pity his mother didn't do the same thing instead of fleeing to the west coast and forgetting that her son even existed. Peggy is pretty sure Alec would have welcomed her back into his life. But she didn't. Instead she chose to start afresh and leave her child to the care system and all its failings. What sort of mother would do such a thing? She knows she wouldn't. Leaning up to reach the box of matches that sits on the fireplace, Peggy opens the box and strikes one, holding it to the scraps of paper that are clasped tightly between her fingers. She watches, enthralled by the rapidity of it all as Barry Wilson's plea for forgiveness and a reunion bursts into flames and turns to ash in her hands. She leaves go and drops the crisp, black flakes back into the grate. Into the fire with all the other rubbish. No more than the old bastard deserves.

# Audrey

It's been a week now. A week since she dropped the papers off at Peggy's cottage. Papers detailing the disappearance of a young woman, along with some snapshots of Alec and the very same woman drinking coffee together. Audrey got lucky on that one. She had initially wanted to follow her daughter to see the kind of places she visited; see what her daily routine was, get to know her some more, maybe even get asked back to Chamber Cottage for coffee and a chat. She had planned on accidentally bumping into her somewhere - in a shop or a cafe. Less invasive than knocking on Peggy's door and giving her the chance to slam it in Audrey's face. But it soon became clear that Peggy didn't actually have a routine or ritual worth speaking of. In fact, she rarely left the house. She took brief visits to the town which saw her snaking up back alleys, always avoiding the crowds. There were times Audrey lost her and had to retreat back to the car, disappointed and frustrated by her daughter's eccentric and often unfathomable behaviour. It worked out well in the end however, Peggy's reclusive ways. It meant that Alec was often on his own for a lot of the time. Twice she saw him with her, this Sheryl lady. Twice they sat in a coffee shop, heads together; talking, laughing, colluding, while her daughter was at home, only a few miles away, by herself, completely unaware what her conniving husband was up to. Audrey sucks her teeth and shakes her head. A complete shit of a man. He was easy to track too, making it so simple for her. He strolled around town without any idea he was being followed and that his affair was being documented. The meetings lasted more than a few weeks giving Audrey plenty of time to work out her plan of attack. She didn't need to follow him for too long. Just a few photographs was all that was required. They told her all she needed to know. She hung onto those pictures, salted them away ready for the time when she would present them to her daughter, show Peggy what sort of a man she had chosen to spend the rest of her life with - a liar and a philanderer. But then the absence of her daughter's face proved too much for her. All the waiting about for Peggy to emerge from that bloody cottage took Audrey's plan in a different direction. She decided to enter into the complex world of social media. It was taxing - having to set up a Facebook account, create a profile, put out friend requests, find Peggy's author page, search out who her friends were - it took some doing. With Audrey's limited capacity for understanding technology and how to navigate her way around social media sites, it was tricky. But she persevered. And by God it was worth the effort. Because then she was able to find out about Sheryl; catch a glimpse into her life, monitor her movements. Read all about her disappearance. That came as a shock initially but, after giving it some thought, all the pieces slotted together perfectly. He had it in him. He was a Wilson after all. Like father like son. She had probably threatened to go public with their affair and he will have panicked, flipped his lid, and now she is gone. Awful clichéd behaviour. Duplicity at its worst. The newspapers are full of such stories. Her daughter's books are full of such stories. The irony of it is absurd.

Audrey flips her laptop up and opens the page set up by Sheryl's sister. She reads it again. She's been missing for a few weeks now. Nobody disappears for that long without a sinister motive. Fingers itching to contact this poor lady and pour out what she knows, Audrey grits her teeth tightly and releases them again, her jaw aching from the tension. She needs to keep it to herself. For now, anyway. She doesn't want to ruin any chances of a meet-up with her estranged daughter. She's waited too long to risk ruining that. It's all she's thought about since retiring. She has focused all her energy on bringing her family back together. She often dreams about visiting Beatrice and taking Peggy with her. The three of them back together again. Just like the old times. She clenches her fists, a gnawing sensation churning around in her gut. She could do with a drink. She hasn't had one for three or four days now, probably the longest she has been without for as long as she can remember. She closes her eyes and waits for the moment to pass, doing her best to ignore the craving. The longing for the sensation that alcohol brings threatens to engulf her - the warm, muggy feeling, the blurring and dullness, the ability to help her through. She has to ignore it, let it pass. Be the stronger force. But it's hard, so very hard, when your days are empty and your life is fuelled only by anger and suspicion. Because that's all she has going for her at the moment. No Peter, no daughters. Nothing worth speaking of. Just a pressing need to unearth the dirty crimes of her errant son-in-law and save her daughter from his iniquitous ways.

She has John of course. He is there for her, in a fashion; popping in and out of her life, calling round to see her when he finishes work, his fluorescent green jacket a sign he has arrived as he passes her living room window. He's a good man. But he's not hers and never will be. Peter was her man, the only one she ever wanted or needed. But a premature death brought on by a heart attack put paid to that. And Peggy even blamed Audrey for that. Putting him under strain with her constant moaning and demands was what she claimed had caused it. That had hurt. Even more than the scathing words directed at Audrey herself. Because for all of her faults she had loved her husband more than life itself and would do anything to have him back. But life's not like that, is it? Life is a chain of events that once set in motion are impossible to undo. Peter is dead and that is that. Her daughters are all she has left and she cannot afford to lose them as well. This is why she has to be so very careful with the information she has about Sheryl, make sure her plan is executed with absolute precision. No room for error. She says Sheryl's name out loud, listens to the sound of it as it echoes around the room, enjoying the sensation it brings as it rolls off her tongue. She's said it so often of late in her head, she feels as if she knows her, as if she is the link that will lead her back to her daughter.

She drums her fingers against the side of the chair, her body rigid with suppressed rage. It's no surprise that Alec keeps a low profile on social media with the flurry of activity surrounding Sheryl's disappearance. He may well be an immoral and thoughtless husband but he isn't an idiot. Audrey doesn't want to do anything too rash however - go around making accusations without all the proper evidence to back it up otherwise Peggy will make absolutely certain they never see each other again. When Audrey does finally confront him, she will also go to the police. She isn't so stupid as to think she can solve this thing on her own. She was once a professional herself and understands the importance of informing the appropriate bodies, making sure all the different strands of evidence are brought together properly, not some half-hearted attempt she has cobbled together herself. But the time has to be right and at the moment she doesn't have enough to go on. She needs more proof, more than supposition and her gut instinct. Until then she will continue watching and waiting, watching and waiting. Waiting for him to make a mistake. Which he will. If he thinks he can hide away in that cottage of his and get away with this heinous act then he can think again. Because she is onto him. She understands his psyche, his movements, has even got his motive sorted. All she needs to do now is work out the final part of the puzzle. Find out where he has concealed the body.

# Maude

He's here again, that young man. Always hanging about he is, getting under her feet. She has no idea what he wants. She's tried asking him but he just laughs and shakes his head then asks her if she wants more tea. More tea indeed. All they seem to do is drink blooming tea. She wonders where they're getting it from with all the rationing and shortages going on at the moment. Stealing it, probably. He looks the type; suspicious looking and shifty. Always has a funny look in his eye, as if he's planning something underhand. She's knows all about people like him. She's met his type before, wheeling and dealing, getting hold of stuff from the black market. Well she doesn't want any part of it and has told him so. She told that Brenda as much yesterday as well but all she did was make a funny face and do a thing with her eyes that made Maude really cross. They all think she's daft - a batty old lady who doesn't know anything about anything. But they're wrong. Because she does know about something that nobody else knows about and she's tried telling Brenda and this lad but neither of them will listen. They pull more of those strange faces and sit her down on the sofa with yet more tea and a plate of biscuits asking her if she would like to watch an old film or listen to the radio when all she really wants to do is draw a picture.

'Here Maude, is this what you've been looking for?'

The boy is standing in front of her holding something out.

She narrows her eyes and stares at the object, 'What is it?'

He does that annoying laughing thing again and wiggles the object about as if she is a small child or some sort of simpleton. 'It's Bobbin. You remember Bobbin, don't you?'

Maude reaches out and grabs it from him - fancy shaking poor Bobbin about like that as if he's some sort of ragdoll. She still doesn't know why he is even here, this young lad. And where's Brenda? Always off somewhere doing something or other. Busy, busy, busy. Always busy doing nothing.

'You'll break his brain shaking him about like that!' she yells, her temper starting to get the better of her. Sometimes it feels as if there is an angry animal inside her trying to get out. When she feels like that it makes her head hurt and she wishes could stop it but she just can't. The angry animal always seems to win.

'Sorry Maude,' he says and sits down next to her putting his hand on top of hers.

She holds her breath in, not sure what he is going to say or do next. Bobbin feels lovely and soft on her lap. She runs her hand over his fur, up and down his back. Up and down, up and down, over and over until she feels the angry animal start to calm down. Her chest is tight and she feels out of breath - as if she's been running round and round in circles. She is dizzy and tired but a picture has come up in her head and if she doesn't talk about it, it will vanish along with all the other things that slip through her brain like water disappearing down a plughole. It's a wonder she can remember who she is most days.

'Can I have the writing thing?' she whispers, trying to keep the angry animal hidden from view, 'and the white stuff to put it on?'

He is annoyed. He tries to cover it up but she can see it in his face. She asks again, 'Please? I would like to have them. I need them.'

'But Maude,' he says in a soothing voice as he drapes his arm around her shoulder and stares down at her face, 'you've done nothing but draw all week.'

'Have I?' Maude looks up, perplexed, a crinkle appearing across the bridge of her nose. She watches, confusion a tight band around her head as the man stands up and shuffles off into the dining room. He comes back a minute later carrying a big pile of those things she can never remember the name of - the white things. Lots of them. They are bunched up between his large fingers as he sits back down next to her. Maude flinches. She can feel the heat coming through the fabric of his trousers and doesn't like it. She doesn't like boys really. Not since that Alfred Byrnes tried to shove his hand up her skirt in the playground. He was a horrible one, that lad. Used to parade around the school yard bothering all the girls. He once pulled Mary Waites' knickers down when she was doing a handstand. He got the cane for that one but it didn't stop him. He still carried on bothering all the girls, doing horrible things to them and making them cry. Including Maude.

'Can you remember now, Maude?' the young man sitting beside her says, laying all the white things out over the sofa. They cover the entire surface, balancing on cushions, some of them dropping off and floating down to the floor like huge square snowflakes fluttering in the breeze.

Maude squints and tries to focus on the drawings. Scratchy lines and scribbling. A house, people lying on the ground, more lines, arms reaching out. And something red. Lots of red.

'What is that?' she asks, pointing to one of the pictures. Something has clicked in her mind and she stops, trying to recall what it is. She sits silently and then smiles and nods, delighted that her brain has decided to work for once and has allowed her to recall what it is that she is staring at on the white stuff, 'That's them!' she half shrieks, staring up at him, 'they were fighting! Pushing and shouting. I saw them. I saw them!'

Maude puts Bobbin to one side, jumps up and hurries over to the living room window, a large bay overlooking the privet that surrounds the house. She points towards the far end of the window, her tiny hand now shaking with excitement, 'Over there! They were fighting!'

He is standing behind her now, his breath close to her ear. She moves away slightly and turns to look at him, unsure what he is going to say or do.

'Over where, Auntie Maude? All I can see is the hedge. And who was fighting?'

'There!' she yells, starting to feel frustrated. Is he one of those stupid boys who sits at the back of class eating chalk? Why can't he see it?

He leans closer to get Maude's vantage point, almost squatting on the floor. There is a break in the privet, a small gap at the bottom and beyond that is a view of the old coastguard's cottage.

'The house, Maude? Is that what you mean?'

She claps her hands and starts to jump up and down on the spot, 'Yes! That's it. I was starting to think you were blind as well as stupid!'

'What happened, Maude? What exactly did you see?'

She sighs and tried to do the eye roll thing that Brenda does with her all the time but ends up feeling a bit dizzy and sick so stops and puts her hands on her hips, 'I told you already. They were fighting and pushing each other.'

'Who? The people who live there?'

Maude nods, her eyes sparkling with pleasure. Finally, they understand her and she is being listened to. Not before time. Sometimes this boy and Brenda are so dim.

'A big fight. And shouting. I opened the window and could hear them being angry.'

'You opened the window?'

Maude stops and watches his face. He looks like the angry one now. And worried. He reaches up over her head and pulls at the handle, tugging at it with his big, long fingers. She watches as he takes a small, silver key out of it and slips it into his pocket, tapping at it as if to make sure it hasn't jumped right back out again.

'Please don't open the windows, Maude. You know Brenda doesn't like you doing that.'

'Oh, pooh to that Brenda.' She puffs out her cheeks and considers sticking her tongue out at him but stops herself, 'Anyway, they had a big fight and she fell on the floor.'

There is a silence as they both stare out at the cottage in the distance.

'Come on,' he says, mildly embarrassed by the whole sorry scenario. Getting involved in other people's domestics isn't his thing. 'Let's see what's on the television, shall we? How about the news? You like the news, don't you, Maude?'

Taking her tiny hand in his, they walk back to the sofa where he gathers up the rest of the papers. Maude slumps down in the seat and places Bobbin on her lap, rubbing her fingers deep into his ragged, patchy fur.

'What if she died?' she murmurs softly, her eyes downcast.

Andrew is searching for the remote and stops suddenly, 'What?'

'The lady over there. What if she died?'

'She definitely didn't die, Maude,' he says resignedly, silently wishing she would stop this carry on and shut up or have a nap or just watch the TV. He's fed up now and wishes Brenda would hurry up back. He needs a break. All of a sudden, the money she gives him doesn't seem so appealing. This whole babysitting thing is bloody hard work.

'How do you know that, Mister Smarty Pants?' She is waving the toy at him and has her head tilted to one side in a childish fashion.

'Because we saw her the other week, didn't we?' *After you escaped and almost wrote their bloody car off*, he wants to add but remains silent. He's tired now. Completely worn out by it all. Where is Brenda? He's ready to go home.

'Yes, well, we'll see,' she adds and turns away from him in annoyance.

Maude sits surrounded by the white stuff, her brain trying to piece it all together. She saw it. She definitely saw it and him saying she didn't won't make the bad pictures in her head go away. It happened. What she needs to do is go over there and see if the lady isn't dead after all. She smiles, suddenly buoyed up by this thought. Yes, that's exactly what she will do. She will take these white things to show the person in that house what happened. As soon as she is on her own, she will find a key to get out of here and she will go over there and show them her drawings and then everything will be all right. She can just feel it. She did it once before so she can do it again.

Maude watches as the young man fiddles with the remote, saying bad things under his breath - rude words - as the picture on the screen flickers on and off. He turns away from her, still muttering under his breath, his eyes angry. She recognises when people are getting mad and doesn't particularly like it. It scares her when they do that because she doesn't know if she is the one that has caused it. Sometimes it's her fault and sometimes it isn't and she doesn't always know the difference. She slowly takes a handful of the drawings and shoves them under the cushions on the sofa while he is busy. She will put them somewhere better later when he isn't looking. He may even go to the place where that Brenda woman goes to. She doesn't know where the place is but it means she can be on her own for a bit and hide the white things, the paper. Maude cackles and covers her mouth as he looks over at her. That's the word! *Paper.* She will take the paper and give it to the cottage people to show them what went on. Her tummy feels all tight and a buzzing sensation fills her head as she tries to cover her smile. She continues to ruffle Bobbin's worn fabric and picks him up to look into his face. She rubs at his nose and pulls him close to kiss his patchy fur.

'You believe me, don't you, Bobbin?' she says softly, giving the cat a gentle shake.

The head flops down and its limbs hang sadly by its side, the stitching stretched and puckered from years of wear. Maude whispers his name then pulls at his arms and watches as they drop and hang lifelessly by his side.

'Bobbin?' Maude says again, mildly rattled, 'you believe me, don't you?'

She continues to stare at the cat, her eyes narrow and dark. Why won't he answer?

'Oh, for goodness sake!' she suddenly shouts, flinging the tatty bundle of fur onto the floor in disgust, 'what would you know anyway?' She feels the angry animal start to move about inside her and takes a deep breath to stop it building. She doesn't even like having it in there. It makes her feel a bit sick and frightened. Reaching her leg out she gives the old toy cat a small kick and watches as it slides across the living room floor, landing in a mangled heap in front of the fireplace, 'I don't even know why you live here,' she says under her breath, 'You're very stupid.'

There is stillness in the room, a slow burning air of immobility, as if everything has been slowed down before Maude reaches her leg out again and gives the cat another strong kick, 'In fact,' she says crossly, 'sometimes it's as if you're not even alive at all.'

# Alec

The lights are far too dim. Not nearly safe enough for female members of staff working late, heading out here on their own, especially if they're parked round the back of the huge storage sheds that house the goalposts and spare chairs and tables that they keep for school concerts and governors' meetings. Alec looks up at the flickering bulb hanging from the top of the canteen wall. It has failed to fully illuminate one of the darkest corners of the car park. It's a part of the school that scares even him; hidden from view, full of shadows. A perfect place for attackers to pounce. Alec pulls up his collar and shivers. He makes a mental note to get the lights sorted next week. Hang the cost and their shrinking budget. Safety first.

The noise is indistinct, so low he barely notices it at first. A gravelly rumble, like the ticking of a distant running engine. He turns and looks behind him, unsure what it is he expects to see. Nothing. The place is empty. Alec continues walking, his senses suddenly heightened, his hearing attuned to every whisper of wind, every ragged breath that exits his body. The sound of his own heartbeat begins to thrash in his ears - a deep, sharp crunching - as a murky, ill-defined shadow appears from round a corner, covering his own grey, fuzzy form. Alec's skin burns as a hand is placed on his shoulder and a voice fills the early evening air.

'Now then, Alec lad, how's it going? Long time no see, eh?'

Alec feels the blood seep out of his body and has to fight the urge to slump down onto the pavement. The voice hasn't altered; the pitch still recognisable with that deep rumble from years of sucking on unfiltered cigarettes. Alec is incensed. The old swine has actually had the audacity to track him down at work and quite literally corner him; he has watched and waited outside, ready to swoop, to force him into a situation from which he cannot possibly extricate himself.

'You're a hard man to get in touch with,' Barry says, a laugh forcing its way out of his belly, contrived and rehearsed. His stomach bounces up and down as he laughs and Alec has a vision of catching him unawares, ramming his fist in there with force, taking the wind out of his sails, squeezing every pocket of breath out of his body.

'I do my best,' Alec replies through clamped teeth.

The whooshing in Alec ears intensifies. He feels dizzy and mildly sick, the wet tarmac tilting and bending under his feet. He walks on, needing the support of the car under his grip, longing for the feel of cold metal under his fingers to stop him falling to the floor.

'I only want a minute of your time,' Barry says, every syllable that falls from his mouth an assault on Alec's ears.

'Fuck off,' Alec says softly and continues walking until he is close enough to his car to almost touch it. He presses his key and has to resist the urge to jump in and mow Barry Wilson down right here in the school car park. Alec turns and stares at him. He's much smaller than Alec remembers, with arms like Popeye and a broad, rotund body. His hair is thinning and he's aged badly. Of course he has, having spent most of his adult life in prison and a series of hostels. You get the face you deserve. Alec notices a few scars down the side of Barry's cheek and wonders if the inmates at Frankland Prison did that on his behalf. He hopes so.

'Come on, Alec son, I know you're pissed off with me an' all that but all I want is a few short minutes with you. Is that too much to ask?'

'Yes,' Alec replies, a pain starting up in his abdomen and reaching up into his neck, winding round and round, strangling him with its intensity, 'it is too much to ask. Now do me a favour and piss off out of here.'

A noise disturbs them. Alec swings round to see Ellen walking towards her vehicle. Joanne the office manager is next to her carrying a pile of papers. They stop and chat by Joanne's car, Ellen's gaze switching between Joanne and Alec's father. Typical. The one evening he leaves on time is the one evening his father turns up. He couldn't have made it when there was nobody else around could he? This is perfect for him, putting Alec in a situation he knows will make him more compliant.

'Aw, don't be like that, Al,' he says just loud enough for the two women to hear.

Both of them turn to watch, a distinct lull in their conversation as they observe Alec and his father in the corner, waiting to see what happens next.

Knowing he will regret it, Alec speaks. It's the only thing he can do to stop this sorry scenario from escalating in front of two members of staff. And Barry knows it. Such a devious, manipulative, worthless piece of shit. He hasn't altered. Alec had always secretly hoped that in the intervening years his father had developed a conscience of sorts, become a changed man - perhaps even missed his only child. Turning his back to the two women to avoid their probing gaze, Alec opens the door and hisses quietly over to his father through a jaw clamped so tightly he feels as if his teeth will dissolve into dust, 'Get in. And don't say a single word. Just get in the bloody car.'

# Peggy

Peggy stares at the text. She's read it at least half a dozen times. Reading it again won't change anything. Her fingers hover over the screen as she wonders whether or not Alec has received the same message. Maybe. Maybe not. It's been such a long time since they've seen any of their friends. She tries to remember when they were last in touch with Polly and Ashfaq or Rob and Olivia. Too far back in her memory to put a date to it. But Rachel has been in contact with them all. Visited them asking about Sheryl. And now, according to Polly's message, the police are starting to take her claims seriously. Sheryl's business as a counsellor can no longer function without her. Patients have started complaining when she hasn't turned up for appointments. Some claimed they received messages cancelling their scheduled time but others have been left high and dry when she simply didn't turn up. And according to Polly and Rachel, something isn't right.

*Have you or Alec heard from her?* Polly asks, *because this is really worrying isn't it? Not like Sheryl at all …*

A knot forms in the pit of Peggy's stomach. What is she supposed to make of this message? What is it they actually want from her? She stopped socialising with them some time ago and isn't sure what it is they need her to do. The sound of the wall clock booms in her head. Her own ticking time bomb. Peggy watches as the second hand moves slowly towards the seven. Where is Alec? He should have been home an hour ago. He's been working long hours since getting this new position but even by his standards this is extraordinarily late. She thinks of his driving, how speed increases when he's under duress. If he has received this message and is currently in the car powering his way along the dual carriageway ... Peggy stands up, blocks it all from her mind. This has nothing to do with her. Why is Polly trying to make it her problem? She's already spoken to Rachel and told her what she knows, told her about the last time she saw Sheryl. What more do they want from her? Peggy slumps down again at the table and watches the hands of the clock as they slowly rotate.

It's 7.30 p.m. when Alec finally spills through the door, a sprawl of angry limbs and frowns. He reeks of drink. Peggy feels her stomach flip. This is a bad sign. Really bad. Alec never drinks after work. Ever. He must have got the text. What other reason could there be for his current state? She nibbles at her fingernails and tries to stem the uneasy feeling that is churning her insides up. What now?

He slams his briefcase down on the table sending Peggy's neat pile of papers into a sprawling jumble.

'Sorry,' he mutters, 'bad day. What are we eating?'

Peggy feels her armpits prickle. With the worry of the message she has forgotten to cook anything. She considers lying, telling him she threw it in the bin since he is so late back. Easier than having to put up with the mood that will no doubt ensue if he's left without any food. Eating was the last thing on her mind. Unlike Alec, she isn't controlled by her stomach and its constant demands for sustenance. A sandwich is usually enough to keep her going. There are days lately when she hasn't even had that.

'Thought we would have a takeaway?' she suggests quietly. 'I can go out and get it.'

The words are out of her mouth before she can stop them. She mentally plans out the route, checks the time. The place will probably be empty. It's midweek, a cold and blustery night. Most people will be at home doing their own cooking. Or at least she hopes so. Regardless, she's offered now, too late to take it back. She stares at Alec. He's in no fit state to go, red eyed and possibly over the limit. 'I could do with the drive out,' she says, hoping he doesn't spot her lies. It's down to her to go. There's no way he can go back on the road smelling like a brewery. Alec losing his license would just be the final nail in their coffin. She watches him, hoping he'll fall for it. His expression is unreadable, his eyes locked and dark, full of frustration and fury.

'Yeah, whatever,' he replies, 'Chinese?'

***

Peggy tries her best to wade her way through the mountain of glutinous food piled in front of her. The smell of the dark brown sticky mound of meat makes her want to wretch. Soy sauce is always too salty and she ends up drinking gallons of water for the rest of the evening. She watches as Alec shovels it into his mouth, flecks of chicken sticking to the corners of his lips. Her stomach threatens to heave. They've barely spoken since she got back and Peggy's skin is on fire, her mind full of itches that she can't scratch. She tries to formulate the words in her head, put them into a coherent sentence but her brain won't function properly. She can't seem to find a way of saying it out loud, of asking what he thought of the message. If he got it, that is. Maybe she is being targeted? She can't think why. Perhaps because Polly and the rest of the group feel slighted by Peggy's withdrawal from their social circle? Surely not? She was hardly the epicentre of their group of friends to begin with. Always on the periphery; an outsider looking in.

'Not hungry?' Alec asks, eyeing the untouched food on her plate.

She stabs at a slice of green pepper and forces it into her mouth, its slimy texture sliding down her throat, greasy and brackish. Her eyes water as she swallows hard and does her best to keep it down.

'Want to pass some of it over here then?' he says, the folds of fury etched into his face beginning to smooth out with each consecutive bite.

Peggy passes him her plate and watches as he devours another meal. She doesn't know how he can do it. Hollow legs. That's what her dad used to say when, as teenagers, she and Beatrice would quite literally eat their parents out of house and home. Like a swarm of locusts they used to descend on the kitchen, stripping the cupboards, bread bin and fridge until they were almost bare.

'Everything okay?' Alec asks as he dabs the corner of his mouth, pushes his plate to one side and leans back in his chair, finally satiated.

'Fine,' Peggy replies, thinking immediately that that is the wrong answer. People only say they're fine when they are anything but. 'I'm good,' she smiles, 'just a bit tired. How about you?'

She sees the change in him, a barely noticeable twitch of his eye, the way he tugs at his collar and twists his neck. Something has definitely happened. Alec runs his fingers through his hair and stands up to take the plates over to the sink.

'He came to see me today.'

Peggy's blood freezes in her veins. Who came to see him? Ashfaq? Rob? Why would they go to see him at work? Or was it at the pub? That would explain the smell of alcohol. He called into the pub on the way home. Not like Alec though. Not like him at all.

'Who did?'

'Who do you think?' he asks as he stares out at the sea, his back turned to her. The tap is turned on and the water gushes into the sink, splashing against the crockery, spraying up the tiles, a fountain of misery.

'I don't know,' she replies cautiously, the atmosphere thick with disquiet and foreboding.

'Him,' Alec mutters, his shoulders hunched as he rests his hands on the edge of the sink. 'Barry fucking Wilson, that's who.'

Peggy's heart crawls up her throat, 'Your dad came to see you? Where? Where did you meet him?'

'In the car park at work,' he growls, 'tonight as I was leaving.'

'Jesus,' is all she can manage. The sides of her face feel slightly numb as she tries to take it in, 'so what did he have to say?'

'Not a fat lot,' Alec replies as he begins to scrub at the pots. Peggy watches, wishing he would stop. This is important, they need to sit down and discuss it; leave everything, forget about domesticity and tidiness and focus on his father. She stares at his back, rigid with anger, watches his controlled movements as he tries to bridle his rage with mundane chores. It's understandable. Barry was violent, a monster by all accounts. The last thing they want is him coming here causing trouble, ripping what little they have left of their marriage apart. Peggy feels a headache coming on. Her mother's recent letters and now this. She feels like her entire skull is being compressed, her brain squashed inside it, shrivelling up like a walnut, rolling about; a small, hard stone knocking against bone. A dull pain settles behind her eyes, the start of something colossal.

'That's why I'm late in,' Alec adds. 'I went to the pub afterwards. Tried to clear my head.'

'Did he go with you?' Peggy is on her feet, small bursts of pain popping behind her eyeballs.

'What? Go with me?' Alec splutters, turning around to face her, 'I'm bloody sure he didn't. I wouldn't socialise with him if he was the last man on earth. Not a fucking chance.'

She nods and pulls at her sweater to straighten herself out, to give her something focus on to stop the eruptions in her skull from making her vomit. She needs space to think, somewhere dark and silent, 'I'm going to have a nap if that's okay?'

'You all right?' he asks quietly.

'Just a bit worn out, that's all. Too long sitting staring at a computer screen,' she lies.

Peggy feels his eyes on her, sees him smile slightly and for one awful minute she thinks he might say he's going to join her. She isn't in the mood for sex. Not now, not after the day they've had. But he doesn't. Instead he dries his hands and heads over to the drinks cabinet in the dining room where he scoops out a crystal tumbler and a bottle of whiskey.

'Purely medicinal,' he smiles as he opens the bottle and pours himself a large slug.

\*\*\*

It's part of her dream. It has to be. The bed sheets are crumpled at her feet and she is freezing. She leans down, grabs at them and sits motionless, listening. Cold fingers trail down her spine. Her scalp prickles. There it is again. A thumping sound - repetitive, relentless. The door. A heavy, authoritative fist is banging on their front door. Again? And at this time of night? Peggy stands up unsteady on her feet, her vision clearer, the pain now more of a residual, dull ache across the top of her head. She visualises Rachel standing there, windswept, forlorn, demanding more answers. She scans the room and looks at the clock. It's only 10 pm. She went for a lie down at what - eight? Probably nearer nine actually. Straightening out her clothes and pulling at her tangled hair, Peggy heads downstairs, her mind a whirl of fear and confusion.

Alec is standing at the foot of the stairs when she gets there, his face a tight wad of turmoil and bewilderment. His hair is ruffled and his clothes are askew. He has fallen asleep in the chair after one too many. Peggy hopes his temper holds as he turns the handle and opens the door.

Something catches in her chest as two burly looking men step forward out of the shadows and speak, 'Evening, sir. My name is Detective Constable Rollings and this is PC Evans. May we come inside? We'd like to talk to you about an incident that took place earlier this evening regarding a Mr Wilson,' the taller of the policemen says. His fair hair is slicked back from his face and his jowls wobble about as he speaks.

Alec stands to one side and motions for them to enter, his hand making a low sweeping gesture. Peggy stares at him then back at the officers who make their way through into the living room as if they are regular visitors here and have called round for a casual chat. She tries to catch Alec's attention but his eyes are glazed and he seems trance like. She hopes to God he didn't finish the entire bottle. Her legs refuse to work properly as she follows him and takes a seat on the sofa. Perching her bottom on the edge, her knees begin to knock together clumsily. She wraps her arms around them to stop the movement and does her utmost to steady her breathing. The two officers perch on a chair each, their black clothes and long angular legs an incongruous sight against the soft, cream leather of the couch.

'So, what's all this about?' Alec asks and Peggy finds herself inwardly heaving a sigh of relief. His speech isn't slurred. He isn't angry at being disturbed. He has snapped into action, an air of professional calm about him, an aura of serenity that, if the truth be told, she finds rather disturbing, considering their current predicament.

'Can you tell me where you were this evening, Mr Wilson?' DC Rollings says, his eyes narrow and unreadable. Peggy's insides shift.

'I was here?' Alec replies looking around and gesturing with his hands as if to say, *where do you think I was?*

'All evening?' the other policeman adds as he taps his fingers against the leather of the chair. Peggy wants to shout at him to sit still, to stop pawing her furniture but instead sits mutely, the veins in her head throbbing, electricity coursing around her body, small shocks of fear jolting through her limbs.

'I came home after work, had a Chinese takeaway and watched television.'

He's lying. Peggy feels a familiar thrum start up in her head. Why is he lying?

'You didn't meet up with a Mr Barry Wilson at any point then?' Rollings asks.

Peggy watches as Alec's shoulders droop and he rubs his fingers through his hair wearily, 'Yes, I did meet up with him. But that was at work. I was only with him for a few minutes. I dropped him off at the end of Albion Terrace. Then I went to the pub.'

'So, you weren't here all evening?' Evans murmurs, a hint of sarcasm present in his tone.

'I was only at the pub for a couple of halves,' Alec says despondently. He stares down at his feet, 'no harm in that is there?'

'There might be if you've tried telling us you were here all evening when you weren't,' Rollings replies sardonically.

'I thought you meant once I got in after work. I was home by seven thirty ' Alec mutters, his poise and self-assured persona disappearing into the ether. Peggy finds herself pitying him. His air of confidence didn't last long. Hardly surprising under such dire and difficult circumstances.

'You haven't asked us why we're here,' Evans chips in. Peggy is incensed. How dare they?

'You haven't given us a chance to!' she snaps. Why are they so hell bent on humiliating him?

'Mr Wilson was admitted to hospital tonight with serious injuries which were sustained during a violent assault. He said you were with him prior to the assault being carried out.'

Peggy watches Rollings' mouth move, sees the glint in his eye. He's enjoying this, loving every minute of it. A man was attacked tonight. A pensioner beaten half to death. And he thinks Alec did it. She swallows hard, sure her fear can be detected by everyone in the room. Her eyes mist over and her fingers tremble. She stares at Alec waiting for his response. The pause seems to go on and on, the tension between them thick and tangible until at last Alec speaks, his voice a hoarse whisper,

'You think I would physically attack my own father?' he manages to say at last.

There is another long silence and Peggy has to stop herself from standing up and ordering them both to leave.

'Well, would you?' Evans is staring at him, challenging him, *goading him*. Peggy wants to slap his face, bring some colour into those pale, lifeless cheeks.

'So, what has 'my father' told you about the attack?' Alec hooks his fingers in the air as he says the words *my father*. Peggy winces, wants to tell him he isn't helping his case. The police don't take kindly to scorn and derision. They can dole out plenty but don't take it well in return.

'The attack is a blank to him. The last he remembers is being in the car. With you. His son.'

Peggy stands up abruptly, the lopsided smile on Rollings' face suddenly too much to bear. This whole thing is a farce. Barry Wilson is setting him up. He has to be. Trying to frame his own son.

Unless … Peggy quashes the thought. Impossible. Unthinkable. Alec hates him. But not that much. Please don't let Alec hate his own father *that much.*

'It wasn't me,' Alec says quietly, 'which I'm sure forensics will be able to prove beyond any reasonable doubt.'

'You don't seem particularly upset about your father's condition, Mr Wilson. Don't you want to know how he is?' Evans' voice filters over, a wave of disdain directed at Alec.

'Ah, I'm pretty sure you guys know all about the man you keep referring to as my father,' Alec tips his chin forward. A small act of defiance. They know. Both he and Peggy are aware that they know. And if they don't, thinks Peggy, then she has every right to throw them out of her house. Such incompetence doesn't deserve their support or co-operation. She stands up and stalks around the living room, anger and frustration boiling up inside her.

'We do indeed. A troubled existence for both of you. You have every right to bear a grudge. I know I would,' Rollings says leaning forward conspiratorially, 'in fact if he were my father, after what he did, I would want to kill him.'

'I think you need to leave. NOW.' Peggy is standing over PC Evans. He looks up at her, unperturbed by her manner, his face a picture of innocence.

Rollings stares over at them before nodding to his colleague. They both stand up. The creak of leather echoes around the room as the chairs readjust to a state of emptiness.

'Don't do anything too rash like leave the country, Mr Wilson,' Evans says and Peggy has to stop herself from running over to him and slapping the self-satisfied smirk off his face.

'Stay where you are.' Rollings' voice booms around the room as he tugs at his jacket and straightens his collar, 'we'll see ourselves out.'

# Audrey

The waiting is driving her half insane. Every minute that passes, every hour, every day, every week is torturous. She can't bear it, hanging about like this. And she deplores being ignored. Deep down, some small part of her hoped that Peggy would relent and get in touch. She'll send another email soon, pester the life out of her until her daughter feels she has no other option than to reply. She should have known Peggy would ignore this, really. Even taking into account the huge rift between them, this is what Peggy does, how she handles trauma. She disappears inside her own head, goes undercover until it's all over, retreats inside her own thoughts and pretends nothing is wrong. Never changed since being a small child. So, until Peggy does get in touch, or Audrey herself approaches Peggy, then she is just killing time, thinking about that poor Sheryl creature and working out what he has done with her. Because she is obviously dead. If not dead, then where is she? People don't just disappear. They need money, food, shelter, all the things we take for granted each and every day. You can't just take off and not need money to survive. Sometimes Audrey can't bear to think about it - the fact that it could be her daughter whose face is currently splashed all over the internet, a headshot of an ordinary looking lady whose entire life was a lie. A woman who lived with a man, not knowing what malevolent deeds he is capable of, not knowing the secrets stashed away in his past.

Just lately, Audrey's mornings have consisted of staring at a computer screen, waiting for her inbox to spring into life but, as with all the other times, the replies haven't been forthcoming. She's had to fill her time in other ways. She's read every book she can get her hands on, even tried writing one herself but gave up after a few attempts at an opening paragraph. She doesn't know how Peggy does it. Far too insular a pastime for her, being stuck inside her own head, rummaging around for ideas, being brave enough to get them down on paper and show them off to the world. She has tried decorating this place. Audrey looks around at the new shade of pale grey on the walls. Better than the burnt orange that she has lived with for the past four years. She doesn't know why she left it so long. Perhaps it's because it doesn't feel like home and she hates living here? This two-bedroom bungalow is a far cry from their detached four-bedroom house on Chestnut Avenue. God, how she loved that place; each and every inch of it. She knew all its nooks and crannies, the strange noises she would encounter at night when the house seemed to come to life; it was as familiar to her as her own skin. After Peter died, the old place seemed to expand, to grow into an unmanageable mess with a garden she couldn't keep on top of, rooms she didn't have the money to heat or decorate. A complete money pit it was, and all the while her finances were shrinking and dwindling away. It had seemed like a good move at the time, re-mortgaging to get the garden landscaped and the roof replaced. Neither of them had banked on Peter's heart giving out like it did, leaving Audrey with hefty repayments. Peter's life insurance paid for the funeral and left her with enough to get by, but it didn't last long. She had already reduced her hours at the hospital before Peter's death and was given a point-blank refusal when she put an application in to go back on a full-time basis. She could have tried for a different position but was too long in the tooth to go through all that carry-on - updating her C.V., getting a profile on LinkedIn. All that nonsense. It was beyond her. So she sold the house and got something smaller. Not necessarily better, but definitely smaller. The house in Chestnut Avenue is where her memories belong - the house where she and Peter had moved to after they first got married, the childhood home of her girls, the place Peggy stormed out of after a huge argument, never to return. Tears burn at Audrey's eyes. Is it any wonder she feels the need to drink? That day. The day when a slow, festering anger that been building inside of Audrey burst out into the open - fierce and unstoppable. She went too far - of course she did. But what parent hasn't blown their top at one time or another? And her fury, resentment and fear were totally justified. You would have had to be blind to not see how completely wrong Peggy and Alec's relationship was. He was an adult for pity's sake and she was just a child. *A child for crying out loud*! Finding the pills was what triggered it. She hadn't reacted straightaway after seeing them there, shoved in a drawer, hidden away amongst a bundle of underwear. For weeks, she had kept it to herself, had lost sleep, was unable to eat properly or think straight. In the end, it consumed her - the thought of them together, having sex, his hands roaming over her daughter's young body … it sickened her. He was a grown man and should have known better. Oh, he was good at putting on a show, telling them his aspirations for finishing his degree, maybe even doing an MA. What tosh. Audrey saw through it all, knew him for the warped individual he really was. She could see beyond his charms, remembered his violent ways, knew exactly what he was capable of. She remembered all too well that feral boy with the wayward look in his eyes; the same look his father had. There were no second chances with Audrey when it came to such behaviour. Trouble would follow him wherever he went. It was mapped out in his genes. He was a Wilson and no amount of schooling or perfecting his appearance and manner would ever change that. In the beginning she had been polite, had done her best to make him welcome in their home, but all the time, in the back of her mind, the memories had lurked. Too vivid and graphic to forget. Leopards don't change their spots. She knew he wouldn't change his. Not with a father like Barry Wilson. The genes will out, as the saying goes.

Peggy had come home that day, so full of it, talking about how happy she was now she had Alec in her life, how amazing he was and how much she adored him, and after the gruelling shift at the hospital, where Audrey had cleaned up faeces, been spat at and told in no uncertain terms by a drunkard to *fuck off and die*, she had flipped. All the worries, the pent-up frustrations, the anger she had kept holed up for so long, had come spewing out. She had said things that she always swore she wouldn't say, and had accused Alec of being a paedophile, her words ringing around the room, bouncing off every wall. Peter was still at work, Beatrice staying out at a friend's house. Just Peggy and Audrey, alone with their anger and accusations rattling off every pane of glass, shaking the very foundations of the house until the entire building felt as if it would come tumbling down around them. But the words and arguments were nothing compared to what happened next.

Audrey rests her head in her hands, suddenly aware of its weight. Heavy. Everything in her body suddenly feels as if it is being dragged down to the ground, the force of gravity too great to keep her upright.

Other authors have pictures of themselves online and in their books, a face behind the words, someone for the readers to make a connection with. But not Peggy, not her daughter. And all because of Audrey.

She can barely bring herself to think about it, that particular event. On the occasions when it does present itself in her mind - because that does happen - it jumps in there, catching her unawares, sending her off-kilter, scaring her with its clarity and intensity, she feels sick to her stomach. All these years on and she still hasn't managed to make it all better. That's when the drink beckons. It's so easy. Too easy. Stuck at home all day, nothing else to do, nowhere to go to, a stream of accusatory, brutal thoughts skittering around in her head. She does her level best to keep them at bay, block them out; wash them away but they are nothing if not persistent; dogged in their pursuit of her sanity.

Audrey had dragged Peggy upstairs and rooted through her drawer, brandishing the contraceptive pills in Peggy's face, hollering at her about sleeping with an older man and Peggy had retaliated by telling her to mind her own fucking business. Audrey hadn't meant for it to happen. It was an accident. A horrible, dreadful mishap. A catastrophe. It's a flashback that will never leave her, haunting her, stabbing at her brain on a daily basis. And try as she might to blot it out, it refuses to go away, staying with her, a stubborn stain of culpability reminding her why her youngest daughter hates her. That day ... Audrey swallows hard and suddenly wishes she had a drink to hand. She looks around, too weary to get up and pour herself one. Her head hurts as she thinks back to that godawful day all those years ago - the day that saw her youngest daughter hurtle out of the house screaming and crying in agony, her face pouring with blood, never to return. And it was all Audrey's fault.

# BEFORE

I am exhausted. So horribly tired. Been shuffling myself forward for what feels like ages but have probably only moved a few feet. Not enough room for leverage. My back hurts and my head is in agony. I think I'm bleeding, can't tell, though. Too dark to see anything. The pain is inside and out, bouncing around my skull, sliding over my skin. So much of it. A dull ache travels up my limbs; cramps in my stomach. I stop myself from being sick. It hurts too much to throw up so I swallow it down. It burns, makes my eyes water, makes my nose run. Snot and spit everywhere. So difficult. I can't even remember which way I've moved any more. Up, down, it all feels the same. I think I've slept at some point. Can't be sure. I'm not even certain how long I've been here. I keep clinging on to the hope that someone will come and get me, open a door somewhere and drag me out. It's hard staying positive when there's this much pain and fear. My throat is sore and I'm thirsty. I tried screaming till I was sick. Hollering, howling, crying for help. It's no use. Nobody came. Not even sure where I am or if anyone even heard. The sound was muffled as if it was just bouncing back at me. I stopped. Need to conserve my energy. Desperate for a drink as well. And the ache in my head is becoming unbearable. Can't decide which part of me hurts the most - my back, head, neck. They're all agony. Sore and cold. Then burning hot, then freezing again. I am tired, my eyes too heavy to stay open. And the darkness, it is absolute. So awful being closed in like this, surrounded by the pitch black. Never known anything like it. And still so few memories. I've tried but can't seem to recall anything. No idea why. Sometimes fragments of thoughts, not even thoughts really, more like images - visions

122

I can't put into words - dart in and out of my brain. They're gone before I can piece them together. All random, floating around, teasing me, stopping me from remembering anything. Can't seem to make the connection. So very thirsty. I have to think of other things, take my mind off it. My sister. I think of Rachel, her lovely face. Where is she? And my dad. His features are blurred, not like Rachel's. I don't think I can remember what he looks like any more. Or the sound of his voice. Or what his last words were to me when I saw him. I'm tired now; really, really tired but I'm too afraid to go to sleep. What if I don't wake up? What if I close my eyes and they stay shut? I tap my fingers against the floor. It's cold. Fingers are numb. I keep tapping till the numbness creeps up my hands. I feel a knot somewhere deep down below my waist, a strange tugging. It tears at my insides for a short while then it's gone. I wait while the feeling seeps out of me and then I realise what it is. Tears flow. I can't stop them no matter how hard I try. The tugging has gone and now a warm feeling covers the top of my legs and spreads up my back. Wet and hot, pooling and gathering underneath me. How did that happen? Why couldn't I stop it?

***

I think I've slept. Hard to tell. Terrible dreams. Fighting, pushing, biting. Nightmares about being unable to breathe. Nightmares about dying.

I shout out again, my throat thick and sore, the thirst raging and all consuming. Need a drink, desperate for it.

'HELP!'

I cough and splutter. No use. Nobody here to help me. How long have I been here? Hours? No, more than hours. Days? Not sure. Not sure of anything anymore.

A terrible pain circles my stomach, griping and clawing at my insides. I try to bring my knees up but can't. Not enough room. The pain increases. So much of it. Then a sudden burst of heat and a terrible stench leaking up from beneath me. Oh God, please no. *Please help me!*

I sob hysterically, unable to stop. The smell fills my nostrils and the pain in my head becomes unbearable as more fluids leak out of my body. And that's when I know for sure. I know that I'm doomed. Forgotten about; left here to die. Still no memories but I no longer care. I just want to sleep. So tired and so much pain. Maybe it will be easier to just let myself go, be swallowed up by the darkness. Easier than fighting it. Just go with it, let death have me. I close my eyes, no longer caring whether or not I ever wake up …

# Peggy

Sleep evades her. Yet again. Her brain is racing, a swirl of activity that makes her want to scratch at her eyeballs and rip her hair out. She listens to Alec snoring softly and wonders how he does it. How is he not up pacing the floor, his nerves in tatters? His father is currently hooked up to a drip in hospital after taking a beating from an unknown assailant. The police have made it pretty obvious they think Alec is the main suspect and here he is sleeping like a baby. Peggy feels her face begin to prickle, a creeping, crawling sensation like an army of ants roaming around under her skin. Is he capable of such an act? Who knows what any of us are capable of when we are under pressure. Swinging her legs out of bed, Peggy pulls on her dressing gown and slippers and heads downstairs. Alec doesn't stir. Such a deep sleeper. She doesn't know how he does it; 'the sleep of the just' as her dad used to say. She pads into the kitchen and fills the kettle before settling down in front of her computer. It fizzles into life and Peggy stares at the screen – 4 a.m. The majority of the nation is slumbering peacefully in their beds. But not Peggy. No rest for the wicked. She listens to the hum of boiling water as she browses the internet, a flash of adverts attacking her brain with their bright, glaring colours and swiftly moving images. She stops for a few seconds then clicks the mouse. It's too easy to do, checking on Facebook, finding the information about Sheryl's disappearance. Reading word after word, each one bleeding and seeping into her bones like poison. She is horrified to see all the comments listed below Sheryl's picture. For some reason, she hadn't quite expected so much interest in the disappearance of a woman none of these people even know. Peggy browses for a while, scrolling down, reading them all - some helpful, some scathing at her taking off like this and putting her family through hell, and other comments truly macabre. Some people have no filter. A world full of trolls. Peggy bites the inside of her mouth. No wonder she would rather stay inside, surrounded by her own four walls day in and day out. So many dreadful people out there, pumped full of vitriol, just waiting to spew it all out. Always armed and ready with accusations and constantly loaded with hatred. She reads the details of Sheryl's last known movements. According to Rachel, she left their father's house at 9 p.m. on Thursday, 22$^{nd}$ September after spending an evening socialising with family. She got a taxi home to Skelton and messaged Rachel to say she had arrived safely. Nobody saw or heard from her again until she sent her sister a text saying she was going away for a while to 'clear her head.' Some of Sheryl's clients received texts cancelling their appointments for the following few days but others were surprised when she simply didn't turn up. There were no more messages until last week when Rachel got another one out of the blue from Sheryl stating that she was absolutely fine and not to worry about her and that she just needed a bit more time to 'sort things out.' Peggy thinks of Alec and wonders whether he even knows of this disappearance and whether or not he received the same text from Polly that she did. He isn't on Facebook so possibly knows nothing of any of this. He's not made any mention of it but then, the news of his father's reappearance has pretty much obliterated everything else. Things seem to be happening so rapidly lately, Peggy is finding it hard to take it all in. It's as if time has suddenly decided to speed up and bring a whole heap of anguish and misery raining down on them all at once. She chews at a ragged piece of nail and considers her options. What good will it do talking to him about this? It won't help to find Sheryl, and Peggy is almost certain Alec hasn't seen her for at least a few weeks anyway. She spits out a tiny bit of fingernail and watches as it lands on the floor, small pieces of her being stripped away bit by bit.

She scans through more of the comments before clicking off the page. Too much. It's all too gruesome to take in. Her fingers hover over the keyboard before she decides to open her latest novel and start the next chapter. The words begin to blur on the screen. She continues to stare at them, reading the same line over and over again before closing the lid with a clatter and pushing her chair back in disgust. It's too early to think straight, her brain is muddled and she is too exhausted to write. What she really needs to do is forget about making tea, head back upstairs and try to get some sleep before the sun makes its appearance on the east shoreline, beckoning them all to rise, ready for the day ahead. A noise suddenly startles her, causing a quick twist in her stomach. She is on edge all the time lately, constantly battling a feeling that everything is about to come crashing down around her. It's coming from outside, the noise. Peggy stands up and stares out of the window that overlooks the sea. The night is a blanket of black velvet, no chinks of light, nothing powerful enough to penetrate the inky mantle of darkness. The roar of the tide is there, the familiar rushing hum that Peggy has grown accustomed to, a backdrop to her days. The noise comes again, alien to her ears, quite different to the snarl of the sea. Outside. It is definitely coming from somewhere outside the house. She pictures Chamber Cottage and its location. High up, exposed to the elements. Windy, dark. It's cold out there for sure but not sub-zero and nothing she isn't used to. It is however, the early hours and the wind is too strong to go out unprepared. Peggy pulls on a coat and slips into her boots. She grabs the torch hanging on the wall next to the door and trudges out there, suddenly wishing she had stayed in bed.

The door is almost taken out of her hand as she slowly pushes it ajar, the roaring wind like a huge, snatching fist forcing it wide open, wrestling it out of her grasp. It bangs against the wall and Peggy flinches as the sound echoes around the cottage. She reaches out and grabs it again, hanging onto it, closing it as quietly as she can. It clicks to and before she can catch her breath, she finds herself being buffeted about by a howling gale, her body bent almost double as it comes at her from all angles, forceful and unyielding, slapping at her face and whipping strands of thick, coiled hair into her face. Peggy turns slightly to the side, the strength of the gusts pushing her back into the wall as she tries to shine the torch around the area by the bins. She's pretty sure that's where the sound was coming from. Even with the torchlight it's almost impossible to see anything. She needs to be careful here. The edge of the cliff isn't so close but the place is littered with potholes and she doesn't fancy losing her footing in the pitch black. She stops and listens, the sound of her feet crunching on gravel, filling the night air. Another blast of freezing wind races in over the horizon and sets the sea into an almighty howl. The force of the squall sends her hurtling into the fence and Peggy feels herself falling onto the floor with a thud. She sits for a short while, trying to catch her breath, the cold seeping up through her bones in a matter of seconds. Clambering back up, she stands with her back against the rough wall, small jagged fragments of concrete digging into her spine. Steel fingers claw at her chest as she hears it again. A low moaning sound emanating from somewhere behind her. She visualises an attacker, crouched, ready to hurtle at her, knock her to the floor, do all manner of unspeakable things to her. It's so dark out here. Nobody around, no-one to help her. The nearest people are Brenda and Maude in the farmhouse over the main road. An exhausted woman juggling a full-time job and looking after a demented old lady. Like they could be of any assistance. And even if the young man is staying over he would be of no use at all. He was a nervous wreck and would blow over in a slight breeze. He couldn't fight off an attacker if his life depended on it. As for Alec - he sleeps the sleep of the dead. She could be murdered right here on her own doorstep and he wouldn't even know. Peggy stops and tries to still her thrashing heart that is jumping around her chest, flapping and banging into her ribcage like a tiny, captive bird. Even in this freezing weather she feels hot, her core temperature a furnace of bulging flames, fear licking and burning her skin. She blinks and steadies her breathing. This is stupid. She needs to calm down and get a fucking grip. She's had far worse than this to deal with before now. What does she expect to find out here for God's sake? This is hardly the first place a madman would hide, is it? Up on a cliff edge in the dead of night. She tells herself that her fear is fuelled by the darkness and the isolation. The noise is probably no more than some sort of wild animal scurrying around, feasting on scraps of food and anything they can scavenge in the dark. Her breath escapes in tiny, fragmented gasps, her throat suddenly dry and tight. Edging her way along the wall, Peggy scours the area with a thin beam of light, the torch heavy in her hand.

'Anybody there?' she calls out, her voice a squeak against the howl of the tide.

A low but definite moan begins to gather momentum. It crashes into her brain and her legs begin to buckle as the sound increases in strength.

'Here,' a voice crackles through the darkness, reedy and brittle, 'I'm over here.'

Peggy wants to weep. Terror twists her insides as she slowly sweeps the torch towards the voice. The yellow light shakes violently as she struggles to hold it still, her knuckles taut, her hands shaking uncontrollably.

'Not there - here!' the voice screeches.

The world tilts and Peggy lets out a scream. She feels herself sliding to the ground as emaciated, ice cold fingers clasp around her ankle and grip on for dear life. Fear blinds her as she hits the cold, stone floor and the voice whispers in her ear, 'You! It's you ...'

# Brenda

It's the dream that wakes her. A terrible nightmare of death and terror and things she can't quite remember clearly enough to put into words. Or at least doesn't want to. Just a jumble of hideous images that will stay with her for the next few days. Nightmares involving falling and screaming and clawing at wet earth to save herself - plunging into a deep chasm, being unable to breathe properly. Dreadful pictures lodged inside her brain. Nightmares are the bane of her life and she is having more and more of them these days. She lets out a trembling sigh. It's the stress of work, she is sure of it. And her break up with Stuart. And of course, her mother. It's always Maude at the centre of things. As if her full-time job as a ward manager at one of the largest hospitals in the north-east isn't difficult enough. And now Stuart is claiming he wants money from her mother's house when she sells it. Such a horrible, odious arsehole he is. He knows how bad things are for her at the moment. She's tried to keep it friendly, be affable and co-operative but he is going out of his way to make the divorce as painful as possible. A pain travels up her neck, lodging behind the rear of her skull, thrashing around her brain. She lies still for a while and waits for the whooshing in her ears to cease, then turns over and longs for sleep to return and engulf her. It isn't forthcoming but then she knew it wouldn't be. Once she's awake, she's awake. Brenda cocks her head and listens out for her mother. She can usually hear her snuffling and snoring in the room next door. It's unusually quiet tonight but then the snuffling takes place just as Maude is settling down. She sits up and flicks on the bedside lamp, wishing she was back at home. She always sleeps better there. Being back in her childhood bedroom wasn't

130

on her list of aspirations at the start of this year. Neither was a messy divorce but there you are. Funny how life can be, waking up one morning realising you no longer want to spend the rest of your life with your feckless, drunkard of a husband, and then being faced with having to watch your mother slip and slide her way into the gaping, ghastly abyss that is dementia. Being a passive bystander, unable to shield her from the horrors that her brain subjects her to every day as it deteriorates and shrivels up until she no longer knows who, or where, she is. Such a cruel, wicked disease.

The wind gathers speed outside, rattling at the windows and sending the sea into a near frenzy. Brenda shivers and pulls on her dressing gown, wondering if she should get up or stay in bed and read until she starts to feel tired again. She could really do with a couple of paracetamol and a glass of water. Her head feels like it's stuffed full of cotton wool and her throat is as dry as sandpaper. It's a good job she is off work tomorrow although under the current circumstances it's actually easier getting up at the crack of dawn and going off to the hospital to do a twelve-hour shift than it is staying here and looking after her mother. Things will be better once she gets this place surveyed and on the market. It's only time that's stopping her from getting things moving, or rather the lack of it. A lick of paint and a few touch-up jobs here and there and she'll put the old place up for sale. It won't fetch a hefty price - it hasn't been properly decorated in years - but it will be enough to employ a full-time carer and it will be worth losing a few grand to not have to spend every day worrying about what Maude is up to in her absence. She will be damned if Stuart is going his hands on a penny of this place so he can piss it all up the wall. Not a bloody chance.

She shuffles her feet into her slippers and tugs her fleecy robe tighter around her midriff then pulls open the door and quietly pads downstairs not wanting to wake her mother. Getting her back off to sleep is nothing short of nightmarish if she wakes in the middle of the night. As well as everything else, dementia has robbed Maude of her own body clock. Once she is awake, she paces the floor crying for her breakfast and demanding Brenda turn on the television so they can watch *The King and I* for the thousandth time that week. Sometimes for a treat they will have a crack at *Fiddler on the Roof* or *The Sound of Music* in order to keep Brenda's sanity intact, but generally *The King and I* is the one that keeps Maude quiet, helps to soothe her and stop her from getting up to anything untoward in the early hours while Brenda snoozes quietly in the chair.

The floorboards creak under her feet as she shuffles along, trying to dodge the noisy ones she knows will let out a squeal. She stops outside her mother's room and considers going in, just popping her head round the door to make sure Maude is okay, but decides against it. She doesn't want to run the risk of waking her and putting them both through any unnecessary stress. Anything involving her mother is an ordeal these days. Brenda is relieved at the silence that greets her as she waits and listens. A guilty thought steals through her mind. She swats it away and admonishes herself for even entertaining the very idea that Maude might have died in her sleep. Because there are days when she wishes it. God, how it would help ease some of the stress in her life to get up one morning and find her mother has departed this life for another one. A life where she can remember her own name and spend her days with Brenda's father; happy and dementia free. And then Brenda snaps out of it and has to deal with one of Maude's rages, or clean up the bed sheets after Maude has soiled herself during the night or be faced with any number of scenarios that her mother's condition throws her way each and every day as Maude's mind slowly shuts down, leaving her a shell of her former self. It's hard to believe, looking at her now, but there was a fully functioning Maude before dementia got its claws into her and tore her brain to shreds. She was an amazing mother and wife, a pillar of the community, a schoolteacher loved and admired by pupils past and present. And now she thinks the Germans are still flying overhead, bombing the shit out of the north-east of

England and that her father is working as a stevedore at the local shipyard. Sometimes Brenda finds herself staring at her mother's face, scrutinising it for signs of the woman she once knew, the woman whose sparkling, dancing eyes once had fire in them. The same lady, whose eyes are now rheumy, glazed, uncomprehending. The woman who spends her days wandering around the house tearing up bits of paper and stripping down to her underwear in the middle of the living room. Dementia - the eater of people, the dark destroyer of the human soul. It has torn the heart out of Maude, and Brenda has to clean up the mess it has left in its wake. If there is a God, Brenda is sure he is up there right now, laughing at her predicament, making her pay for every teenage misdemeanour she ever perpetrated.

She quietly heads downstairs, figuring it's better to let sleeping dogs lie. At the bottom of the stairs Brenda stops, flicks the light on and opens the door into the living room. She stares at the sight before her and feels the blood drain from her head. The living room has been completely ransacked, cushions overturned and thrown on the floor, papers scattered everywhere. A lamp in the far corner of the room is turned on and Brenda stops, barely able to breathe as a cold blast of wind whips around her legs, stopping the blood in her veins. Tugging at her fleecy robe and struggling to control her breathing, Brenda shuffles towards the kitchen, fear consuming her. The draught increases in strength the closer she gets. A ribbon of fear wraps itself around her head. What if there is someone in the kitchen? Poised to attack behind the door, knife in hand with demonic intent? Heart jumping around her chest, Brenda takes baby steps past the dining table toward the open door that has started to creak as it moves slightly in the gathering breeze. She can barely breathe. Her chest aches and her skin is clammy. Reaching out she uses the flat of her palm and quickly pushes the door fully open, steeling herself for a blow. The door slams into the wall, the clatter causing her toes to curl. Brenda stares through at an empty room. No burglar, nobody rooting around looking for items to steal so they can feed a raging crack addiction. Nothing amiss. Except for the back door which is wide open, a gaping mouth allowing the night to creep in and drape itself around the room like a heavy shroud. She doesn't know whether to feel relieved or horrified. Why is the back door wide open? Stepping forward, Brenda quickly slams it shut and locks it, scanning the room as she turns to head back into the living room. The thought of somebody prowling around makes her queasy - somebody down here, searching, touching their things, turning the place upside down while she and her mother were asleep upstairs. Something flickers in her mind, flames licking at her exhausted brain. *Maude.* Taking the stairs two at a time, Brenda tears upstairs, visualising a madman leaning over her mother's bed, peeling the covers back to reveal her tiny, frail body. A helpless victim, unable to defend herself. Bile rises in Brenda's throat and tight fingers grasp at her windpipe leaving her struggling to breathe properly as she opens Maude's door, no longer caring if she wakes her or not. She will sit up all night watching any number of musicals as long as her mother is safe. Light from the landing spreads over the bed in the centre of the room. The room spins. Vomit rises. The bed is empty. Brenda stalks across the floor, her footsteps now heavy and panicky. Flinging open wardrobe doors and dragging drawers out onto the floor in a blind panic, Brenda begins to scream out,

'Mum! MUM!'

Her voice reverberates around the bedroom, bouncing off walls and accentuating Maude's absence as Brenda tries to stop her hysteria from bursting out and sending her into a complete meltdown. She has to keep cool and composed, use all of her professional training, remain calm in the face of adversity. There is a rational explanation behind all of this. There has to be. Terror yanks at the back of her brain, scaly fingers squeezing all logic out of her thinking process. She fights it off, wishing she had a decent husband or a sibling to help her. It's not easy being alone, having to make all the decisions, facing all the terror on your own without anybody to turn to for help. She stops, sweat coating her face, fear prickling at her scalp.

The rest of the house. She begins to search it, stalking from room to room before it suddenly dawns on her.

'Fuck!'

Tearing down the stairs, Brenda wrestles with the lock on the back door, her palms clammy as she attempts to turn it, the cold metal handle slipping out of her grasp until she eventually manages to snap it open. She hurtles out into the freezing night air, her breath misting up in small, grey wisps before trailing off into the ether.

'MUM!' her voice disappears into the night - a small, inaudible whine drowned out by a sudden howl from the sea down below.

'Mother! MAUDE!' She grabs her dressing gown and gathers it up, holding the folds of fabric in her clenched fists as she gallops across the garden, desperately scanning the area for any signs of movement. It's useless. Her eyes strain against the darkness. She needs a torch but can't even think whether or not there is one in the house. There must be. They had them when she was a child growing up here but can't recall seeing one anywhere while she's been staying here and she doesn't have the time to go searching. Her mother is out here somewhere. Brenda thinks of the cliff edge and the black sea below and feels hot pins stab at her face. It was only a matter of minutes ago she was wishing her mother dead and now ... a heaving breath catches in her throat. She swallows hard and rubs at her eyes wearily. She should call the police. Maude is a tiny, vulnerable old lady. Even without taking into account the location, she could freeze to death out here. And to think she was initially furious with Andrew for letting her escape out here weeks back and now here she is, in the same position, except this time it's worse. It's four in the morning and Maude is nowhere to be seen. An involuntary sob escapes before she has chance to stop it. Hot tears begin to flow, misting up her vision. She rubs her face with her sleeve, a gelatinous mixture of snot and salty tears smearing over the fabric leaving a glue-like residue.

'Come ON, Mum! Where the hell are you?' Her voice wafts through the night, a thin streak of nothingness. She turns back to the house. She has to ring the police and she has to do it right now. Every second she wastes puts Maude further in danger. Whether it be from the sharp night air or a fall down a rabbit hole or, God forbid, a tumble over the edge of the cliff down to the deep, treacherous water beneath. Brenda's breathing increases, coming out in heaving, rattling gasps, her chest heavy with despair.

'MAUDE!' This time her voice has some substance to it; a bellow that travels across the garden, filtering through the hedgerows and piercing the night air. A lull in the weather has caused a momentary silence. The sea has ceased its almighty crashing; the wind has dropped to a slight whisper and Brenda can at last hear the echo of her call trilling in the distance. She stops, a hiccup caught in her throat as she listens. Did she imagine it or is there a sound coming from somewhere beyond the garden? Or is it just that she is *wishing* to hear something and her imagination is playing tricks on her?

'MUM! Where ARE you?' She waits, her ear attuned to the reverberations of her own calls.

There it is again. An indistinct but definite sound. Unable to keep hold of the yards of material bunched up in her fist, Brenda shrugs off her thick, fleecy robe. It drops to the ground at her feet and gathers in a soft mound. Wearing only a thin nightgown and a pair of slippers, Brenda takes off at a gallop, darting out of the garden and into the blackness beyond. There is no light anywhere, the opaqueness of the night complete, but she'll keep on going, follow the sound until she reaches her.

'MOTHER!' She screams Maude's name over and over again and stops only to listen for a response. It's there - faint and light, a whisper on the wind, but somebody, somewhere is calling back to her. Heart pounding at her ribs like a battering ram, she sets off once more, not caring whether she falls over; not concerned about the danger that may lie ahead. She has to find her mother - poor, tiny, helpless Maude who somehow managed to find her way out of the house and is currently stumbling around in the dark on top of a cliff, wearing God knows what and with God knows who. The faster Brenda runs, the further away the sound seems to get. She stops and hollers once more, 'MUM!'

This time the answer is closer. She is able to make out hazy sounds and form them into a vaguely coherent response. *Thank fuck for that! She's alive ...*

'Here,' the voice shouts as Brenda pounds across the grass, over the gritty, uneven road, onto more grass, through the gorse bushes that snag and tear at her skin, leaving her bleeding and crying out in pain, and eventually onto the long stretch of gravel that leads to the old coastguards' cottage near the border of the clifftop. *Near the edge* ... RIGHT NEAR THE FUCKING EDGE! Brenda feels her legs buckle at the thought of Maude staggering and falling, limbs flailing, fear consuming her as she cries out for the daughter that wasn't there, the daughter who didn't save her.

By the time she reaches the perimeter of the cottage's garden she can barely hold herself upright. Tears are blinding her and her arms and legs are slick with blood where the thorns have torn and ripped at her exposed skin. She stops, adrenaline coursing through her system, masking the pain. It'll hit her later, when she stops, when this is all over. She touches her upper arms and sucks her breath in. She may even need stitches and a tetanus injection. No time right now. She'll sort herself out later. Right now, she needs to find Maude, who will be freezing and terrified and possibly in need of medical care. How the hell did she get out? Brenda can't bear to think about it. Her fault of course. She must have left the key in the door. No way did she leave it unlocked. She stumbles forward, driven on by guilt and fear. Moving round the back of the cottage, Brenda lets out an involuntary gasp of relief. An open door. The back door is ajar and coming from it, Brenda can see a long shaft of light that is penetrating the darkness, flooding the step with a spread of yellow. Something catches her eye, a movement, noises, a bundle of shadows. Brenda moves forward, her chest tight with fear and trepidation at what she may find there. Her eyes are drawn to the flickering movements to one side of the light. She stares down, horror gripping her as her eyes land upon an opaque shape on the floor. There, huddled in the dark, is a writhing mass of limbs. Brenda steps forward, dizzy and sick with fear to see two tiny bodies at her feet ...

'Mother?' she whispers, her voice hoarse and ragged.

The shriek cuts her in two as Maude's voice splits through the darkness, an edge to it that freezes her blood. 'She's dead!' The tiny voice cries, 'She fell down and now she's dead!'

Brenda feels her head spin as an icy hand reaches out and grabs her nightie bringing her crashing down onto the floor in an undignified, painful heap.

# Alec

It's rare for anything to wake him but the almighty racket going on outside Chamber Cottage has dragged him from the deepest of slumbers and he is absolutely fucking furious. What the hell is going on out there? It sounds like a pair of caterwauling feral creatures right outside his bedroom window, a series of howls and squawks that has filtered through his brain, into his dreams and ripped him from the comforting arms of sleep.

Alec throws back the quilt, suddenly aware that Peggy isn't there. He reaches over and touches her side of the bed. It's cold. His brain freezes, caught between the dark realms of sleep induced thoughts and stark reality. He sits for a few seconds trying to make sense of it. Is it morning and she's already up? He swivels his head round, stares at the clock and waits while the numbers come into focus. It's almost four thirty in the morning. *Four thirty?* Where the hell is she and what in God's name is going on outside his house? The somnolent fog inside Alec's head begins to clear as he stands up, pulls the blinds to one side and peers out of the window. Nothing out the front but an impenetrable blanket of blackness and the usual rush of the sea. He pulls on a pair of joggers and a t-shirt and stalks out onto the landing to peer out of the window that overlooks the side garden and rear of the cottage. The noise is amplified there. Voices. Shouting. Then screaming. *Shit!* Alec stumbles downstairs, feet twisting and turning under him, his chest pounding. *What the fuck is going on?* Images of a gang of intruders, high on drink and drugs, bursts into his brain as he prepares himself for whatever is going on out there. And what about Peggy? What have they done to her? Fire rages as thinks of her tiny frame, how inept she would be at fighting anybody off.

Alec looks around as he races into the living room, his head spinning. Everything is normal. Nothing out of place. Eyes wide, he heads into the kitchen, steeling himself for a blow. That's where they'll be - whoever *they* are. Peggy's laptop is in the centre of the table, its usual place. Another tidy room. The hairs on the back of his neck stand to attention as voices sift through from what he can now see is an open door. How did he not notice that before? *An open door ...* He listens, a creeping sensation working its way up his spine as he hears Peggy's voice, pleading, cajoling, and then another screeching voice. Something registers in his brain, a familiarity about that sound that he can't quite place. Alec pauses, his temples pounding, then hurtles outside, ashamed of his reticence and fear. The cold air bites at his bare arms. He lets out a low grunt as he trips and falls over the pile of bodies on the concrete step to the side of the door.

'Jesus!' His cries silence the other voices as he stumbles over the gravel, pulling at his joggers and dancing about in bare feet, sharp gravel pricking the sensitive skin on the soles of his feet. 'Fuck!'

'Alec?' Peggy's voice is mingled in with a cacophony of sound that has begun to swell once more.

He stares down at the pile of bodies spread over the floor. Sucking in his breath at the pain that is stabbing at him, Alec leaps back onto the step, away from the tiny, jagged stones.

'What the hell is going on here?' He leans down and grabs the arm of another lady and pulls her upright, his face full of fire, 'and who the fuck are you?'

The ashen-faced woman starts to shake, her large body barely covered by a short, cotton nightdress. Rivulets of blood snake down her arms. She looks as if she has been clawed by something. *Or somebody.* She opens her mouth to speak but is drowned out by more shrieks from the small, wiry corpse-like shape on the floor. 'Home! I want to go home Brenda. TAKE ME HOME.'

'All right Mum, please don't shout. We're going home now,' she says sharply. Her voice is brittle as she flashes a glance Alec's way. 'Come on, Mum, let's get you up.'

Lifting her arm up, she shrugs herself free of Alec's clutches, her body trembling violently. Blood covered hands reach down to haul the tiny shadow upright. Alec immediately recognises the shape before him. It's her - that old lady, here on his doorstep in the early hours of the morning. *What the fuck?* Peggy drags herself up from the floor and dusts herself down with shaking hands as the old lady slowly straightens up. Peggy's hair is a wild, dark tangle of curls and her eyes are sunken into her face; grey hollows set deep in her skull. She rests her hand on Alec's arm and he can feel the tremor from her ice-cold fingers, tiny vibrations pulsating through her skin.

Alec stares as the old lady unfurls her skeletal frame and stands before him. Her eyes have a sharp, wild look about them, not the look of an uncomprehending, demented old woman but someone who has a purpose, a hidden, simmering anger. An agenda he can't quite fathom. She thrusts something towards him and for one sickening moment Alec fears it might be a knife or a piece of glass. Any sharp implement designed to hurt or maim him. He takes a sudden step back and watches as she shoves a piece of crumpled paper into his hand. Her palm is cool and crisp like parchment, which for some reason completely repulses him.

'Here,' she croaks, 'this is for you.'

Alec quickly pulls away from her, this ghost of a woman with eyes like coal; the old woman from the farmhouse; the lady who makes his skin crawl. He stares down at the screwed-up paper before straightening it out and squinting at it in the dim light.

'I'm so sorry,' her daughter says, her voice cracking as she speaks, 'I have no idea how she got out. I can't apologise enough for this. It's all my fault. I take full responsibility.'

'She could have been killed out here on her own,' Peggy's voice has a sour edge to it. She is ashen and Alec can see she has taken a blow to her head as she fell. Fortunately, it looks as if the old lady was underneath her and she afforded Peggy a softer landing than if she had fallen on the concrete but he can see that her head is still sore and she is exhausted and shaken up. In a rare moment of pity, he slides his arm around her and pulls her close.

'I'll take her straight home and call by in the morning to see if you're okay. I'm a nurse and I can drive you to a medical centre or your doctor's surgery if you would prefer that.'

Peggy hangs onto Alec and shakes her head vehemently, 'I'm fine. Just need some sleep, that's all.'

Alec stares at the paper, his eyes scanning the unrefined scribbles and marks on there, drawn by the hand of a manic old lady. He looks up to see the pair of them begin to walk away, the elderly woman shuffling along in a pair of fluffy slippers and her daughter in a short nightdress. He shakes his head at the insanity of it all. *This is fucking madness!*

'Hang on a minute!'

Brenda turns around to face him, her eyes stricken with fear at what he might say.

'What exactly *is* this?' Alec brandishes the paper in the air, his fingers clutched tightly round it as he waves the drawing about angrily.

'I'm really sorry. Sometimes mum gets an idea in her head and it just takes hold. She won't settle until she sees it through. Completely delusional, I know, but that's just how she is.' Her voice sails through the darkness of the night, the final words almost drowned out by a sudden blast of wind that nearly takes the paper right out of Alec's grip.

'That doesn't answer my question!' he barks back at her, 'I want to know why your mother is out here bothering me and my wife AGAIN.'

'Just leave it Alec, please.' Peggy's voice is no more than a whisper, an exhausted plea for him to calm down. But he can't. He's awake now and no amount of pleading will make him calm the fuck down. His head is raging, a bubbling cauldron of anger, frustration and fury at being dragged from his bed at such an ungodly hour. This is the second time this silly bitch has allowed her mother to practically terrorise him and Peggy and if she thinks she's going to get it away with it like she did last time, then she can bloody well think again. Enough is enough. Who is this strange little shrieking woman with her clumsy, overweight oaf of a daughter anyway?

Alec sees the woman's face darken. He waits while she decides how best to respond to his question then watches incredulously as she turns away from him and practically drags her mother off over the grass verge and onto the path that leads towards their house. He considers heading off out there after her, giving the pair of them a piece of his mind but knows how Peggy would react to such an outburst, so stands quietly instead, his fist curled into a tight ball, the paper scrunched up inside it.

'Just let them go, Alec. Please.'

He feels her eyes on him, the pleading expression for him to keep his temper in check. Like a reprimanded child, frustrated by his lack of liberty and angered by the current situation, Alec grabs Peggy's hand, pulls her inside and slams the door behind them both.

# Peggy

She can't even think what day it is. It's light outside and rain is battering at the windows; tiny torpedoes hammering at the glass. It feels like sharp slivers of ice are cutting deep into her soul. Another cold and miserable day. Alec is sleeping soundly. It's the weekend. It must be. She reaches over and stares at the clock then slumps back down, slinks under the duvet and shivers, a jumble of horrible images all jostling for space in her head. Did last night actually happen? Or has her frazzled brain added bits on to make it seem more outlandish than it actually was? Peggy closes her eyes again and tries to remember. One thing is certain - the young man was right - the demented old lady possesses the strength of ten men. It took Peggy a good five minutes to get the old woman to release her ankle from her wiry clutches. She moves her foot gingerly dragging it over the cool bed sheets. It's sore and tender. Peggy feels sure she must have a handprint of her skeletal fingers imprinted on her leg, such was the ferocity of the grip. The pair of them had huddled and wrestled there on the cold step for what felt like an age, Peggy always aware of the old lady's tiny, willow-like frame, doing her best to make sure neither of them broke any bones. And when the old woman did finally stop writhing about, Peggy tried her best to calm her down, to stop her shrieking like a wild animal in its death throes. She hadn't been able to get a great deal of sense out of her, but Peggy was able to pick up a few phrases that she had kept repeating like a mantra - *Shouting and fighting, shouting and fighting,* punctured with the occasional scream of *She fell! I saw her, she fell!* No amount of soothing and cajoling would stop her, even when Peggy offered to take her inside and give her a hot cup of tea and a biscuit.

Nothing worked. She just went on and on, screaming into the darkness. There seemed to be no end to it. Eventually Peggy shut off to her shrieks and accusations, told her brain to ignore it, that sooner or later the old lady would wear herself out.

Peggy turns onto her side and rubs at her face wearily. And then of course there was the piece of paper that she gave to Alec. Not the childish scribbles they had both been expecting; nothing like that at all. It was a dreadful picture, a complete shock for something produced by someone in her state, more like something drawn by the hand of a psychopath. Pictures of broken bodies, blood spurting out of them at all angles. Peggy shivers and feels hot fear begin to rise inside her, bubbling like lava. She thinks of the incident with Alec's father and the subsequent visit from the police and can no longer bear it. Throwing back the quilt, Peggy practically catapults herself out of bed and heads straight into the shower where she scrubs at her skin until it is almost raw. She needs to feel clean, to rid herself of the horrors of yesterday. This is all too much and she's not sure she can bear it any longer. The water pummelling her body is the only escape from it all, the only place she feels safe. Steam billows up in front of her face, misting up her vision. She continues to wash and scrub, turning the temperature up as high as she can until it begins to burn her skin and she can no longer stand the pain.

Alec is still in bed, snoring softly, as she dries herself, rubbing vigorously with the towel. She dresses and heads downstairs, pushing away the thought that there will be two policemen sitting at her table waiting to arrest them both, grinning madly, ready to haul them both off to the police station to question them over the assault on Barry Wilson.

Heat pulsates from her reddened body as she fills the kettle and stares out to sea. How easy would it be to walk into the water, away from it all, and never return? Be pulled away by the tide, sucked into the vast, black sea where nothing will exist for her anymore. No worries, no fears, no Alec. There was a time when she couldn't comprehend why people would do it to themselves, but just lately … well lately she has let her imagination run riot. She has a possible future mapped out in her head and she doesn't care for it. Not one little bit. It terrifies her. The visit from the police and the event last night. Her mother badgering her. Then there's the matter of Sheryl. *Jesus*. Talk about everything happening all at once. It's ludicrous, what's going on right now, as if some kind of conspiracy has been dreamt up by the powers that be to send her insane. If she doesn't get a grip and sort her head out, it might just work.

Behind her, the kettle clicks off. Perhaps they need some time away together, just her and Alec, somewhere in the middle of nowhere where there are no phones, no technology, no distractions. And no policemen or lunatic parents waiting in the wings. Surely, they can afford a short break to salvage what's left of their marriage? They can use the Visa card to pay for it. What's a couple more hundred pounds debt, on top of the thousands they've already got, going to do to them? Peggy's agent has high hopes for her latest book. Besides which, isn't it worth it just to have some time away from all this stress? The money they thought they were going to have to spend on the damage to the car is still there. Maybe that's how she can sell the idea to Alec. Use a little bit of psychology to persuade him they need a short holiday. Just a weekend. That's all she's asking for. A couple of days somewhere in a little cottage in the middle of nowhere. She manages an ironic smile. Isn't that what they've got right here? And look how shit that is. She lets out a puff of air, feels a sharp pain take hold in her neck. All she is doing is running away. People are her problem, not the location. And even if they do go off somewhere, all this will be here waiting for them when they get back. All of their problems - her mother, Sheryl's disappearance, Alec's dad. The police. None of them are going to simply vanish into the ether in their absence. No, she needs to stay here and face whatever comes their way. She tries to visualise Barry Wilson's beaten face, a mass of purple bruises and angry, red cuts; his mouth swollen and distorted. Perhaps he lost some teeth in the attack as well, that's if he had any to start with. Then she thinks of his ailing, old body hooked up to a drip, his bed surrounded by policemen while a frenzy of reporters wait outside the ward, hanging onto the idea of getting a good story, something worth reporting on. A story with a bit of substance to it. A local man, *a teacher, no less,* viciously attacks his own father. Wouldn't they all just love that one?

Peggy bites her lip and thinks about how well Alec handled the whole thing, how calm he stayed while her nerves were jangling. How did he do that? And why did he lie about where he had been?

'Any breakfast on the go?' His voice startles her. She swings round to see him standing there, fresh faced and smiling. *Smiling!* She must have woken him up. He was out for the count earlier. Peggy decides to not mention the idea of a weekend away. Pointless, really. What would they gain apart from a break from the accusations currently being thrown their way?

'I've just boiled the kettle. You make some coffee and I'll rustle us up some scrambled eggs, if you like?' She is surprised at how chipper she sounds. A far cry from how she actually feels but then she has always been good at covering up, tucking the lies deep within her, keeping them hidden.

'Sounds good. I'm starving.' Alec rubs his hands together and grabs a couple of cups from the dresser.

How is none of this getting to him? Is there a side to her husband she doesn't know about? Or maybe it's just that his childhood gave him an air of resilience whereas Peggy's own childhood appears to have damaged her for life. Another reason to hate her mother. Not that she needs any more reasons. One look in the mirror is enough to remind her of why she left. Peggy's scars are all too visible, unlike Alec, who carries his on the inside, keeping them safely tucked away from prying eyes.

Cracking eggs on the side of the bowl, Peggy has a sudden flashback. She does her utmost to suppress it but no matter how hard she tries, it won't leave her. That day, all those years back. She was just a kid, too young and naive to defend herself. Manipulative to the core, her mother knew exactly what she was doing, tackling her about the whole issue of the contraceptive pills when only the two of them were in the house. No allies, nobody around to stop it escalating. Which it did. Of course it did - this is her mother, after all - causing arguments is her forte; her defining feature.

Peggy grabs a fork and whisks the eggs with a strength she didn't know she possessed. She adds a sprinkling of salt and continues to beat the fork around the bowl, enjoying the feel of the metrical tap of metal against glass.

It wasn't her fault. She was no more than a kid, yet she has carried the guilt around with her for so many years, believing the burden of blame should be placed firmly at her door for dating an older man - for having sex with an older man - the man she eventually married. It has taken her a long time to realise she did nothing wrong, but it's too late now. The damage has been done. Her face is testament to that fact.

'There you go.' Alec slides a steaming mug of liquid her way. She takes it and downs a long slug, savouring the burning sensation and slightly smoky taste as it travels down her throat.

'Won't be long with this,' she murmurs as she pours the yellow liquid into a pan and turns the gas on.

Grabbing a wooden spoon, Peggy continues stirring the eggs, her mind still firmly focused on that day. If she didn't know better she would say that her mother had done it on purpose. After all, nobody in their right mind would wrestle with their child and push them that hard when they were next to a glass door would they? It was ludicrously stupid to do what she did. Dangerous. Her mother was lucky the police didn't press charges. And the only reason that didn't happen is because Peggy didn't go to the hospital, which is why her face now looks as though it has been through a shredder. Had she gone for treatment and got it stitched, perhaps her life would have turned out differently. Perhaps her mother would have ended up in court. Who knows what would have happened, but, as it turned out, Audrey got off scot-free because the child she scarred for life ended up protecting her from the authorities and the powers that be. Even Alec still doesn't know the truth of that day. He has no idea her mother called him a paedophile and he also has no idea that her mother pushed her, face first, through a plate glass door. He doesn't know any of it because Peggy didn't tell him. What she did tell him was that she and her mother had argued and she had fallen and that she had left home and now wanted to live with him. He had agreed and from that day forward the incident was hardly ever mentioned. He tried to get her to see a doctor about her face but the more he pressed her, the more stubborn she became. Doctors would ask questions and as much as she loathed her mother, she wasn't about to report her for child abuse. No, the punishment she meted out to Audrey was far worse than that. Peggy made sure she severed all contact with her mother. Beatrice tried to persuade her to come back and talk but Peggy refused. It didn't take Bea long to realise that living with their mother wasn't an easy ride and shortly afterwards she too moved out to stay in a tiny bedsit with a friend. Which left their father to battle it out with Audrey on his own. Peggy feels a lump lodge itself in her throat, hard and painful. She swallows it down. A solid stone of guilt. Perhaps if she had stayed around, he would also have had an easier time of it, but as it was, Audrey half-nagged him death about everything and anything. He was all she had left to go at. And go at him she did. The house was never modern enough, the garden never tidy enough, his salary never large enough. The list of her complaints and his purported misdemeanours was endless. On the odd occasion when Peggy managed to get through to him on the phone, she could hear her mother's shrieks in the background, asking why he wasn't out mowing the lawn and demanding he hand the phone over so she could speak to her daughter. So, they started meeting for coffee instead, she and her father. Funny thing is, he never asked Peggy about that day. It's as if he knew all about it, and no words were needed. He knew exactly what they were both up against when it came to dealing with Audrey. Nothing more needed to be said.

Peggy continued to watch from a distance, dismayed and helpless as her father was cornered into borrowing money to renovate the house, putting him under massive strain both financially and physically. There seemed to be no end to his list of chores - go to work, earn more money, paint the house, dig the garden. On and on it went, until one day when it all ceased. That was the day he stopped. They put her father deep in the ground and all of a sudden, the world became a lesser place without him. After that, Peggy gave up on Audrey altogether. The bits of information her father had given her about her mother was all she'd had to go on. After his death, she had nothing. No contact, no news about how she was getting on. Nothing at all. And that suited her just fine. The one thing Peggy did find out about her mother via an old neighbour was that she had turned into an old soak. That little piece of information didn't surprise her one little bit. She had always liked a good drink, claiming the stress of work drove her to it.

Peggy turns as she feels hot breath on her neck, 'Almost ready?' Alec is standing next to her leaning over the hob, his eyes fixated on the food. He has taken her by surprise, his words cutting into her thoughts. She stares at his side profile and for one dreadful second has a vision of him smashing a fist into his father's face, blood spurting from Barry's swollen mouth. She closes her eyes against it but is bombarded with images of Alec driving his foot into Barry Wilson's stomach, the old man's internal organs shifting and rupturing with the force of it. Is Alec really capable of carrying out such an act? Then she thinks about Sheryl and suddenly feels faint. They still haven't spoken about her and she isn't even sure if Alec has received any messages about it. If he has, he certainly hasn't mentioned it to her. She decides to remain silent about that one. Talk of Sheryl will never come to any good.

Peggy lifts the pan off the hob. She no longer feels like eating anything and the smell of the eggs is starting to make her feel nauseous. Dishing the food up, she has to muster up all her strength to shove a few mouthfuls in without vomiting. She notices how thin her hands are as she places her cutlery down on her plate.

She really must start eating again. Her clothes are falling off her, lately. Alec mentioned it just last week, said it in an accusatory way as if she was doing it on purpose. Another one of his wife's bids for attention.

Her head begins to throb as a noise filters through from the hallway. They both stop and stare, their eyes locked in anticipation. Both she and Alec know what this is - *who* it is that is knocking at their door at this time of the morning. Alec continues to stare at her, his fork hanging mid-air, a slight tremble visible in his hand. Peggy's heart begins a steady thrum up her neck. This is it. This is the part where everything begins to unravel. She stands up, her legs like lead, and shuffles along the hallway, her innards squelching with dread as she opens the door to see them standing there, the two of them with their shiny suits and faces devoid of all emotion.

'Good morning, Mrs Wilson. Is it all right if we come inside?'

Peggy stands to one side and watches Rollings and Evans as they saunter past her, ready to rip her life to shreds with what they are about to say.

# Maude

They're angry with her, Brenda and that tall, gangly lad. When she woke up, her back hurt and her head was aching. She was cold too. Really, really cold. Now she's up and has had her breakfast and they are staring at her and shaking their heads as if she's done something wrong. She can't remember doing anything bad but she can tell by their funny looks and sharp voices that she's in trouble. Maude looks down at her feet. They've warmed up a bit now but as she stares at them she can see the black bits, all dry and grubby, smeared in between her toes and over the soles of her feet. Reaching down, she rubs her fingers over her toes. Why has she got mud on her feet?

'Brenda! Dirty feet. I've got dirty feet!'

'I'm not surprised you've got dirty feet. You're lucky you're not dead, never mind getting all het up about a bit of mud, mother.'

There it is again. That angry, mean voice she uses when Maude has done something bad. She can't remember doing anything but she did have a funny dream last night. She dreamt she was running and running, out in the cold and there was a lady in the dream but she doesn't know who it was. She thinks a man was there too, but can't be sure of it, and she doesn't know who he was, either. It wasn't this tall boy - that much she does remember. It was someone older. Not like her, somebody more like Brenda. It was dark in her dream. Too dark to see anything properly. No wonder she can't remember who they were.

'You must stay in the house today, Mum. I have to go out to run some errands so Andrew is here to look after you.'

'Andrew? Who's Andrew?' she asks as she digs at her toes with slightly yellowed fingernails, 'Anyway, I don't need looking after.

Can look after meself. I'm not daft you know.' Maude continues picking at the dirt. It's making her itchy and she doesn't like feeling itchy. 'Can I have a bath? My feet smell.'

This seems to amuse the pair of them and Maude watches as Brenda and the boy laugh together. Maude joins in. She likes it when they all have fun together. Better than them being angry with her. Better than her being angry with them. She doesn't like getting annoyed and upset but sometimes she just can't help it. Things happen in her head, things she can't explain - bad things - and then the next thing she knows, stuff is getting thrown about, ornaments and sometimes even furniture, and she is crying and everything is just a mess. But laughing is fun. This is better. She enjoys a good laugh; it makes her tummy ache and her mouth go all funny at the sides.

'Come on, Mum, let's get you sorted,' Brenda says, while shaking her head and smiling. Maude has no idea why she's doing that but she doesn't mind. Everyone is happy and that's good. If Brenda is in a good mood then everything will be just fine.

***

'Where has she gone?' Maude asks, her face just centimetres away from the young man's. He moves back in his seat. Maude shuffles in closer. She needs to know where Brenda is and he isn't answering her so she moves in as near to him as she can. She doesn't like being ignored.

'She won't be long. She's just gone for some paintbrushes. Don't worry,' he says, in a tone she doesn't care for.

'I'm not worried,' Maude whispers as she fiddles with a strand of hair that has attached itself to one of her buttons, 'I just want to know where she is so I can tell her about my dream.'

'Well,' he says, sitting up straight, 'why don't you tell me about it? I like talking about dreams.'

Maude eyes him cautiously. Is he being - what's that word again? - sarcastic, yes that's it. Sarcastic. Because she doesn't like sarcastic people. They make her feel unwanted and sad. As if they are laughing at her. And nobody likes being laughed at. She stares at him and watches as he starts to look away. He seems all right, this lad. Maybe she can tell him what she remembers? Thing is, she's not even sure if was a dream or if it actually happened. This morning she was sure it was a dream, but now - well, she can't be certain. She always gets muddled first thing in the morning, but once she's eaten and had another nap, everything always seems much clearer in her head. As if a thick fog has lifted and she can see properly once more. That's the thing, you see, she has to say these things as soon as she remembers them, otherwise they disappear into the dark places in her head. And right now, her head is clear, which is why she wants to say it straight out, get the words out. Not keep them sitting in her brain where they'll just melt away with all her other thoughts, get sucked away down that big, fat drain never to return.

'It wasn't a dream at all,' Maude says clearly, her voice making the young man suddenly sit up and pay attention, 'I saw it all. I remember now. And if I don't tell somebody then I won't be able to settle.'

Her eyes feel light in her head as if they're about to roll straight out of her skull and up into the sky, like tree blossom floating along on the breeze. No aching head or fluff clogging up her thoughts. Clear. Everything is suddenly so very, very clear.

'Well, I'm all ears, Aunt Maude, why don't you tell me all about it?' His voice is soft, gentle. It eases Maude, makes her feel wanted. And she does really want to tell him what she remembers, before she forgets it all and the words refuse to come out properly.

'I got out once before,' she whispers breathlessly, excitement at being able speak clearly beginning to overwhelm her.

'You got out again?' he says a little too loudly. The boy's eyes are wide, and rather than scare or annoy Maude, it makes her want to laugh. He reminds her of her little brother, a cute one he is.

'It was before. Not like last time,' Maude says quietly, 'and you weren't here. Brenda was asleep in the chair. Right over there,' she says, pointing at the recliner in the corner of the room, 'I had the window open but couldn't hear everything they were saying so I decided to have a wander. Shouldn't have really. Think I had ants in my pants,' Maude says, letting out a giggle, 'but anyway, the key was in the door, so off I went. I followed the voices, went to where the shouting was coming from. It was really loud. And she was crying as well.'

'Who was crying?'

'Over there. A lady over near the cottage,' Maude replies and rolls her eyes at him, her finger pointing towards the window. She's sure he's a bit slow, this lad. Takes him an age to pick up on anything she says.

'Did you go into the house, Maude? Please tell me you didn't just walk straight in?'

'Course I didn't!' she cries in disgust, 'It was outside. They were outside arguing, so I watched them. Loads of swearing and shouting. Really dirty words. Shouldn't be allowed to use words like that in public.'

He smiles and nods his head in agreement, 'You're absolutely right, Maude. It shouldn't be allowed at all. Anyway, what happened next? Did you come back home?'

'Course I came back home. But not before I saw it.' Maude rubs at her eyes. They're starting to ache again, that dragging feeling she gets when the mist begins its heavy descent into her brain, clogging up her thoughts and memories. The lightness didn't last long. It's becoming briefer and briefer these days. Soon she won't feel or see anything at all.

'Saw what, Maude? What is it that you saw?' he whispers, leaning in closer to catch what she is about to say.

'I saw her fall. All the blood as well. It was everywhere. And then I saw the worst thing. Because the blood wasn't the worst thing, you see …'

The boy gets a crease above his eyes, a long line across his forehead, and his eyes are wide as saucers, 'Maude, are you absolutely sure about this?'

She smiles smugly and wriggles in her seat like a small child. Now he's listening to her. All of a sudden, he is interested in what she's got to say. Not before time either. She's been trying to tell them all for weeks and weeks about this and nobody listened. Nobody was interested. Well now they'll listen to what she's got to say, won't they? All of a sudden, her words are important to them.

'Of course I'm sure,' she barks, 'do you want to know what happened or not, young man?'

'Yes, sorry,' he nods quickly, 'carry on. So, what was worse than the blood, then?'

Maude places her hands in her lap, trying to get the words right. She locks her fingers together and concentrates as hard as she can. She doesn't want it to come out all wrong, otherwise he won't believe her. And she wants everyone to start believing her because what she's about to say is true, she saw it happen. She knows that now. It wasn't a dream at all. It was real life. She witnessed it. Not a programme on the TV like those ones Brenda watches, where people get punched and beaten and stamped on, and then get back up and run away. Not like that at all. This was a murder. A real life murder. And there was a body. She saw it all. It actually happened. Right near her house as well.

'She died. Her head was full of blood. I saw it, I really did. But the bad bit is worse than that …'

'Go on,' he whispers, his face pale, his skin suddenly clammy. Maude watches him. He looks a bit frightened and small beads of sweat are standing out on his top lip. She clears her throat before speaking again,

'She was put in a big hole. Right under the house. Over there,' Maude points again towards the window and Chamber Cottage in the distance, 'that little house over there where the woman and man live. There's a dead body underneath it.'

# BEFORE

A terrible smell. It's everywhere. Can't escape from it. And still no light. No idea of time either. Head hurts so much. Kept being sick but have stopped now. Vomit in my hair, under my head, over my face. Urine all over me too. And excrement. Piles and piles of shit pouring out of me. On my clothes, my hands, covering my entire body, spreading like poison, filling my nostrils, making me retch even more. A vicious circle of fluids leaking out of my body. Soon there will nothing left of me. Just a dried-up corpse slowly rotting into the ground. Worm fodder.

Thought I saw somebody earlier. A person standing over me, smiling. Just a vague outline. Couldn't make out their face. I tried but my head hurt too much and my eyes were gritty. Then they disappeared. Think it might have been a dream. Can't be sure.

Keep thinking they will find me; somebody will open a door and get me out. But deep down I know it's not going to happen. I'm going to die here. Sometimes I wake up and wonder if it's actually happened and I'm already dead. So dark and dingy here, it's hard to tell. Perhaps I am. I see things. Didn't see anything when I first woke up here but now I see lots of things. People, events, my memories played out in front of me like a show. I hear stuff too. Voices whispering, calling my name, drifting around me like ghosts. I'm not scared. Not of the ghosts and not of dying. Can't be any worse than this, can it? A black, cold, lonely hole filled with a vile stench. If there is a hell, I'm already in it.

My eyes close. A wave of pain hitting me. A burning, throbbing arrow of pain shooting up my back and circling round my head, almost splitting it in two.

A cough, then more vomit spilling out of me, a sea of bile and acid, swilling round my mouth, threatening to choke me. I turn my head to one side and let it flow. I no longer care. Too exhausted, too thirsty, too much pain.

One good thing though. I'm starting to remember. Not all of it. Just bits, fragments, floating around like tiny pieces of a jigsaw all meshing together in my head. Had been at Dad's house then went home. Messaged Rachel. Always worrying about me living on my own. Silly sister.

Stinging eyes, more tears.

Lovely, silly Rachel.

I try to remember some more but am so tired. Need to sleep. Try to stop my eyes closing but they're heavy.

So very, very heavy.

A face appears in my mind before I disappear into the darkness of my own head. I think about it as I fight to keep my eyes open.

Then it happens. It crashes into my brain like a clap of thunder. I can remember it all. It comes to me in a flash, everything that happened. But why now? Maybe I'm going to die and it's all an illusion. I squint and cough out the remainder of the bile from the back of my throat. It burns as it travels up, stripping what little skin I have left from the back of my gullet. But it doesn't matter because this is real. I know it is. It's definitely real. I want to laugh, cry, scream out loud, but am too tired to move.

Maybe this is it. Maybe this is the part where I go to sleep and I don't wake up. Perhaps that's why my memory has allowed me to see who it was that did this to me, given me the identity of the person who put me here in this godforsaken hole. A person I thought cared about me. Someone I loved, who I thought loved me too, has put me in this hideous place to die.

More tears come, streaming uncontrollably with a mixture of snot and vomit. I thought they cared. I really thought they loved me. How could they do this to me? *How could they?*

'*What are you doing here?*'

'*What do you mean, what am I doing here? I've come to see you, obviously.*'

*A long pause, deep breathing, the sound of the wind howling in the background.*

'*You shouldn't be here. What if somebody sees you?*'

'*Well then, perhaps you should ask me in.*'

'*You know I can't do that.*'

'*Why not?*'

'*You know fine well why not. Now please leave.*'

'*I got a taxi here. They've just left a few minutes ago. I'm not going anywhere anytime soon …*'

*An enigmatic smile, a hand leaning on the door, a foot on the step, moving closer. Two bodies almost touching. Heat pulsating through the fabric of their clothes.*

'*Go away. You need to leave here. NOW.*'

*A voice echoing around the countryside, slicing through the sound of gulls overhead as they circle, swooping and diving, scavenging for scraps of food.*

'*I've just told you, I'm not going anywhere. I have no transport. What are you going to do, force me?*'

'*If I have to, then yes, I will force you to leave.*'

'*Go ahead, then. Force me. You know you won't do that. We both know you won't do it.*'

*Eyes searching for an answer, scrutinising every movement, looking to see if they mean what they say.*

'*What is it you want from me?*'

'*Just you. That's all I want. Only you.*'

*A roll of the eyes, deep scornful laughter.*

'*No, you don't. You just don't like being told you can't have what you want.*'

'*That's not true. We're meant to be together, you and I. You know it and I know it. You're just too stubborn to admit it, that's all.*'

'*You don't know me at all, do you? I've told you before, I'm married and that's that.*'

'Not happily though, are you?'

'What's that supposed to mean?'

Dark eyes staring, provoking, edging closer to the truth.

'Exactly what I said. You're not happily married, are you?'

'Go away. Get off my doorstep.'

'See? It's true. You can't deny it, can you?'

'Leave here right now.'

A hand reaching out, then slapped away. Smiling. Caustic laughter.

'Tell me you have a happy marriage and I will walk away from here and you will never see me again.'

A long pause, quick movements, a door being closed. A foot jammed in to keep it open.

'SAY IT!'

'Why are you doing this?'

A deep sigh. A flood of salty tears, running, spilling onto the floor beneath their feet.

'Because I love you. I can't live without you.'

'Try …'

'No. I don't want to. You need me, you need to admit that. Walk away from this marriage. Stay with me. Please …'

# Audrey

She gathers the papers up and tucks them tightly under her arm. She is going to sift through them all, put them in order and get everything straight in her mind. Dates, times; she needs to be sure of them all before she calls the number on the news page. The police are involved now. Not before time. Why would they think a few garbled text messages are a reliable indicator of whether somebody has taken themselves off or whether they have been taken against their will? What about bank accounts and other ways of checking on someone's movements? Mobile phones for instance? Isn't there some way of tracking them? Triangulation, they call it. She's looked it up, done some research into it. The police have been pretty shambolic throughout, really, relying on family and social media to find a missing person when they should have been out there themselves trying to find her, banging on doors and questioning people. Audrey knew all along that something sinister was going on. Pity nobody else did.

The first time she followed him, he actually met up with her, this Sheryl. *The very first time!* Just goes to show how long it had been going on for. They probably met all the time, walked around town as if nothing was wrong, then checked into a seedy little hotel somewhere and spent the afternoon having sex, pawing each other's bodies. Disgusting. She did see them slide through a door on a side street in town. She waited. Hung about outside, ready to confront him but was questioned by a neighbour as to why she was standing there, so Audrey left. Lost her nerve and went home.

She doesn't blame Sheryl. He was the married one - is the married one. He should have known better. She was probably taken in by his good looks and charisma. Because there's no denying he's a handsome man and, from what she remembers, quite the charmer too. As her mother used to say, certain people can charm the birds out of the trees. Alec is one of those people. A way of hiding his sins. Tuck them away behind a smile.

Audrey heads off to bed, wondering if people are aware just how easy it is to track their movements and pry into their lives using social media? It's been a real eye opener going on there, seeing just how much some of these young people are prepared to reveal of themselves online. Quite literally in some cases. Photographs of young, scantily clad women pouting at the camera like porn stars. And then there are those who flirt outrageously with their comments, making suggestive remarks, using those silly faces. Emoticons they're called apparently. Ridiculous things. They make grown people look like children.

Audrey flicks the light off and wonders what future generations will make of this method of communication. Will they, too, think it immature? or will it all actually continue on in the same vein and spiral out of control completely with people using it to convey all kinds of warped messages to each other? She read an article recently about teenagers sending naked images of themselves; snapping away on their phones and handing them over to anyone and everyone who will accept them. They are then bandied about all over the internet, reaching thousands of people worldwide, if not millions. Shameful stuff. It's as if the world has gone mad. Nothing left to the imagination anymore, no secrets, nothing left to hide.

Placing the pile of papers down on the bed, Audrey sighs and bites the insides of her mouth. She's forgotten her drink. It's in the kitchen, next to the cooker, where she left it. A small one before bedtime won't hurt her, will it? Just a wee nightcap to make sure she gets off to sleep properly. It's not as if she has to be up in the morning. No job to go to, no family to care for. Just her, here in this place on her own ...

She pads through to the kitchen, exhaustion beginning to swamp her. It's the computer that causes it, staring at the screen for hours at a time, trying to fathom out how all of it works, getting to grips with the bloody printer which insists on jamming up every third sheet of paper, trying to stop everything on the screen from disappearing for no apparent reason. She hates computers and tried to steer clear of them at work as best she could, so her skills aren't as sharp as they should be, but she'll get there. She'll make sure of it. She needs to be on the ball, get her facts straight, get all this paperwork in order so she can nail that psychopath; get him away from her daughter. Set her free.

It's unusually warm in the kitchen as Audrey searches around for her crystal tumbler. She could have sworn she left it next to the oven. Obviously not. Her hand sweeps over the clutter on the kitchen surface. A little bit of tidying up before going to bed wouldn't have gone amiss but tiredness got the better of her. No matter; she has all day tomorrow to sort it. All day, every day, actually, so there's no rush, no need to keep it pristine. Nobody but her here to see it. She shoves a handful of envelopes to one side - only bills and receipts anyway - and pushes them out of her way. Underneath the mass of paper sits her glass, still full. Audrey smiles and picks it up, taking a sip as she heads back through to the bedroom. She can drink it while she reads in bed. Perfect.

She pads back through to the bedroom. It's at times like this she doesn't mind being on her own so much. As long as she keeps herself occupied, has a project on the go, she can manage, stop the misery descending and obliterating everything.

Pulling her clothes off, she slips into her nightgown and climbs between the sheets, holding the glass up over her head as she wriggles down and gets comfortable. She smiles at the decadence of it all and takes a good long swig of the whiskey, enjoying its deep, fiery tang. It travels down her gullet and lands in her stomach with a punch. That's the bit she really likes - the afterkick. It gives her a real buzz. Makes her want more of it. She stares at the glass. This is the last of her single malt. She needs to enjoy it while it lasts. Tipping her head back, Audrey closes her eyes just for a second, and slowly drains the remainder of the drink.

***

The smell takes her breath away, attacking her nostrils and the back of her throat. She wakes up gagging for breath, her mouth dry and as hot as hell, her chest burning. She sits upright, spluttering and coughing and tries to look around the room. Something isn't right. Her eyes are stinging and she feels as if she can't breathe properly. Tugging at the covers, Audrey leans over and tries to switch the lamp on. Letting out a shriek, she pulls her hand back and waves it about wildly, pain coursing through her palm and over her fingertips. What the hell is going on? Scrambling around for her slippers, she stands up and then is somehow pushed back onto the bed. A wave of something hot and tight hits her in the face. A blanket of acrid smoke billowing in from the passageway trails its way through the room, rapidly obscuring her vision, filling her lungs and making it impossible to breathe properly. Audrey forces herself up again and then, fighting through the blackness, is able to stagger over to the door only to be beaten back by a burning wall of flames that is ferociously licking its way towards the bedroom. On instinct, she slams the door shut and falls back on the bed, tears streaming. She tries to scream but ends up coughing so hard she feels as if her throat is about to close up. It's impossible; she can barely breathe. Everything is too dark and so hot. So very, very hot and her throat is raw.

How is this happening? Has somebody done this on purpose? Images fill her head - did she leave the fire turned on? No, she checked, she's sure of it. Has somebody been in her house? Oh, sweet Jesus! Who would do this? Kids? Surely not. This isn't the most salubrious of areas but neither is it what can be classed as particularly common or rough. Another thought punctures her brain, a possibility for this horror she's being subjected to. No. Please, no. He might have a mean streak but he wouldn't do something as drastic as this would he? Not to her surely? Has he noticed her following him - is that what this is about? Adrenaline suddenly kicking in, Audrey lunges herself towards the window and whips the curtains back before hammering on the window. She is not going to sit here and let the flames engulf her. She needs to get out. The glass is black with soot and her fists burn as she pummels against it relentlessly. Smoke expands in her lungs and she has to stop to catch her breath, sucking in what little oxygen is left in the scorching room.

Gasping and crying, Audrey flaps her hands around. The key. She needs to find the key for the window lock. *Dear God, where is the bloody key?* Sweeping her hands along the sill, Audrey feels something small and hard under her palm. She grasps at it but loses her grip and cries out as it falls to the floor. Behind her, somewhere in her house, she hears an almighty shattering sound and lets out a small, dry shriek. Falling to her knees, Audrey scrambles about, her nightdress getting caught under her legs. She tumbles forward, a tangle of fabric and limbs, and hits her head against the wall. A searing pain shoots up through her skull stopping her in her tracks. She waits for the pain to ease up and the dizziness to go and then clambers about. No stopping. No time to wait. She has to do this. Gulping madly, her eyes streaming and chest struggling in the dense wall of smoke that is expanding by the second, Audrey taps her fingers around the carpet. She has to find this stupid, bloody key. She has got to get out of here, come hell or high water. A sudden roar from somewhere in the house sends her into a frenzy. She spreads her arms out, sweeping the entire area. What little energy she has left is draining away from her leaving her exhausted and barely able to move. It's getting closer. She can sense it. And pretty soon it will burst through her door, a barrier of flames, ready to envelop her in its hot, angry clutches.

Audrey sobs weakly, her strength sapped. She dips her head in one last ditch attempt to locate it, her fingers pulling desperately at small tufts of carpet, its stringy fibres already singed and beginning to burn. Then suddenly she finds it - a tiny, hot, jagged piece of metal, the object that stands between her and safety. The thing that will save her life. Gasping for air and gulping wildly, Audrey nips it tightly, the nickel plating searing her finger ends. She mustn't let go. She cannot lose it again. This is her last chance. She can hardly breathe and she is terrified. Heart jumping against her ribcage, she rummages around for the keyhole, her hands trembling and quaking. She has to do this, she has to stay calm but it's so difficult. Desperation begins to claw at her, muddying her thinking, turning her brain to jelly. Looking down at the tiny piece of metal, Audrey slowly turns the key round and round in her fingers staring at it in confusion. Holding it tightly, she tries to insert the wrong end into the lock. With burning palms, she quickly realises her mistake and removes the key away from it but cannot for the life of her work out how to put it in properly. Its shape is a complete mystery to her. Her head aches and she can't seem to think straight anymore. She fights the fatigue that threatens to drag her entire body onto the floor and holds the small key aloft, staring at it with gritty, exhausted eyes. Holding it by the flattest, widest part, she places the pointed, serrated edge into the narrow slot of the lock and wants to cry out when it fits perfectly. Turning it slowly, Audrey feels like screaming and hollering and putting her fists through the window when it jams as she attempts to rotate it. Taking what feels like her final breath, she holds the key as tightly as her fingers will allow. She is sure her skin is melting and her lungs are shrivelling up inside of her but she needs to do this otherwise she is going to die, be burnt to a crisp right here in her own home. With rapidly failing dexterity, Audrey clamps her fingers together and, as carefully as she can, twists the key, paying no attention to the heat and the burning metal that doesn't want to move. She keeps on turning it, ignoring the sticking points, forcing it to shift until at last it slips free and the button depresses. Audrey grabs the handle, oblivious to the heat, and in one frantic, clumsy manoeuvre, pushes the window open. An almighty, welcome gust of cold air swoops in, coating her in its iciness, pushing oxygen into her burning, air deprived lungs. She tries to cry out but nothing will come. Her mouth forms into a dry, cracked, desperate O shape as she leans out of the window, her skin feeling as if it is about to drip off her bones like molten metal.

'She's here!' A man's voice filters through the air, deep and warm. Music to her ears.

Audrey slumps forward, her arms hanging over the sill, head lolling. She thinks her eyeballs are going to explode, about to burst into tiny fragments and float around in her head. She starts to mumble, her words febrile and delirious, then she stops. It hurts too much to say anything. Her brain feels as if it's burning up. She can't think about anything except how to breathe. And even that is excruciating.

'Come on, love, we've got yer,' the voice says. Big, strong arms are placed under her head and around her waist, and Audrey feels herself being dragged through the window, over the hot metal frame and out into the cold, night air.

'Are they on their way?' another voice says, 'Feels like bloody ages since I rang!'

Gentle hands place her down on the grass, cool and soothing, 'You're gonna be all right now, love. Take some deep breaths. The fire brigade are on their way,' the person with the strong arms says. His voice is soft, like dripping honey. A blanket is laid over her body. Something spongy is placed under her head. She wants to cry but hasn't the energy.

'Fucking 'ell! Give 'em another call,' a voice shrieks from somewhere behind her. Guttural and emotive. Full of anguish.

'Give 'em a chance, man,' a woman's voice says, pleading and desperate, 'we only rang them a couple of minutes ago.'

An unearthly shattering sound surrounds them and Audrey feels herself being pulled away across the grass away from whatever is happening.

'FUCK!'

'Get back everyone! GET BACK! The fucking window has blown out!'

A ferocious roar fills Audrey's ears and if she had the energy she would howl and scream. Her house is being destroyed. Everything gone. All turned to ash. Her entire life ruined. Everything she owns going up in smoke.

'Ring them again! Jesus fucking Christ. Give 'em another call, will you?'

At that, a sound pierces through everything; a cacophony of unsynchronised sirens, wailing and screeching as they edge closer, the noise nightmarish and distorted in Audrey's head. Is this what it feels like when you die? She senses hot breath on her neck as the honey voice comes again, 'Just stay still, love. They're here now. Everything's gonna be just fine. Stay still and don't try to move.'

She couldn't move if she tried. She has nothing left. No energy in reserve, no breath, no house, no family. Nothing. Audrey blinks, her eyelids dragging over her irises and pupils like sandpaper. She may as well be dead. It would have been easier if she'd just thrown herself into the flames, let the fire take her away from it all.

Her last thought before breathing apparatus is placed onto her face, is Peggy. The words *stay safe* rattle though her brain as a row of hands hoist her onto a stretcher and she closes her eyes against the huge wave of pain that threatens to engulf her.

# Alec

They can't arrest him. He hasn't fucking well *done* anything. What are they going to charge him with for God's sake? Hating his own father? Since when has that been a crime? In fact, it's a pre-requisite, especially if Barry Wilson is the father in question. Such a horrible, lying bastard. Never changed.

The two police officers sit at the dining table, their expressions unreadable. Who the fuck do they think they are, these people? Marching into his house, sitting here at *his* table, wielding power with their authoritative air and superior smiles. This is his house. He's the one in charge here.

'Well, here we are again,' Rollings says with a slightly southern drawl as he eyes up the eggs and coffee and smiles, revealing a row of uneven, yellow teeth. Alec curls his fists up under the table and cracks his knuckles, enjoying the sensation it affords him as he feels the release of tension flood through him. He imagines the softness of Rollings' skin when it connects with his fist and pictures his decaying teeth exiting his head as the punch takes hold, Alec's knuckles embedding themselves in his podgy, pale flesh.

'Yes, here we are again,' Alec replies, trying and failing miserably to keep the sarcasm out of his voice. He sees Peggy flinch and wants to smile. He has no idea why. It's not as if this particular incident is even her fault. It's the frustration that's driving him. The frustration and pent up anger; years of it, simmering and boiling away inside of him, eating at his very core. A cauldron of childish fury directed at anyone who is unlucky enough to get in its way. A dark, unfortunate upbringing has resulted in him having two policemen sitting here in his kitchen, glaring at him as if he's something they've just scraped off their shoes. How is that his fault? Being born into a destructive, violent family, being beaten and then abandoned. How is any of it his fucking fault?

'Don't let us stop you,' Rollings says as he continues to stare at the food. He taps his fingers on the large, oak table, a solid, dull beat full of menace. 'Thought you would have already eaten, actually. I was just thinking you look like the kind of guy who's always up early. A go-getter if you know what I mean.'

'Sorry, no,' Alec says through gritted teeth, 'I don't know what you mean. Would you care to elaborate?'

'Shall I make some more coffee?' Peggy's voice cuts through the charged air of simmering anger, 'Nothing too flash,' she says, a definite tremor in her tone, 'we don't have one of those fancy coffee machines that grinds the beans and everything, but we have got a Tassimo machine if anyone's interested?'

Alec watches as Evans looks to his superior for the nod to say he can go ahead and agree.

'Sounds perfect, Mrs Wilson. Black, no sugar.' Rollings smiles.

'How about you?' Peggy asks, staring at PC Evans. She actually feels sorry for him, Alec can tell. The way she's looking at him, all doe-eyed. Always one for the underdog is Peggy. Typical.

'Same for me,' Evans replies dryly.

Alec doubts it, imagines he probably has cream, sweeteners, the works, but sees it as too much hassle so goes along with whatever his boss says. Alec wants to laugh out loud at it, a grown man under the thumb of his superior. Like a baby.

'Nothing for me,' Alec whispers grimly. He turns to look at Rollings and holds his gaze, their eyes locked together, 'So, I'm assuming you didn't call up here just for coffee?'

'Indeed, we didn't,' he replies, a darkness spreading over his face. Alec feels his insides shift slightly, an iron fist slowly squeezing his intestines, making him woozy and sick. A disquieting veil settles in the room, bleak and heavy. Peggy is at the stove, setting mugs out, humming slightly. To an untrained eye, she appears like an everyday woman making coffee for a small gathering of friends but Alec knows better. He can see the slight tic at the corner of her mouth, the nervous quiver visible through her t-shirt, the way she keeps sweeping her hand over her right eye …

'Ah, that's perfect, thank you.' Evans takes the cup from Peggy's grasp, steam billowing up in small wisps and circling round his face.

Peggy hands Rollings his coffee and sits down next to Alec. A thin sheen of perspiration is coating her face, tiny droplets sitting in an arc around her hairline and slowly trickling down her temple.

'We were at the hospital first thing this morning,' Rollings adds, enunciating every syllable for effect.

Alec feels a bubble of air catch in his throat. He swallows hard and forces it down. Why is he dragging this out? Why can't he just come right out and say whatever it is he's got to say?

'How is he?' Peggy asks. She keeps her eyes firmly fixed on the policeman, never once glancing Alec's way.

'Well,' Evans says as he blows a cloud of steam away from the rim of his mug, 'considering the severity of the attack, he's making quite good progress.'

'Still got a long way to go until he's fully recovered, however,' Rollings adds, staring at Alec as if this piece of information will somehow impact on his conscience. Alec knows what he is about, this Rollings guy. He's trying make him squirm, see how far he can go before Alec snaps. Well, it won't happen. He's bigger than such a scenario. He is better than that.

'So, what happened while you were there, then?' Alec asks. He's had enough of this dramatisation now, this contrived, badly acted piece of nonsense. It's about time they explained their presence in his house. He's been more than cooperative, remained calm in the face of adversity and their accusatory bollocks. It's about time they just bloody well came out with whatever they're here to say.

'Well, as it turns out, your father's memory has miraculously returned.' Rollings pauses, watching Alec closely. He raises his eyebrows and takes a sip of his steaming coffee. Alec meets his gaze and watches how the policeman casually drinks the boiling liquid. Burning and black - just like his soul.

'And?' Alec asks tightly.

'And it looks like he met up with a couple of acquaintances after you dropped him off.'

The silence is deafening. Peggy's eyes are wide as they all wait for the next part.

'He's a real character, your dad, isn't he?' Rollings adds, waiting for Alec to agree. Alec is rigid. He will not become embroiled in this - this *banter* about a father he despises, with a policeman who is virtually a stranger to him. He simply will not do it.

'So anyway,' Rollings says through clenched teeth, obviously annoyed at Alec's lack of response, 'they got into a scuffle over some unpaid debts. Apparently, your father owed them quite a bit of money. Still does.'

'Really?' Alec says sarcastically, as he pictures himself driving his fist into Rollings' tired, flabby face.

Evans slurps his coffee, the noise not dissimilar to the last dregs of water being sucked down a drain.

'It all got out of control and they ended up beating your father pretty viciously after he told them he didn't have the money to pay them back.'

Another heavy silence descends as they all wait for Alec to say something. Instead he stands up and holds out his hand for Rollings to shake then offers it to Evans who almost spills his coffee as he reciprocates.

'Well, thank you for stopping by and informing us of this latest development. I do hope the offenders are brought to justice.' Alec can see Peggy, all nervous and edgy as he steps out from behind the table and indicates, with an outstretched arm, that the officers now need to leave.

They both stand, eyeing each other cautiously as they slowly make their way out of the room and back into the hallway, the two steaming mugs of black coffee barely touched.

'Would you like to know what ward he's on so you can pay a visit?' Evans asks. Alec isn't entirely certain but thinks he can see a glint of sarcasm in his eye, a sparkle of something dark, something slightly malevolent, as if he's enjoying this.

'Not really,' Alec replies stiffly, 'but thanks for the offer. If I feel like going to see him, I'm pretty sure I can find out that information for myself.'

Evans purses his lips and nods approvingly, suddenly seeming to comprehend Alec's hatred of his father; a man beaten black and blue by more people he has wronged with his actions - a man who deserves all he gets.

'We'll be in touch if we need any further information,' Rollings adds, for no other reason than because he can. It's as if he has to have the last word to exert his control over this situation. Alec suppresses a cackle. It must have half-killed him, having to come all the way up here to exonerate a man that only yesterday they thought was guilty of nearly killing his own father. He should feel sorry for them really, these two guys. It can't be easy, having to admit that you were wrong, that all your instincts and policing skills are completely and utterly way off beam. If anything, these men deserve his pity.

'I look forward to it,' Alec adds, unable to disguise the edge that has crept into his voice, 'and don't worry, chaps, I don't plan on leaving the country.'

He makes sure the door slams just loud enough as they leave, to let them know what he thinks of them and their shoddy detective work. What a complete bloody shambles. Only when he's certain they are far enough away does Alec relax and let it all out; all the pent-up hatred and anguish, all the worry and horror he has been subjected to comes out in a torrent as he leans back against the wall and howls.

# BEFORE

Everywhere. They are everywhere - crawling over me, under me, around me, their dry, scaly feet skittering over my face, sitting on my stomach, sniffing at my legs, their long tails swishing over my face. They're going to eat me, I just know it. They hang about, gorging on my vomit, drinking up the urine, bathing in my excrement. The noise gets to me - more so than the feel of them. The scratching and scurrying sets my nerves on edge. It's a sign that they're on the move, ready to bite. Hungry rodents who will stop at nothing to fill their bellies.

Hoped I'd be dead by now but it hasn't happened. Too long. Death is taking too long. So much pain. Every limb, every organ, every inch of skin hurts. It's indescribable. Woke up earlier, disappointed at still being alive. No chance of getting out of here now. I know that for certain. All hope vanished. Everything gone. A dull ache travels up my spine. I try to shift to alleviate it, to move away from the rats and the shit and everything that has leaked out of me, but can't seem to do it. No energy. Too tired to move. Too exhausted to breathe.

Lots of memories though, thousands of them buzzing round my head. Seems like the weaker my body becomes, the sharper my thoughts are. Loads of recent things swimming in my head - nights out with Rachel, laughing with Polly when she fell over drunk, her ringing me the next morning asking me how my hangover was. Such good times; fun times. Then memories of being in town with Alec. Him taking me to a coffee shop and talking to me about Peggy, thinking I was her friend. Asking me about her issues, why she won't leave the house, the fact that she doesn't love him anymore. Me watching his mouth move, unable to give him any real answers. Unable to give him the answers he so craves. The answers he deserves.

Pain bites at me as I try to move, as I try to get away from the pool of urine under me, the cold, wet liquid that is seeping into my pores, covering me with its stink. Agony pierces me, pummels my back, stops me from getting away from it, so I lie here, like a dead body; wet, immobile, rotting in my own blanket of death.

Why did this happen? Why like this? I remember the cottage, the howling wind, the seagulls overhead. The beautiful, blue sky and the sound of the sea. Couldn't get inside. Wouldn't let me in there. Kept me on the step. Like a stranger. Like a *nuisance*.

I try to turn my head but can't. Pain shooting up and down my skull, around my neck, behind my eyes. Vomit rises. I swallow it back. Wouldn't have thought it possible for there to be anything left inside of me. I'm a dried-up cadaver - all but dead anyway. Forgotten about, unloved. Left to rot.

I remember banging my head. I was hit, pushed, told to go away but I wouldn't. Know now that I should have. Shouldn't have gone there in the first place. Should have let things be, got on with my life on my own. Managed as I was before. Not impossible. Better than this. Better than being here. Better than being dead.

I wasn't wanted. Thought it was mutual, thought we would be together. How wrong I was; so very, very wrong on that score. Everything will continue without me, friends will mourn, family will cry but everything will go on as before. *They* will go on as before, carrying on with their lives as if I never existed. But one of them will know. They put me here and they will *always* know. That will be their own personal hell.

It's hot in here. No rats at the minute, but they'll be back. Perhaps I'll be dead by then. Hope I am. Don't think I can last much longer. So many strange feelings, so much hurt.

I close my eyes, overcome with a strange sensation. My head is light. Everything feels different. As if something momentous is about to take place. Maybe I'm thinking too much. Trying too hard. I need to stop raking over things in my mind. Panic grips me once again. Been quite calm lately. No choice really. Only the rats and mice have set my heart racing, but now I feel frightened. Really scared. Terrified, actually. It's getting hard to breathe. Not enough air. There are people here. I know them, these people - my nan, my grandpa. My mother. A wall of familiar faces hovering around me, smiling, beckoning me to go with them. The pain begins to leave me, leaches out of me in great waves. I visualise it, drifting out of my skin, sharp needles of torture slipping out from under me. Then I am filled with a feeling of euphoria, a sensation so powerful it makes me want to weep. No more panic or fear, no more darkness. I am suddenly overwhelmed with it all. I have never felt like this before in my life. The tears now begin to well up. Not tears of sadness or fear, but tears of joy. The closed-in space around me begins to widen and I can move. I look down and grieve for the woman I was before I finally take the step to the other place. The place where I will be free.

# Brenda

'Hang on a minute, Andrew, I'm just getting in the car. Give me two seconds, will you?' Brenda bends down, throws her handbag onto the passenger seat and slides into the driver's side, closing the door with a thump. What a shift. Only ten days to go and she has two weeks off. It can't come soon enough. The thought of what she will do with her mother while she has a weekend away with a few friends hangs heavily in her mind. She banishes it. One thing at a time, Brenda, one thing at a time. She grapples with her seat belt and then retrieves her phone, tucking it under her chin as she puts the key in the ignition and turns it. She wants the heater on. It's bloody freezing and she can't wait to get warm. Her fingers are like ice as she fumbles about with the dials, turning it up to full.

'Right, sorry, I'm with you now. What's that you were saying?'

His voice is a crackling squeak through her mobile as the engine kicks in and the heater roars into life, blasting her with a stream of cold air. She shivers and closes the vents. *Jesus!* All she wants is some warmth.

'Sorry to ring you, Bren, but she's being all weird.'

Brenda has to stifle the laughter that she feels bubbling. Can you get weirder than Maude when she's at her weirdest? Is that actually possible?

'Okay. In what way?' She wants to ask is it that Maude thinks the Germans are about to march in and take over the whole of the north-east? Or is it that she keeps asking why she can't go to school? Or perhaps it's that thing she does where she gets on her hands and knees and crawls around the living room pretending she's a fairground donkey asking if anybody would like a ride on

177

her back for tuppence a go? So many weird moments to choose from, Brenda feels spoilt for choice. If it wasn't all so scary and bizarre and hysterically funny, she would cry. But she doesn't. She won't allow the tears to escape, because if they do, she fears they would never stop; a saline river of dread at her predicament; at the husband who keeps threatening to bleed her dry, at a mother who is slowly but surely turning into the child that Brenda never had, at the whole sorry, amateur dramatic performance that is her life at this moment in time.

'She was going on about a body under the house,' Andrew says as Brenda rubs her hands together, her attention waning by the second. There is nothing her mother can do or say that will surprise or shock her. She's seen it all now, so this particular incident had better be good. She is tired, cold, hungry, and wants to get home before the traffic starts to build up and all the rush hour crazies hit the road and hinder her progress.

'A body under the house?' Brenda replies, the words hollow and meaningless to her. When it comes to her mother's activities, everything she says and does takes on a whole new meaning. To Maude, dead bodies under the house is simply an extension of the whole WWII thing that is still raging in her head. She's said it before - *dead bodies everywhere! Bombs exploding killing the whole street ...*

'I know it sounds daft now, but at the time - when she was going on about it, she seemed like, well, really clear about the whole thing and it was a bit scary ...'

Brenda suddenly feels sorry for him. It's a really crap job, caring for an old aunt who has the mind of a seven-year-old. She doubts there are many young lads out there who could do what he has done over the past few months. He has been quite brilliant at it, despite everything Maude has thrown his way. Quite literally as well, on more than one occasion. He has done a sterling job and saved Brenda's sanity, stopped it from slipping out of her grasp and sailing off into the blue yonder.

'Okay, well, how is she now?' She feels a waft of heat begin to emanate from the top of the dashboard and leans forward to open the vents. Heat. Letting out a sigh of relief as a blast of warm air hits her, circling around her legs and thawing her freezing toes, Brenda stares at her reflection in the mirror. God, she looks old. Overweight, tired, and just bloody old.

'She's asleep now. After she was going on about it she quickly fell into a really deep sleep. I had to prod her a few times, make sure she wasn't — well, anyway, she's out for the count on the sofa at the minute. And I hate to say anything but one of my mates rang earlier asking if I fancied going—'

'Andrew, you have been utterly brilliant. I'm on my way home now. As soon as I get there you can get yourself off. I've got your money here, so you go and see your mates and have a good time. You've bloody well earned it.'

'Right thanks,' he says, stumbling over the words. Brenda visualises him biting his nails nervously, his soft, pale face flushing up at having to ask for time off and for the money she gives him. She wants to weep. Poor lad. She feels so sorry for him. Stuck there with Maude for hours at a time. The whole thing makes her want to hammer her fists on the steering wheel and cry out to the whole world about how unfair it all is. Then she thinks of the people she saw this morning, the victims of car crashes, the beaten women, the cancer patients, and tells herself to get a grip. Because right now, that's the only thing that is keeping her going, helping her to put the whole sorry scenario into perspective. Despite the long shifts, despite the cutbacks that have made her job a thousand times more difficult than it already is, despite all of it, work is the only thing left in her life that she can rely on. That and poor old Andrew.

'I'll be there in under half an hour, Andy. You get your stuff sorted and you can get straight off.'

'Cheers, Bren.' His words are soft and thoughtful, making tears prick at her eyes. She blinks them away. *She will not cry!* She flings her phone onto the seat and watches as it topples onto the mass of litter spread in the well of the car. Ignoring it, she swings out of her parking space, suddenly keen to hit the road and get home to see her mother; the woman who, in the past six months, has turned her life upside down, the same woman who gave birth to her and is now the woman who has been reduced to no more than a child. The very same woman Brenda right now wishes were the dead body under the house.

# Rachel

It never felt right, the tone of those messages. She should have pushed the police further when she first reported her sister missing, told them that something was amiss. But would they have believed her, when all she had to go on was a hunch? Would the local, overstretched police force have taken her seriously when she had no more than gut instinct telling her that Sheryl was in trouble? Probably not.

*'I'm taking some time away to sort my head out ...'*

*'Don't worry about me. I'll be in touch soon ...'*

It didn't even sound like her. *Sort my head out* isn't a phrase Sheryl would ever use. When Rachel had replied and asked what she needed to sort out, the message simply said,

*'Relationship issues.'*

That didn't ring true either. As far as she is aware, her sister isn't even in a relationship. If she is, she is doing a damn good job of hiding it. God knows she has had some real humdingers in the past so maybe she's keeping quiet about it until she's sure it will work out? Rachel doesn't think so, but then again, after Sheryl's previous car-crash relationships, anything is possible. Her last boyfriend turned out to be the local big guy in town, a drug dealer with his own brand spanking new Mercedes and a host of dodgy minders to watch his back. That one didn't last long after the police swooped on his flat in a dawn raid, breaking the door down while the rest of the neighbourhood slept. He is currently serving seven years in prison. Not long enough in Rachel's opinion. The one before that was a serial philanderer, somebody who simply couldn't keep it in his trousers. Everyone knew about his ways and tried to tell Sheryl, who ended up in complete denial. And the one prior to that - well Sheryl kept pretty quiet about that one actually. Rachel has always suspected it was a woman but said nothing. Not that it matters. Sheryl's love life is her business. She just wishes her older sister would find somebody - a soul partner - like she has in Dominic. Sheryl always seems to stumble from one catastrophic relationship to another. She has a knack for forming disastrous relationships with totally unsuitable partners. Funny how she can spend her days advising others how to navigate their way through difficulties in their lives and yet can't manage her own.

Rachel thinks of her sister's job. Sheryl's clients are her lifeblood. She lives to help them and would never just abandon them the way she has. It's unthinkable. Rachel knows that Sheryl has some savings but with no money being earned, how are her bills getting paid? What about her rent and her other outgoings? She has badgered the police to check Sheryl's bank account to look for any suspicious activity and only hopes they've done the appropriate checks and realised that something is terribly amiss. Because it is. She can just feel it. Somebody has taken her sister and the same somebody has used Sheryl's phone to send these fake messages, to fool everyone into thinking she is safe. Well it won't work. The police may have fallen for it but Rachel can see straight through such a cruel and devious trick.

She stares at the screen, at Sheryl's smiling face beaming out at her from the police incident page and feels her stomach tighten. *Where are you Sheryl? Where the hell have you gone to?* The most difficult part, apart from the obvious, has been keeping it from their dad. It's fortunate that he rarely leaves the house and doesn't know how to operate a computer. The one thing they've nagged him about for years, not getting a laptop, has suddenly become a fortunate state of affairs for her. He thinks Sheryl has gone away on holiday with some friends but it won't be too long before he begins to question why she hasn't rung him. He's disabled, not stupid.

Rachel leans back in her seat. This is all so surreal. Nightmarish. This is the type of thing that only ever happens to other people, not to her. Not to their family. She stands up, suddenly imbued with a sense of purpose. The police might be doing their bit now, after not taking her seriously, but what's to say she can't continue doing her own investigative work? Better than sitting around waiting for clues to fall in her lap from the darkening sky above. That won't bring Sheryl home, will it? Sitting here alone with only her thoughts for company will solve nothing. All it does is make her feel helpless and frustrated. She has two days off work. She should be making the most of them, getting out and about, tracking Sheryl's last movements.

The first place she will visit is the town. That's where Sheryl goes for her shopping. It's where her office is, for goodness sake. She practically lives there. She will ask people if they've seen her, she will put posters up on lamp-posts, plaster them across shop windows, do whatever it takes. She won't stop until somebody, somewhere, tells her that they saw her sister, spoke to her, passed her in the street. Anything, any little thing at all that will tell her what happened to her big sister. She will move heaven and earth to get her back. And she is going to start right now.

# Peggy

'Hello?' A sharp crackle howls at her from the handset. Peggy pulls it away from her ear and glares at it as if the inanimate object in her hand is solely responsible for the disturbance. More crackling, then a voice; muffled, distant.

'Peggy? Is that you?'

She freezes. Recognises the voice as her own. It's been a long time since they spoke. Too long.

'Bea?'

She sees Alec's head turn, notices his frown. They never got on, not really. Too much alike. Both opinionated, both fiery.

'Can you hear me? I can hardly hear you. Wait a second while I get sat down.' Peggy listens as her sister shoos the cat off her seat. A miaow of protestation, a rustle of fabric as she settles herself and then a modicum of clarity as she speaks once more, her voice so much like Peggy's own it sends a tingle of recognition down her spine. 'Right, that's better. I'm sorted now. You've probably guessed why I'm ringing.'

A pause ensues while Peggy tries to go through all the birthdays and anniversaries in her mind. She hasn't guessed at all. She has no idea at all why her sister is calling her and now alarm bells are ringing in her head, loud and clear, making her light-headed.

'No,' Peggy says quietly, loath to admit defeat, 'no idea at all. Maybe it's just to say hello since you rarely contact me?'

She wants to bite her tongue as soon as the words leave her mouth. Too late. They're out there now. Harsh and loaded with a healthy dose of bitterness.

'Yes, well, the line runs both ways,' Beatrice replies softly, her tone suggesting she is used to Peggy's sarcasm.

'I'm sorry,' Peggy whispers quickly, as if the words are poisonous and saying them will confirm to the world what she already knows to be true, that she is tainted. Venom running through her veins, hot and unstoppable. A beast lurking within, waiting to strike.

'So,' Beatrice continues, as if nothing has just taken place, 'I take it the hospital haven't rung you, then? Or the police?'

'Why would they?' Peggy's vision blurs and the room begins to sway. The police. Again.

'You haven't heard?' Beatrice's words send her brain into complete disorder, a stream of disorganised thoughts jockeying for position in her head. Pieces of a puzzle all trying to slot into position and failing miserably.

'Heard what?' she tries to keep her voice even but in her head it sounds as if she is underwater. Her throat feels thick, coated with a bitter substance that is stopping her from speaking properly.

'About Mum,' a sigh at the other end of the line. 'Look, it's early morning here and we've just had the call. God knows why they didn't ring you first.'

*Because mum and I haven't spoken for twenty years? Because she always preferred you over me?*

'But anyway,' Beatrice continues, 'at least they managed to get hold of one of us.'

'Who did?'

A sigh, as if she is stupid. Peggy suddenly feels as if she is ten years old all over again. She had forgotten how good her older sister is at doing this, making her feel inadequate, making her feel as if she needs putting in her place.

'The hospital. They called me twenty minutes ago. Mum is in hospital after being involved in a fire.'

The words rock Peggy, hitting her like a slap in the face. *A fire?* 'What? Where?'

'In her house - her bungalow. They didn't tell me all the details but from what I've gathered, the place is gutted. She was in the bedroom and the door was closed. That was the only thing that stopped her from dying. Silly old bugger had disconnected the smoke alarm after the batteries ran out.'

The room rotates as Peggy tries to stand up. She needs to move about. She has a terrible tingling sensation in her legs and has an overwhelming urge to shake them about; to keep them moving. It feels as if concrete is being poured into them, fixing her to the floor.

'I - I don't know what to say, Bea. I really don't ...'

'How about, how is she? That would be a good start.'

Peggy feels her cheeks burn, senses a twitch starting up in her eye, 'Is she okay? I mean is she badly injured or disfigured or anything?' Once again, the words come tumbling out without any real thought behind them. They just appear, unbidden. Perhaps they're always there, Peggy thinks, watching, waiting, ready to tumble out when the time is right.

'Disfigured? Why would you say that, Peggy? Are you trying to be funny or something?'

'NO!' Her voice rises in pitch, echoing across the kitchen, sending Alec hurtling towards her, his eyes wide with concern, 'I just meant is she okay? Not badly injured?'

'Well, why don't you go to the hospital and find out since you're close by and I'm over five thousand miles away?' And with that the line goes dead. An interminable silence follows as Peggy lifts the handset away from her ear and stares at it, bewildered. She holds it aloft as if it is diseased, something she needs to get rid of quickly.

'What the hell was all that about?' Alec is standing close to her, his breath slightly sour as it drifts near her face.

'It's Mum. She's been in a fire.' Peggy looks up to the ceiling and bites her lip. She feels as if she wants to cry and is bewildered at her behaviour, but then she has done a lot of things lately and has no idea why. It's as if everything is spiralling out of control, her life is being slowly but surely sucked down a huge hole; a swirling eddy determined to get her and she is powerless against its strength; caught up in its greedy clutches.

'Where is she? Which hospital?' Alec moves away and is back in an instant. Peggy looks at his hands. He is holding two coats out towards her. She should take one of them and they should go. But she can't seem to move, no matter how hard she tries. She is glued to the floor, unable to shift into a gear that will set her body in motion.

'Peggy!' he shouts, his voice booming around the kitchen, a stray bullet bouncing off walls until it eventually pierces through her thoughts, sending a pain searing across the top of her head.

'I don't know!' she cries, 'I didn't get a chance to ask. She hung up on me.' Beatrice hates her. She can just tell. Her own sister, the only remaining family member worth speaking of, now despises her.

Alec grabs the phone out of her hand. She watches, dazed as he dials 118 118 and asks for the number of the local hospital. After that it's all a bit of a blur. She tries protesting, telling Alec that there's no point visiting, that her mother will only turn them away but each time comes up against a brick wall. And he is so damn difficult to argue with. His reasons are solid, his emotions intact whereas hers are running free like water, spreading far and wide, leaving her unable to function as she normally would. Before she knows it, they are strapped in the car and heading onto the main road, leaving a trail of dust and stones in their wake.

'You weren't like this with your father,' Peggy says sulkily as she slinks down into the seat, her chin almost touching her collar. She is a child again, being dragged from her play and taken to places against her will, a passenger on a journey she does not want to be making. Trees pass her; conifers, oaks, sycamores, their leaves a dark smudge in her peripheral vision, their trunks a line of huge thick, brown beams. She wants to go home where it's safe, where nobody can see her. Home, where her problems and worries can be contained, stacked up in order. Then she thinks of the cottage and realises she is better off out here on the road, away from it all. She is a nomad, wandering through a desert, nowhere she can call home, no safe place to rest.

'Don't, Peggy,' Alec warns, his back as straight as an arrow, 'this is completely different and you know it. This is your chance for you and your mother to start again. A fresh start.'

She wants to cry out to him that he has no idea what he is doing, what horrors he is about to unleash. She wants to tell him that she and her mother are completely different people with no common ground worth speaking of and that her mother hates him. She wants to scream at him that Audrey Penthorpe, his own mother-in-law thinks he is a murderer and a paedophile. But she doesn't. She remains silent all the way to the hospital, praying to whichever god may be listening, that by the time they get there, her mother will already be dead.

# Audrey

She can hear voices, quiet murmurings of ghosts hovering over her, their words a stream of whispers floating in and out of her consciousness. She doesn't recognise them, knows this isn't her bed. *What is going on?* There was a man - that much she does remember. He had a deep voice, thick hands. Why can she remember his hands? What was he doing to her? Something over her face. Heat. Coughing, choking. Lying outside on the grass. Sirens.

The voices over her fade away and she is left in silence to ponder over where she is and why she is here. She tries, makes a concerted effort to piece it all back together but something hard and sharp is pushed into her arm and before she can begin to analyse anything, she feels herself descending, slowly falling into a deep vacuum of emptiness where darkness reigns supreme.

When she awakes there are more voices surrounding her. She doesn't open her eyes. Easier that way. At least she can pretend she's still asleep, pretend that none of this is actually happening.

Another voice. A lady. She sounds young - mid-twenties perhaps. A thin, sibilant tone with a strong northern accent.

'We'll know more when she wakes up but as far as we can tell, apart from some minor burns on her face, she only suffered smoke inhalation. She's a very fortunate lady, your mother.'

*Mother?!*

Audrey lies quite still, hoping they can't see the pulse that is starting up in her neck at the sound of their words, see the quiver of fear on her skin.

'We need to find some accommodation for her. A member of the team from Social Services has been here but we were hoping that since she has family ...'

A voice she thinks she knows cuts through the air, and she has to exercise all her strength to not sit upright and rip out the cannula that is attached to the back of her hand, to tell them to ignore him but she can't seem to summon up the strength.

'She can come and stay with us. It's not a problem.'

*Yes, it is! It's a huge problem.*

'We've got a spare room, haven't we?'

The voice is met with silence until another voice she doesn't recognise dips in, 'We need to assess her when she wakes up. The doctor should be round shortly.'

Then the sound of something being put at the end of the bed. Notes, perhaps? A clank of plastic hitting metal; the soft shuffle of comfortable shoes, the tell-tale squeak of nurses' footwear, moving away from her. More silence. Awkward, loaded with a sentiment she can't put her finger on. Within a couple of seconds, she can hear the sigh of movement on vinyl seats and pictures them, the two of them sitting close by, watching, waiting, willing her to open her eyes. What will she say to them? How is she supposed to react? Trying to calm her breathing, she waits a few seconds, then slowly drags her eyes open. It is surprisingly painful, as if a film of sandpaper is wedged between her eyelids. And that's when she sees it - a vision of beauty, an angel framed by a halo of light filtering in from the window beyond. *Peggy.* Her back is upright, not slouched as Audrey imagined, and her dark hair is scraped back from her face in a thick ponytail. She is slim: no, thin. Very, very thin. Even more so than when she last saw her at the beach, and her eyes are downcast, her dark lashes glossy against the backdrop of autumnal sunshine behind her. Audrey wishes she could stop time, keep this perfect vision intact, hang onto it for forever. A keepsake to tuck away in her mind.

'Hello Audrey. Just take it easy, don't try to sit up. The doctor will be here shortly.'

The moment is gone, shattered into a thousand tiny fragments by the sound of his voice. Her blood turns to sand as she slowly tilts her head and sees him sitting there at the side of her bed, smiling, his mouth drawn into a grimace, his perfectly straight teeth bared as if in anger.

She nods and turns her head back to Peggy. She could stay like this for hours, just staring at her, taking on board every aspect of her daughter's beautiful features. And they are beautiful. Even the scars. They are part of who she is, not something she should be ashamed of. She wants to say hello, to reach out and feel her daughter's soft skin against hers but hasn't the energy and also fears the repercussions of such a move. She needs to remember that Peggy hates her with every fibre of her being. Audrey has to earn that love back, show her that she wants to do everything she can to make it up to her, to catch up on those lost years. Which she will. Once she is better and out of here, she will do whatever is required. Because it will be easier now. The connection has been made. Peggy is here, everything is tangible. Anything is possible now. It's all hers for the taking.

# Rachel

The town is busy, which, in a way, is a good thing. More people to question, more faces to search for answers. The downside is that she is getting hard stares from certain prim-looking characters every time she puts a poster up. One old lady has already asked what the hell she thought she was doing defacing public property; ruining bus stops and lamp-posts that are paid for by tax payers' hard-earned money. Rachel showed her the pictures of Sheryl, explained the situation but was met with a scowl and a stream of reasons why she should get herself off home and leave the police to carry out the job properly and not be out here stepping on their toes, messing up their work. Rachel wanted to ask what work, since they haven't taken her claims seriously and believe her sister has gone off on some kind of weird sabbatical to find herself just because of a few stupid text messages. But she didn't. She smiled and nodded and accepted the old lady's speech with good grace, waited till she was out of sight, then continued plastering the posters around town, stopping passers-by, showing them her sister's smiling face only to be met with a sad shake of the head before they moved on and continued with their day.

She refuses to give in, despite getting nowhere. She absolutely will *not* forget about her sister and leave her to the hands of the local police efforts. If it takes her till midnight to make some headway with this, then she will stay here to do it.

Newsagents, she discovers, are the most helpful.

'Aye, course you can, love,' the man behind the counter, in the tiny tobacconists, says to her when she asks if she can put a poster up in his window, 'put it right in the middle so everyone can 'ave a good look, see if they recognise 'er.'

She thanks him profusely and moves on, going from shop to shop, some saying they would love to help but company rules state no posters, while others suck on their teeth a while before agreeing and allowing her to stick it up with the other bits of paper in the window, offering Xboxes and washing machines for sale.

The heavens open as Rachel grabs another handful of posters out of her backpack. Scurrying out of the fat droplets, she stands in a bus stop with her wad of papers.

'You know her, then?' a voice says behind her. Rachel swings round to see a man in his thirties staring at her with interest.

'Yes. Yes, I do. Do you?'

His voice is soft as he speaks and he has a slight southern accent. Rachel tries to control her breathing and keep her anticipation under wraps. He may simply be making conversation. She shouldn't get her hopes up. This might go nowhere, a complete dead end. She'll no doubt go up plenty of those whilst searching for Sheryl.

'Yeah, kind of,' he smiles at her, a lopsided affair. He is unshaven and a slight sheen of grease covers his dark hair. She stands stock still, waiting for him to elucidate. A bus growls to a halt next to them. She stands to one side to let him pass but he waits and shakes his head, 'This one isn't mine.'

Rachel nods knowingly and watches as a throng of people filter onto the bus, jangling pockets full of money to find the right change. And then they are all gone, leaving her and this man alone under the cover of the green shelter. Bullets of water pelt the Perspex roof as the shower gets heavier, increasing in strength, dark clouds above releasing a torrent of rain on the town.

'She was my counsellor. I used to see her once every few weeks but stopped once I got back on my feet, y'know?'

Rachel nods that she does know and smiles at him, 'So you haven't seen her for a while then, I take it?'

He nods and shrugs. 'She was brilliant. Really helped me through some tough times but I stopped going earlier in the year. No need to continue, really.'

The rain continues to pelt the shelter and Rachel stares up at the clouds overhead, trying to stop the tears from escaping. When she looks back at him he is holding out his hand for her to shake. She takes it, his grasp firm and warm despite the plunging temperature.

'I really hope she turns up. She's an amazing woman.'

'Yes. Yes, she is,' Rachel says, the lump in her throat a hard stone of anguish.

A roar behind her sends her a shiver up her spine as another bus pulls in, throwing a spray of water into the gutter. She watches as a river of rain snakes its way down the glass, a mesh of dirty streaks, dark and dreary, like the mood she is carrying inside.

'This is mine, I'm afraid,' he says as he apologetically sidles past her clutching a fistful of money. He waits while a stream of people file off then turns to give her one last half-hearted smile before jumping aboard and disappearing inside. Rachel feels ridiculously bereft, as if the only link she had with Sheryl is gone. A town full of people and nobody knows anything. Fighting back tears, she steps out into the rain, a torrent of water washing the streets, thundering down on people sending them scurrying into shop doorways for shelter.

Head down, she picks up her pace and turns up a side street, ignoring the door to the practice where Sheryl's office is based. No clues in there. Just a room where she met some of her clients. At least now the police have finally decided to move their arses they can access the files, look into some of her patients. A lot of them have gone through major issues in their lives and may have gotten too attached to her, done something stupid. God, she hopes not. The very thought of it makes her feel sick to her stomach. That's always Sheryl's problem. Too soft with people, too gullible when it comes to a sob story. Stopping, she thinks better of it and pulls out another poster, then sticks it up on the battered old door that leads to Sheryl's office. Water runs down her back as she presses it firmly onto the wet surface, cursing the British weather under her breath.

'Related to you, is she?' The voice takes her by surprise. She turns to see a woman behind her, dyed blonde hair piled high on her head and a silver stud through her lower lip. She is in her late twenties and is scrutinising Sheryl's picture so closely her eyes have narrowed to tiny slits. The rain appears to have no effect on this striking creature. Rachel stares at her flawless complexion and lacquered hair and nails. A tiny drop of rain slides down her forehead and over her eyelid, clinging to the dark lashes before she shakes her head slightly and blinks it away.

'Yes, she's my sister.'

'Thought so,' she replies pensively, 'you can see the resemblance. Same shape nose. Ski slope. Not like my hooter.' She brings her finger up and strokes the soft cartilage below her eyes as if to prove her point. 'I see her about here quite a bit. She comes in the cafe where I work. Not seen her for a while though.'

Rachel feels her heart start up and has to take a deep breath to stop a squeal escaping.

'Hope she's okay. Seemed like a nice lady. Always left me a tip.'

She starts to walk away and Rachel reaches out to stop her. She wants to huddle somewhere warm and dry and demand that she tell her all she knows about Sheryl, beg her to start at the beginning and leave nothing out. But the studded lady has pulled away and is losing interest, her phone already pressed to the side of her head.

'Was she with somebody or on her own?'

She stops and turns, her brow furrowed in confusion, her blonde hair threatening to topple down over her face as a blast of wind takes her by surprise, rattling its way past her in a rush, 'Huh?'

'Sheryl? My sister! Was she alone or with somebody when you saw her?'

The woman shrugs and turns away then says something into the phone and turns back, her voice almost drowned out by the gush of the rain as it pounds the cobbled alleyway, 'With someone! Always with someone. Sorry gotta go.'

And with that she is gone, her feet galloping through the puddles, her hand cradling her phone to her shock of white hair as she disappears out of sight. Rachel spends the next hour traipsing through town, sticking the last of the posters up anywhere she can - walls, windows – she'll stick them on people's backs if she has to. Only when they have all gone does she decide to head home. Soaking wet, her hair drips into her eyes, her beige raincoat now a dark grey colour as she trudges wearily back to the main road. She is too tired to make the mile-long journey home. Walking here seemed like a good idea at the time, given the lack of parking facilities but now she is bone achingly tired and freezing cold. She hasn't the energy to walk back. Even her teeth hurt.

She passes the taxi rank and takes no time at all to make her decision. Swinging the door open she peers in and gets the nod from the driver. Shaking off the excess water, Rachel climbs in, grateful for the wall of warmth that hits her as she slides down in the seat and straps herself in.

'Busy day, eh, love?' the driver asks as he glances in his rear-view mirror and swings the car out onto the road.

Rachel grabs a tissue from her pocket before wiping her face and blowing her nose, 'Yes you could say that.' She stuffs the tissue deep in her pocket, leans her head back on the headrest and struggles to stop the tears from flowing. She only hopes somebody comes forward, recognises Sheryl from the posters, otherwise it will all have been for nothing.

'Shopping day, was it?' he asks as they head out of town, the car swinging through the narrow side streets.

'No, no shopping today,' she replies wistfully, staring out at the many cars parked one after another after another. A constant line of vehicles stacked up, all going nowhere.

'Oh, okay,' he says and remains silent.

'I was out looking for my sister,' her voice warbles as she speaks. She swallows hard, doing her best to keep it together.

'A little one, is she? Got lost in town?'

'What? No,' Rachel half cries, her patience and energy waning by the second, 'she's my older sister and she's a missing person. I've been out putting posters up around town. See if anybody remembers seeing her.' Her words are sharp, clipped. She can't help it. Desperation is setting in. She's exhausted, wet, freezing cold, and beginning to fear the worst.

'Sorry to hear that,' the taxi driver says quietly and Rachel can tell he doesn't know what to say to make any of it better. Nobody does. 'Are you alike?' he asks softly, 'I mean I was thinking if I knew what she looked like I might have seen her, y'know? Be able to help maybe ...'

Rachel wipes away a lone tear that's managed to escape, 'Some people say we do but I don't think so.'

'Right,' he answers and she sees him take a long look at her side profile, 'I dropped a lassie off a few weeks ago around here. Looked just like you she did.'

Rachel's head buzzes. She swallows hard and tries to think straight. She can't afford to get too excited, to jump to the wrong conclusions only to be let down. Again.

'She had long blonde hair a bit like your colour,' he says, 'and she asked to be dropped off back there in town.'

He has her attention now. Rachel shuffles round in her seat and watches him as he drives, 'Whereabouts? I mean where did you drop her?'

'Just next to the coffee shop. You know the one with the tables and chairs outside that are always blowing over?' Rachel nods. She knows it well. Everyone does. Their flimsy furniture is often to be found clattering its way down the street when the wind gets up, which is pretty often round these parts.

'She said she was meeting someone,' he adds and Rachel feels her chest tighten.

'Can you describe her?'

'Like I said, longish blonde hair, blue eyes. Oh, and the one thing I do remember was her tattoo - a long snake that went all the way up her arm.'

Rachel feels herself being squashed, her hopes diminished with his words. Sheryl has no tattoos. She is terrified of needles.

They sit for a while. Her silence gives him his answer, 'Not your girl then, I take it?'

She shakes her head and turns to stare out of the window so he can't see her face, streaked with tears.

'Right,' he whispers as he begins to tap his fingers on the steering wheel as if he is thinking, trying to conjure up a mental image of the missing woman, 'sorry 'bout that. Wish I could have helped you more.'

'Just here is fine,' Rachel says as they round the corner of her street. The rain has eased up and she suddenly needs to get out of the car. He has turned the heater up and she feels as if she is choking.

'You sure, love? You're soaking through. I can drop you off at the door, no extra charge …'

Rachel feels more tears start up at his words, 'That's really kind of you but I feel like walking the last bit. I need to clear my head, it's been a long day.'

He nods knowingly and stops the car. She opens her purse and rummages inside for a handful of change, suddenly wishing she had kept one of the posters or had a picture of Sheryl in her bag or purse to give him.

'Well, I hope she turns up,' he says, as Rachel sloshes a handful of coins into his palm, 'it must be a right worry for you.'

\*\*\*

He considers driving back and looking for her, trying to work out which house she went into after he manoeuvred his way out of the road, but doesn't have the time to go knocking on every door trying to find her. He only made the connection after driving back through town and spotting the posters she had put up all over the place. And they were *all over the place*. Windows, walls, doors, lamp-posts, bus stops - a woman's face grinning out at the sea of faces that pass through the High Street carrying out their daily routine of collecting groceries or going to work; hundreds of them, all on their way to somewhere else. He recognised her straightaway, remembered their chat as he took her on the winding path up there. Said she was visiting a friend and would ring him for a cab back again in a few hours. Had a bit of craic with her, he did. She seemed like a right nice lady.

He swings the car round and tries once more to work out which way the young lassie headed but it's such a long road and they all look the same after a while, these big old semi-detached houses. He'll drive back through the High Street en route to his next pick up and get the number written on the poster. He can ring her later, after his shift, tell her what he knows; which is probably not much, but better than nothing, isn't it? Funny thing is, it stuck in his head that pick up, mainly because of the location. He's never been up there before, that old cottage on the clifftop - wasn't even sure anyone lived there. For some reason, because it's so close to the edge and stands on its own, he presumed it was empty.

The radio crackles into life as the taxi driver three points in the road and turns back towards town hoping they find each other, those sisters. Dropping her off up there was probably nothing of any importance anyway. Right now, he has work to do. A full night of pick-ups ahead of him. He yawns and listens as an order is barked through about doing an airport run to Newcastle and then taking someone into Durham City. It's going to be a long one. He turns the music on and shakes his head before leaning over and turning on the sat nav. What a bloody shift.

# Alec

He had to offer. There was no other option was there? But now Peggy is sitting beside him in the car, her body frozen in anger, her face a mask of fury.

'You can't honestly tell me you're prepared to watch her go into a home while we have a spare bedroom for her? After what she's been through?'

Her voice is a shriek, a howl of a fury that Alec feels sure could shatter glass. He visualises the windscreen being ripped out by the sheer power of Peggy's vocal chords at full pitch.

'What *she's* been through? What about what we've been through - what she has *put* us through?'

His forehead furrows, a deep line etched between his dark brows, 'Peggy, that was years ago. You were a teenager, for God's sake.' He takes a corner too quickly and swears as he lifts his foot up off the accelerator, 'and to be honest I never have understood why you've remained so angry with her all these years.'

He glances her way briefly, their eyes meeting just for a second, a rapid, knowing look before he shifts his gaze back to the road.

'Haven't you,' she says through gritted teeth, her words more of a statement than a question.

'No actually, I haven't,' he replies, determined not to be dragged into an argument about her scars. He's not prepared to put up with any of her woes. Not any more.

Rain spatters the windscreen, a stream of thick tears spreading over the glass as Alec drops a gear and heads up the steep incline to Chamber Cottage. The place is deserted. No tourists, no dog walkers, everyone at home or in shops in town sheltering from the rain.

'I think it's the least we can do considering she has nowhere to live, don't you?' Peggy doesn't answer but then he didn't expect her to. It was purely rhetorical. Peggy's attitude is really starting to grate on him, the way everything is always about her. Audrey is a lonely old woman. No more than that, and if he's being honest, having somebody else around will alleviate the tension in their house. He hoped that he and Peggy were starting to make a go of things but living with her is like being on an emotional rollercoaster. So many ups and downs he actually gets dizzy with it all. And of course, still no sex. Nothing. Zilch. No wonder he can't keep his eyes off Ellen at work, who actually follows him around like a lost puppy, giving him the come on with her tight skirts and high heels. Sleeping next to Peggy is like being in bed with a block of ice. In a bizarre sort of way, he's actually looking forward to having Peggy's mother here with them. He's had nothing to do with her since he was a kid. And that part of his life was pretty shitty. Audrey's memories of him will be of a skinny, lonely kid - the scruffy one from the council estate at the end of her road who used to roam the streets at all hours, uncared for, unloved, unwanted. All he remembers of her is an aloof, middle class lady who wore expensive jewellery, high heels and make-up whereas his own mother wore the same threadbare clothes day in and day out and cut and dyed her own hair.

Alec sniffs and pulls at his collar as he feels the heat rise around his neck. Peggy thinks she's the only one with problems. Peggy and her issues. He's lived with them for so long now, they've become an integral part of their marriage, like an extra limb that refuses to work properly; a heavy appendage attached to everything they do, uncoordinated and clumsy. Superfluous to requirements. He remembers Sheryl's advice about his marriage and shakes the words away. All in the past. All over with now. No more visits there. No more Sheryl.

# Peggy

She hears the low drone of the engine as they make their way up the twisting bank that leads them home and listens intently to Alec's words. They hang heavily in the air between them, sharp icicles piercing her thoughts, freezing her brain. For a reason she can neither fathom nor articulate, Peggy cannot bring herself to tell him. Twenty years and she has never been able to tell him the full tale of that day - the day her face was ripped to pieces, the day her world changed forever. She doesn't even know why. To protect him from her mother's words? Perhaps. But then there's lots of things she keeps tucked away in her mind, secrets she shouldn't have that she will never tell him about. She's becoming quite good at it, this lying business.

'You didn't have to live with her, see how devious she can be, watch how she ate away at my dad, nagging him half to death, day after day after day,' Peggy barks. She feels her skin grow hot and starts to unfasten her coat.

'That still doesn't explain not talking to her for all this time, Peggy. Don't you see?' he says, a pleading expression in his tone. 'This is your chance to start again. Wipe the slate clean.'

They pull up outside the cottage and he yanks the handbrake on. 'This is your chance to do the right thing.'

She is sapped of energy. Exhausted by it all. Twenty long years of hating and loathing has taken it out of her.

'Where will she stay?' Her voice is a whisper, a loose stream of words that roll around in the still air, meaningless to her. They're just sounds escaping, things she knows she has to say to placate him.

'Jesus, Pegs, what is wrong with you? We've got a spare bedroom, you know we have!'

She nods, suddenly too weary to put up a fight. His mind is made up. This is a fait accompli and she is no more than a passive bystander, a watcher of her own existence as once again, her mother steps in and takes over, ripping what little life she has left into tiny pieces. She probably planned it all. Realised her emails were being ignored so decided to do something more drastic to get Peggy's attention. And once she's in the cottage with them, living her life, up and recovered, there's no telling what she will say or the lengths she'll go to, to make sure she is heard. Such a wicked, calculating, old bitch, lying there in a hospital bed, hooked up to drips, garnering sympathy from anybody who is stupid enough to give it to her. Alec was the worst, sitting there all quiet and awash with compassion. If only he knew how much the pensioner in the bed hated him. If only he knew what she thought of him, how she would gladly see him hang. He has no idea, not a bloody clue. Because Peggy has kept that from him too, destroyed the newspaper clippings and all the photographs Audrey sent her. Funny, isn't it? How their lives are all intertwined, a negative spiral of hatred and culpability - she blames her mother for all her ails and issues, her mother blames Alec and Alec blames her. All locked together in a ring of accusations and hate.

She wrestles with the door handle, her palms suddenly clammy. This is a done deal so she had best get used to it. Whether she likes it or not, Audrey is coming to stay with them. After twenty odd years of silence, Peggy and her mother are about to be reunited.

*'So, this is it, then? The end of us, so to speak?'*
   *'Yes. You know it is. You need to leave now.'*
   *'Hold me. Please. Just one last time.'*
   *A step forward out of the house. An arm stretching out. A shove.*
   *'Don't do that. Don't ever push me away.'*
   *A noise somewhere in the distance. Heads turning to look.*
   *'What is that? Is somebody out there?'*
   *'There's nobody out there. You're imagining things. It's time for you to leave now.'*

*Another distant scraping noise.*

*'You need to let me in now. Someone is watching.'*

*A smile. A slight of hand, an arm being grabbed.*

*'What are you doing?'*

*'LEAVE.'*

*It all happens so quickly - the tangling of limbs, the jostling, the slipping. Then the crack of bone on concrete. A rapid burst of blood, dark and thick, gathering around them. A guilty stain - spreading, pooling, growing by the second. And the blood; so much blood ...*

*Everything else is a blur. Panic. Absolute blind panic taking over, muddling logic, rubbing out all reasonable thought. Think, think, THINK!*

*A sudden idea. A way out of this whole situation; a way out of the accident, the harassment, the threats. An end to it all.*

*A glance around. Nobody to be seen. All alone.*

*It's heavy, the body. Pulling it round the back of the house. Relief that at last it's all over. Fear at what is just beginning.*

*Tugging at the weeds covering the hatch. Years of growth concealing it. Wrenching at the handle, fearing it will stick. It doesn't. Staring in at the darkness within - at the deep well of nothingness. Her final resting place. The place where it all ends.*

*And then after it's been done, nothing left to do but clean up, wash it all away - the blood and the memories. Scrub at everything until it's all gone ...*

# Audrey

It's not how she imagined it. She pictured something older; something very cottage-like with tiny rooms, low ceilings, and dark wood beams, dusty antiques littering every surface and dark corners full of cobwebs, but in actual fact, it's surprisingly modern.

'I'll take these through to your room Audrey,' Alec says as he wrestles her bags out of her hand leaving her and Peggy in the silence of their diminutive kitchen, the smallest room in the house.

The journey in the car passed relatively quickly, the silence eased by the radio presenter whose chirpy demeanour seemed to rub off on everyone, Alec was even whistling at one point when his favourite song came on. Anybody watching would have thought they were a happy family on an outing, not three people who hadn't spoken for over twenty years.

'I suppose I should show you where everything is?' Peggy murmurs, her eyes looking everywhere but at her mother.

Audrey clears her throat, a hacking cough still present after the fire. Her mind freezes. She knows what it is she wants to say but for some reason the words won't come. They stick in her gullet, hard and painful, lodged in place. Perhaps it's for the best as they would probably come out wrong anyway. She would end up spewing forth a load of pent-up bile and ruin everything. All she needs to do is bide her time, take it easy for a few days and do her best to be as pleasant as she can to the people who have given her somewhere to live while her insurance company sort her claim out. This set up isn't ideal - far from it - but it's better than being stuck in a hotel and it also gives her the opportunity to get things moving with Peggy; show her she isn't the harridan

Peggy thinks she is. She needs to soften her approach, show some humility and gratitude towards them. Be the biddable, amenable person everybody always wanted her to be. Only then will her daughter start to take Audrey's claims seriously.

She spends the next half hour following Peggy around, being shown where everything is kept - towels, shampoo, all manner of toiletries Audrey has never heard of.

'This is where I write,' Peggy states flatly as she points to her laptop, which is placed in the centre of the oak dining table. 'It's my full-time job, which means nine to five every day,' she adds and stares at Audrey, her eyes dark with resentment.

Audrey nods and tries to look humble, 'Don't worry, I won't disturb you. The only thing I ask is that I can use your phone to ring the insurance company, if that's okay? The sooner I get things moving the better.'

Peggy nods and shrugs her shoulders. Audrey feels her soul sink a little. This is going to be hard work. There is no way Peggy is going to make it easy for her. Not that she expected her to. Twenty years is a long time. A lot of love lost. So much to make up for.

'Right, well I think I'll head off out into town and leave you two ladies to it, if that's alright?' Alec is standing behind them, car keys in hand and a jacket slung over his arm, 'Got to pick up a few things for my course tomorrow.'

Audrey stares at Peggy and then back at Alec.

'You're still going?' Peggy's voice is almost a screech and Audrey feels her skin burn at the intensity of it.

'Of course I'm still going,' Alec replies, his eyes suddenly narrow, 'Why wouldn't I be?'

Peggy shrugs and glances briefly in Audrey's direction, before resting her gaze back on Alec, her eyes dark, full of hidden shadows, 'I just thought that maybe under the circumstances, you would postpone it?'

A small gasp barely audible but it is there, 'Under *what* circumstances, Peggy?' Audrey watches as he tightens his grip on the keys, his fists reddening with the extra exertion. She finds herself wondering how often this happens. How often does her daughter ask a reasonable question and have to put up with this - this show of anger that is so obvious it is palpable?

'Well, you know,' Peggy says more quietly this time, 'with all the changes we have here, I just thought ...'

Audrey feels her face heat up. She should say something, ease the moment, make her daughter feel less nervous, but fears that whatever she says will be mistaken as sarcasm or spite and doesn't want to risk losing Peggy completely, so instead slowly retreats to her room, claiming she is tired.

She listens to the hushed tones of their voices from below as she lies on the bed, a small double that overlooks the swelling sea. This is a short-term move. It's not for forever. It was quite obvious from the very outset that Peggy wasn't keen on having her mother move in with them but oddly enough, Alec seemed really positive about the whole thing. Audrey can't think why. They barely know each other, although she has a damn sight more background information on him than he will ever realise.

The last thing she hears before sleep drags her away into its darkest realms is the rush of the sea far below, the angry roar of the tide as it sprays against the rock, lulling and soothing her with its ferocity and menace.

She quickly becomes immersed in a dream where flames lick at her ageing body and she is trapped in a room with Peggy and Sheryl. Sheryl is mouthing something at her, trying to shout to her across the burning room but she is unable to make out the words. Audrey steps closer, the acrid stench of melting flesh filling her nostrils. She reaches out to Peggy who is crying, her eyes wide with fear. Sheryl continues to shout to her, the words becoming clearer as Audrey advances, the flames no longer a threat to her. Then suddenly everything goes quiet. The fire is gone and she is standing in a room with her daughter and a woman she has never met but knows very well.

'You need to know something,' Peggy is saying to Audrey as Audrey reaches out her hand and tries to touch her daughter.

'Yes, tell her,' Sheryl says, her voice a desperate squeak, 'tell her,' she is saying.

'Tell me what?' Audrey cries suddenly, feeling terrified. She doesn't want to hear what is coming next. She has no idea what they are going to say but is consumed with complete and utter dread.

'It's both of us!' Peggy shouts, tears now pouring down her face.

'What about both of you?' Audrey asks, her stomach a tight fist of fear as she stares at their faces.

Suddenly the flames start up again, a huge wall of orange and red; thick, angry flames cutting into their skin, melting their arms and faces like candle wax.

'It's the two of us together,' Sheryl shouts, the skin around her mouth dripping away from her face, exposing the bone underneath.

'Please tell me what's going on!' Audrey shrieks, barely able to stay upright in the intense heat.

'We're both together now,' Peggy says, her voice no longer recognisable as she turns to face her mother, the skin above her eye gone completely, leaving nothing but a wide socket staring at Audrey, white and reproachful.

'What do you mean you're both together?' she screams, her words sticking in her gullet like gravel.

'Can't you see it, Mother?' Peggy says, all too calmly, her face white with exposed bone, 'Can't you see what's happened? We're both together now. We're both dead.'

***

Audrey wakes coated in perspiration, blood rushing in her ears. She sits up and is overcome with dizziness as she tries to stagger off the bed. Is this how it's going to be now she has survived a fire? Will she be overwhelmed with images and nightmares that tear at her already frazzled brain night after night?

Shuffling to the bathroom, she splashes cold water on her face and listens to the silence beneath. No voices, nothing but the sound of the sea thrashing the very cliff that they stand on. Soon it will be over. This whole sorry situation. She will make it all go away. Only then will Audrey be able to rest, to say that she did her level best to see justice was done.

She dries her face and stares in the mirror above the sink. A much older woman stares back at her. Bags sit beneath her eyes; lines curl round the edge of her mouth and her expression is that of rejection. It's been her partner for so long now she can barely remember a time without it. Well, not for much longer. This is her chance, probably the only one she'll get - her last chance in life to put it all right, to make everything better, back to how it should be.

'Come on Audrey,' she mutters through gritted teeth, 'pull yourself together, old girl. No more bad dreams or worries or fear. You've got a missing person to find.'

# Peggy

They both stand at the door and wave him off as if they are a close family saying goodbye to a long-lost relative. Peggy has no idea why her mother has taken it upon herself to do this; to stand so near to her, to hang around in the doorway as if she has lived here for years. As if this is her home. She is so near, Peggy can feel her hot, sour breath on her neck, the pulsating, rhythmic waves of poison escaping from Audrey's lungs, polluting the air around them.

'So where is it he's off to, again?'

Peggy stares at her mother, aghast. Did her brain turn to mush in the fire? How many times does she have to be told something before it finally sinks in? 'We spoke about this last night. He's attending a headteacher's conference in London. Remember?'

'Ah yes, that's right,' Audrey replies as she pulls pieces of loose cotton off her blouse, 'a headteacher's conference. Even though he's not a headteacher. Because he's not, is he? He's the deputy. Not the head.'

Peggy has to use all her self-restraint to not turn around and punch her own mother in the face. Since arriving she has taken every available opportunity to insult Alec. The way he makes tea, the type of programmes he watches on television, his taste in music; every bloody thing has been a problem even though he has been the perfect gentleman in her presence. He has waited on her hand and foot, been charming, pleasant; gone out of his way to make Audrey feel welcome and yet still she insults him, constantly on the lookout for chinks in his armour.

'No, he isn't a headteacher, but then you already know that, don't you, Mother? I'm not sure why you're asking, unless of course it's to demean him and make disparaging remarks about his position within the school,' Peggy barks as she closes the door and pushes past Audrey.

'Oh, it's neither of those things, dear,' Audrey replies coolly as she follows Peggy back into the living room, 'I was just asking that's all. Just making conversation.'

Peggy finds herself too irate to speak. Her heart is thumping wildly in her chest as she watches her mother sit down on the sofa and pick up a piece of embroidery. Even the way she moves her fingers, holding the needle with her bony fingers, her dextrous, quick movements as she pulls at the cotton, the tight purse of her lips as she concentrates; it all annoys Peggy beyond reason. It's going to be a long few days, just Peggy and her mother alone together in this cottage. Solitary walks on the beach will suddenly seem very appealing if her mother continues with her barbed comments. Regardless of the blustery weather and the forecasted rain, she will trudge on and on until she drops with exhaustion rather than spend time in here, with her own mother.

'I was just thinking about all the posters that have been put up in town,' Audrey says casually as she tugs at the fabric, pulling it tight, her mouth a thin, firm line. 'Such a terrible state of affairs,' she adds, 'somebody going missing like that, don't you think?'

Peggy wants to scream. Her mother is doing it again. She has done it all her life, throwing out casual remarks that have the power to explode, sending shards of red-hot metal around the room, injuring unsuspecting bystanders with their hidden meanings and thinly veiled threats. Peggy knows all about the posters. She saw them as they travelled through town to pick Audrey up and again as they came back. Sheryl's face everywhere. Alec didn't seem to notice them, his thoughts were elsewhere - work, Audrey, his father. Hardly surprising really considering the goings on they have had with the police recently. He has more than enough on his plate. It must have been Rachel who put them there. Peggy tries to control her breathing, which suddenly feels laboured and erratic. She stares down at her nails, ragged and torn where she has bitten them down to the bone. There's been no further communication from Polly or any other of their friends but then she didn't expect to hear anything else. It's been such a long time since either she or Alec saw any of them, they're no longer on their radar. They are the forgotten friends; the lost ones.

'Do either of you know her? This lady who has simply disappeared into thin air? This is a small town. I thought everybody would be talking about it.'

Audrey stops sewing and stares up at Peggy who is standing by the window, her back to the raging sea outside. A silence takes hold. Their eyes lock briefly before Audrey turns her attention back to the needle in her hand. She stabs at the material, her mouth puckered, her eyes dark and judgmental.

'Okay, Mother, we can dance around each other for the next two days,' Peggy says, her voice raspy with anger, 'or we can come straight out and talk about this and clear the air. Take your pick.'

Audrey widens her eyes and Peggy wants to laugh. She shakes her head and looks up to the ceiling. Even her mother's mock astonishment is badly executed.

'Talk about what? I just happened to mention about what everyone in town must be talking about. A missing lady. As I just mentioned, this is a small town. People disappearing round these parts must be a pretty rare occurrence. If it were me and I lived here I would be out there searching for her, doing whatever I could to help out. That's all. I'm just surprised that such an occurrence seems to have passed you both by. Perhaps it's to do with your location - stuck up here on the cliff edge. Removed from it all. Quite a lonely existence for you I should imagine...'

Peggy clamps her teeth together, grinding them back and forth until it hurts. She releases her jaw and wiggles it from side to side. A shooting pain travels up the side of her head as she speaks. She closes her eyes against the wave of nausea that accompanies it and exhales loudly before speaking.

'Look, if you must know, neither of us has seen Sheryl for ages. And without wanting to sound cruel or uncaring, it isn't really our problem. According to the police and her sister, she's sent some text messages saying she wants to be left alone for a while so, quite frankly, I'm not sure what all the fuss is about.' Peggy brings her hand up and drags it through her hair. She is always shocked at how knotted and tangled it is. No amount of brushing ever frees the curls that lock together, leaving her with a web of tight coils. She rests her fingers in there, hoping her mother can't see how much she is trembling. This is one conversation she does not want to be having. Not here with her mother sitting opposite her. Not ever, actually.

Peggy turns to see Audrey staring up at her; the thin skin around her eyes is creased and her jaw is hanging open ever so slightly. The fabric sits on her lap and she is completely motionless as she scrutinises Peggy's face. She feels the floor begin to sway. Her words ring in her head, a clanging reminder of what she has just done; what she has just given away.

'You know her?' Audrey gasps, 'Oh, I had no idea! You must be terribly upset about it. I mean everyone must be beside themselves with worry.'

'Everyone meaning me and Alec you mean? Come on Mother, why don't you just say it?' Peggy can barely contain her anger. She can feel it bubbling up, growing inside her, ready to explode, 'I mean, while we're at it why don't we talk about those notes you sent me, eh? And the emails. Let's have a chat about those, shall we? That's what you want isn't it? That's why you're here. It's probably why you started that fire, so you could worm your way in here, have your say. Ruin my life all over again …'

Peggy stands breathless, astounded at her mother's cool demeanour while she feels as if her brain is about to combust. She had hoped for some sort of reaction with that particular statement but she watches as Audrey continues sewing, her thin fingers ploughing a line through the fabric - *in, out, in, out, in, out.*

'I don't think now is the right time, Peggy. You're too tetchy, too angry,' Audrey says icily.

Peggy stares for a while, notices how straight her mother's hands are, how tightly she is grasping the needle, sees the tic in her jaw, how it pulsates while she concentrates on the task in hand and it's only then that she realises this is all an act. She isn't half as calm as she appears to be. Right now, her mother is anything but relaxed. She is giving the appearance of somebody detached and untouched by their conversation but as Peggy watches, she can see the skin stretched across her knuckles, taut and white. Audrey's legs are crossed tightly, her calves perfectly aligned, but Peggy can see a slight twitch of a muscle. She wants to laugh, to yell that she can see beyond it but instead remains silent, watching the agility with which Audrey's fingers dart across the cotton, creating a pattern of colours on the cream coloured fabric.

'I'm not sure when the right time will be,' Peggy says as she turns to stare out of the window. A splattering of rain hits the pane of glass. She peers up at the sky, at the grey clouds bunching up into a sinister mass overhead. A proper storm gathering up. No beach walk today if this keeps up. Just Peggy and her mother stuck here with their wicked thoughts and accusations. She breathes heavily, her fingers clasped tightly as she does her best to keep her temper in check. Today is going to be a very long day indeed.

The knock at the door takes them both by surprise, sending an electric pulse down Peggy's spine. She is rather pleased to see her mother lose her grip on the fabric, and watches with undisguised glee as it floats onto the floor, landing at her feet in a crumpled, multi-coloured heap. Not so graceful or poised after all.

'I take it by your expression, you're not expecting anyone?' Audrey says tersely as she grabs at the material and snatches it back onto her lap.

'No. No visitors expected today,' Peggy replies as she stalks off into the hallway thinking how easy it would be to take her mother on a walk with her in this inclement weather. Nobody else around to see them. One hard push and she could send her off into the sea never to be seen again. Until the tide decides it has had enough of her, that is, and washes her back to shore a mile down the coast. Even in death Audrey would still have the upper hand, presenting her broken and battered body for all the world to see. *There must be an easier way,* thinks Peggy as she pulls the door open and feels her knees buckle.

# Maude

Her head hurts. She stares up from her horizontal position on the sofa and sees Brenda and that boy staring down at her. She has a terrible pain locked somewhere deep inside her brain and it's making her feel dizzy and quite sick. She can't think where she is or how she got here. Her thoughts are fuzzy and muddled, as if the top of her skull has been sawn off and stuffed full of candy floss, all her memories coated in a sticky mess that stops her from remembering things properly. It scares her, feeling this way. She wishes she could go home, see her parents again, climb into her old bed - the one she shared with her brother and sister - and nuzzle her nose up to the soft, warm sheets. They don't have much money, her parents; hardly any at all in fact, but her mother always makes sure they're clean and well cared for. Not always well fed, but then everyone is permanently hungry at the minute, aren't they? It's the war that's to blame for that. Her dad keeps telling her so. She would like to see her parents and wonders when they're going to come for her. She didn't want to be evacuated but that's just how it is. All her friends and family scattered far and wide. She does miss them though. This Brenda lady is nice and everything and that boy - well he's a bit dim and mutters a lot but apart from that it's okay, really, but she would rather go home and face the bombs. She's had enough of being here now. As her mam said to her dad as she reluctantly handed her children over to the powers that be; better to die together than to live apart.

She can hear them talking and picks up snippets of their words, tries to put them together so she can understand them but it's all such a muddle, so difficult to think straight.

'I'm sure she was just getting confused,' Brenda says softly.

'Probably,' the boy replies as he bites at his lip, 'it just came across as real and quite scary.'

'Yes, well she does that sometimes, Andrew. Besides, I daren't go across and mention anything after the last couple of episodes. They already think we're harassing them and the man there thinks I'm mad, judging by the way he looked at me last time.'

The boy laughs and then Brenda joins in with him. Maude doesn't like them doing it. She feels sure they're laughing at her. She tries to sit up but her head swims and her eyes hurt. They feel too big for her head, like oversized marbles sitting in her skull, ready to split it apart. Even blinking hurts.

'It's okay Mum, just take it easy,' Brenda says softly and places a cool hand across Maude's forehead. It feels quite lovely; the firm touch that gently brushes the pain away. Maude lies back down and doesn't struggle. She hasn't the energy for fighting. Not today. Everything is cloudy and difficult, her limbs heavy, her brain useless and foggy.

She listens to them talk some more, trying to piece all the bits together so she can understand what's happening. Something about a board and a man coming to look around once the walls are done. What's happening with the walls? More bombs perhaps? She hopes not. She came here to get away from the Germans and all the fighting. Something else about losing money. It doesn't matter, that bit, anyway. Maude doesn't have any money to lose. She opens her eyes and scans the ceiling, trying to remember how she even got here. Nothing makes sense anymore. Like how did she even end up lying here on this sofa? And whose sofa is it? Suddenly overwhelmed with the effort of trying to figure it all out, Maude starts to cry. She tries to stop it, to wipe the tears away and control herself but the more she tries, the harder the sobs come out, until she hears someone screaming, crying and realises it's the sound of her own voice echoing round the living room; a guttural, howling noise that permeates everywhere; every crevice, every dark, shadowy corner.

'Want to go home! I WANT TO GO HOME!'

Her chest hurts and her head pounds and every single part of her body aches and is trembling. She can no longer hear Brenda and the boy. All she can hear is the sound of her own screams ringing in her ears and no matter how much she tries, she simply cannot stop it all. Everything is disappearing out of her brain. She has no idea where she is, where her parents or brothers and sisters are and all she knows is she is desperate to get back home. She wants everything to stop. All of this anxiety and anger and confusion. She has suddenly had enough.

'It's okay, Mum.' The voice cuts through her cries and she feels a pair of warm arms around her back but it doesn't stop the fear as she rocks back and forth, wishing she could close her eyes and make it all go away. That's all she wants now, all she can focus on - for everything to disappear, all the bad dreams and the scary thoughts and worry about missing her family and whether or not they're all dead; buried under a pile of rubble after another air raid. All she wants is for it to all come to an end.

\*\*\*

Maude isn't at all sure how long it went on for. She has a vague memory, a fleeting thought that at some point she may have fallen, tripped when she got up to go somewhere. The toilet perhaps? But when she wakes up again she is in a different bed. Not the one that that Brenda woman always makes her sleep in, but a white one that is cool and scratchy and when she opened her eyes, the first thing she saw was a big window with no curtains. Her room has curtains so she can't be in her own bed. The noise, as well - lots of scraping and banging and buzzers and bells going off in the distance. The sound of feet shuffling and people talking. It makes her head ache and her stomach go into an uncomfortable, painful shape.

Maude looks up at the many faces looming over her, staring at something on the top of her head. A man reaches out and traces his fingers over the top of her skull. Usually she would react, shriek, try to back away from his touch but she is sapped of all energy, her body a lead weight. She hears their words but none of it means anything to her. All gibberish. A stream of incomprehensible sounds. She can see Brenda amongst them and that makes her feel better. She's a nice lassie, that Brenda is. Always smiling. Always quick to cuddle and say lovely things to her when she gets angry or scared.

'... would recommend a home ...'

'... her needs too great ...'

'... very frail ...'

A home? Maude perks up. She likes the sound of that. At long last she is going home. And not before time. Brenda has been really good to her and everything but to be able to go back home ... well that sounds so lovely, so perfect. Music to her ears. To be back in her own bed, back home with the sooty smell of their open fireplace, back to playing in the street with her friends; watching as Alfie, her brother, clambers over the piles of rubble, looking for pieces of shrapnel after the Germans have wiped out half of their street. She lets out a small sigh of relief as she closes her eyes and drifts off into her own little world. Back home sounds just fine to Maude. Back home is where she wants to be.

# Rachel

She should have asked to speak to him last time she was here. She knows that now. These things are always easy to figure out with hindsight, aren't they? She should have stayed around, asked for his number, not been so easily fobbed off or taken Peggy's word for it that they hadn't had any contact with Sheryl for ages. If it hadn't been for that taxi driver, she would still be stuck at home worrying and biting her nails, or out plastering up more pictures or sitting talking to the police, asking them what the latest developments are and why they aren't putting more effort into finding her sister. On her last visit to see them they claimed they were trawling through all the CCTV footage trying to track Sheryl's last known movements but it appears that so far, they've come up with nothing and yet here she is, a cashier at the local bank with no knowledge of police procedures whatsoever, out and about knocking on doors, doing their work for them and already she has a lead. At their last meeting, she asked them about looking into Sheryl's clients and they reckoned they were onto it, but Rachel somehow doubts it. They're still taking those bizarre text messages as an indicator that Sheryl is safe and sound and has taken it upon herself to disappear. They are making all the right noises, saying they will begin an investigation, but doing very little. Apparently, you have to have learning difficulties or be an alcoholic or a drug user - anything that is deemed vulnerable, before the police begin to pick up their pace and put any effort into finding you. If you are one of the Sheryls of this world - happy, successful, able to make your own way through life - then you are pushed to the back of the queue. Not considered a priority in this world of budget cuts and understaffing.

She brings her fist up and hammers on the door as loudly as she can. There's a car parked up here. Somebody is in. She is absolutely determined to sort this thing out and won't leave until she gets the answers she wants to hear. She will *not* be ignored or lied to this time. Her sister deserves better than this. She deserves to be found.

The woman who opens it is a complete mess. It's the same lady as the last visit but she is thinner; much thinner than the last time they spoke and dark crescents of exhaustion hang heavily under her eyes. Her hair sits on top of her head, a crop of unruly, black curls that she has piled up with a comb and slides. It refuses to stay put and keeps falling down over her pale, wan face. Her right eye bulges slightly. Rachel noticed it last time she was here - a web of razor like scars that criss-cross around her socket and up over her forehead, asymmetrical and uneven, as if they have refused to heal properly.

Rachel holds her breath before speaking. She needs to get this right. She needs to be courteous so she can get inside the house. The last thing she wants is for the door to be slammed in her face. If that happens she'll be left with no other option than to go to the police and she feels almost certain they won't take her seriously or follow up on her claims. Not a priority. This is something she has to do herself, a way of gathering as much evidence as she can before going back to them. The taxi driver's comments may amount to nothing but she's not prepared to take that chance and dismiss it. Every bit of news, every morsel of gossip, every rumour or tiny piece of information may be the thread that leads Rachel to her sister.

She stares at the lady before her and feels herself being scrutinised, the dark eyes taking in everything about her appearance. She stands tall, unwilling to be the victim this time, unwilling to let this liar get the better of her.

'Hi, I hope you don't mind me calling round again. I was just wondering if I could have a quick word?'

Rachel feels something catch in her throat as, without warning, Peggy steps forward and quietly closes the door behind her.

Not what she was expecting. The action of somebody who is on their guard; somebody with something to hide. They both stand facing each other on the step, their eyes locked together as the wind pushes at Rachel's back. She pulls her collar up, hoping to draw attention to the icy temperature as she shivers dramatically. Peggy's eyes stay locked on hers, full of shadows and vaguely threatening.

'I told you everything I know last time you were here,' Peggy murmurs, her voice a low whisper against the backdrop of the furious, thrashing waves far beneath them and the roaring wind that is howling round them.

'It's just that I got a call from somebody who said they saw Sheryl come up here at around the time she went missing so I was just wondering if we could go inside and talk about it a bit more?' Rachel tries to keep the edge out of her voice but it's so difficult under the current conditions. She is freezing and can feel her frustration growing by the second. Why is this woman being so awkward and uncooperative? What on earth is she hiding?

'I said it before and I'll say it again. I haven't seen Sheryl for a long time now. Ask our friends, they'll tell you the same. We haven't socialised with anybody for months and months.'

'And what about your husband?' Rachel asks, refusing to give in. She will not leave here until she gets some answers. The answers she wants; the answers she desperately needs to hear.

'My husband isn't here today. He's away working, so I'm afraid I can't help you with that one.' Peggy crosses her arms, a defensive stance. A fortress against Rachel's barrage of questions.

She feels a wave of thoughts and ideas rush through her brain. She has to get this woman on her side. She cannot blow this opportunity. If she has to, she will present her trump card, but would rather do it inside because when she does say it, at least Peggy can't turn around and slam the door in her face. She would have to ask her to leave or physically drag her from the house. In the first scenario, Rachel will simply refuse, and for the second one – well, Peggy is half her size. It simply will not happen. She won't allow it to. Rachel isn't going anywhere until she finds out more information about Sheryl's relationship with Peggy's husband.

A movement behind Peggy takes Rachel by surprise, a clicking sound followed by a low, solid creak as very slowly the door begins to move. A faint hissing sensation takes hold in Rachel's head as another woman appears from the shadows and stands in the doorway, her arms folded, her face the picture of surprise. She is an older woman, perhaps in her sixties, Rachel guesses. She clears her throat and steps back before beckoning Rachel inside.

'Close the door, Mother. I'm handling this.' Peggy's voice is cold. Her back is rigid as she speaks, her gaze still fixed firmly on Rachel.

The woman in the doorway talks as if Peggy hasn't uttered a word and Rachel makes her move before anybody can stop her.

'Come on in, dear. I'm sure we can sort all this out in the warmth of the living room with a nice cup of tea. You must be nithered out here in this awful weather.'

# Peggy

Nausea rises and her head feels as if a furnace is raging in there. This is why she came outside, to stop this happening, to ward off this woman, to send her on her way before Audrey could intervene and yet here she is, ushering her inside into the warmth. *Into Peggy's house!* Were it not for the fact that this Rachel lady has a new piece of information and could blurt it out any time, Peggy would order her out, tell her to be on her way whilst telling her own mother to shut her mouth and keep her outlandishly stupid opinions to herself. But instead, she watches, mute and barely able to move as the two of them slide past her, chatting away as if they have known each other for years, before sitting down at the dining room table, Rachel rubbing her hands together dramatically as if she has just been subjected to Arctic conditions.

'Milk? Sugar?' Audrey's voice chirrups across the kitchen as she busies herself lifting mugs down from the dresser. Peggy is speechless.

'Yes, for the milk and no to the sugar, thank you,' Rachel croons, blowing on her hands. This is ridiculous. She has to stop this, to say something and eject this creature from her house before her world begins to crash down around her.

'As I was saying outside before my mother decided to take over, there's only us here for the next few days, so if you'd like to leave me your number again, I'll call you if I find anything out or come across any new information.'

She is met with a wall of silence.

Unable to take it any more, she marches over to where Audrey is standing and grabs the cups from her mother's hands, sending them tumbling to the floor where they smash into tiny pieces, the fragments spreading around their feet, sharp, tooth-shaped splinters of porcelain staring up at her accusingly. Her head swims.

'Peggy!' Audrey half shrieks, 'what on earth are you doing?'

Peggy tries to speak; she has all the words formulated ready, but they refuse to come out. Her throat feels tight, fear constricting her windpipe as she stares over at Rachel sitting here, in her house. She swallows hard, sure she is going to pass out at any second. Hanging on to the kitchen top, she stumbles across to a chair and slumps down wearily. She cannot allow her to speak, to let her say whatever it is she has come here to say, not while her mother is here listening, hanging onto every single word.

'Are you okay?' Rachel's voice filters through the thick haze that has settled in Peggy's head. She wants to cry. The voice sounds genuine, caring even. She doesn't want to hear it. She doesn't want to hear anything at all. This is wrong. So horribly, horribly wrong.

'I'm fine,' she manages to croak, 'just tired. I've not been sleeping well lately.'

A short silence. The sound of water gushing and more crockery being rattled. Murmuring from behind her.

'There. All sorted and swept now,' Audrey says in the sing-song voice that makes Peggy want to weep with despair. A cup of steaming tea is placed in front of her. She takes it gratefully and gulps a large mouthful down, enjoying the burning sensation as it travels down her throat. Fiery liquid washing away her sins. No more than she deserves.

'The thing is,' Rachel says as she takes a sip of her tea and winces at its temperature, 'I was talking to a taxi driver and he said he remembers giving Sheryl a lift up here around the time she disappeared.'

Her words crash into Peggy's brain like a boulder, sending her off course. She feels as if she is drowning, the weight of the huge waves dragging her out to sea, salty water lapping around her ears, blocking everything else out.

'So, I'm a bit confused because you definitely said you hadn't seen Sheryl for ages, didn't you?'

The air in the room becomes thin. Invisible fingers clasp themselves around Peggy's windpipe, further restricting the flow of air. She begins to gasp. She needs to get outside, to breathe properly, to feel the rush of the breeze on her face, to hear the incessant roar of the tide, to just get away from this woman and her words; her accusations. She wants to get up and run away from it all but her limbs refuse to work properly. Were she to make an attempt to stand, she feels sure she would collapse in a sorry heap at Rachel's feet.

Another awkward silence ensues. Peggy sees Rachel and her mother look at each and then back over at her. Her face burns as she takes another gulp of hot tea and swallows it before finding the strength to speak, 'I'm really sorry, Rachel, but I'm not feeling too well. My mother will take your number and we'll call you later, but right now I need to lie down so if you wouldn't mind leaving us?'

With that she stands up as slowly and carefully as she can and waits for Rachel to do the same. The floor sways violently as Peggy hangs onto the edge of the table. Fury begins to build. She wishes this woman would just follow suit and get the message and simply go.

Nothing happens.

She stares hard at her as Rachel continues to drink her tea slowly and deliberately, her movements precise and ordered until eventually Audrey breaks the silence, 'How about I give you a call later, Rachel, when my daughter is feeling better? If you'd like to write your number down, I'll let you know when you can come back and we'll talk about this thing properly. Clear the air. It must be very distressing for you, so the sooner we sort it out the better.'

This seems to work, to snap her into action. For once Audrey's authoritative tone and demeanour are a welcome force.

Peggy watches, dazed, as her mother leads Rachel out of the room and into the hallway, a look of protestation on her face and locked into her body language. Her exit is an unwilling one, irritation and displeasure oozing from every pore.

She strains to listen to the hushed tones of their voices out in the passageway but her ears seem to be full of cotton wool and her head feels as if it's in a vice that is being tightened second by second. Her senses are no longer functioning as they should be. Everything is coming undone. She is unravelling bit by bit, the tapestry of her life slowly falling apart with every passing second.

By the time Audrey comes back into the room, Peggy is sure she is going to pass out.

'Sit down, Peggy,' Audrey says sharply, her eyes dark and narrow, her mouth a mean streak of disapproval, 'I think now we really do need to talk.'

# Alec

He dumps his bags down on the floor and lets out a long sigh. Such a long drive. It seemed to go on for forever, with so many hold ups and road works along the way. Why do they close all the main roads at the same time, resulting in the biggest snarl up of traffic he has encountered in a long, long time? He unzips his case, grabs his phone and sits on the edge of the bed, his head buzzing and his neck stiff after sitting behind the wheel for so long. Yawning loudly, Alec kicks off his shoes and scrolls through his messages. He needs to contact Peggy, let her know he's arrived safely, and send a few work-related emails as well. Rotating his shoulders to free up his spine, he takes a deep breath and stares hard at the screen, eyes blurring as he takes them all in. His skin suddenly hot and prickling with anxiety and unease, Alec slaps his hands over his head. *Jesus.* This has *got* to stop. She's done it again, misread his subliminal messages and taken things too far. Partly his fault, admittedly. He has, after all, quietly lusted over her since taking up his new position and very possibly presented her with the opportunity to carry on like this, but now it all needs to come to an end. He can't let it continue like this. This is by far the most inappropriate text she has ever sent. They've exchanged anecdotes, the odd smutty joke, but this ... this is too close to the bone for his liking. This could lose him his job. They're colleagues, no more than that and it needs to stay that way. At least she has taken the plunge and is leaving next year to do her teaching degree. That will put an end to it all, but that's a long way off and, in the meantime, they have to work together. It's going to be a difficult and long year if this kind of behaviour continues.

Alec stares at the message and bites at his lip,

*Missing you here at school. We should make up for it when you get back. Can't wait to see you again but in the meantime picture me here naked in bed ... Love Ellen xxx*

He quickly hits the delete button and sends a message to Peggy to let her know he has arrived. A short text, no emotion, no gentle, loving phrases; a perfunctory message to let her know he is here safe and sound. His fingers feel like blocks of wood; thick and clumsy as he presses the buttons, guilt seeping out of every pore. He finishes the obligatory missive to his wife and throws the phone on the bed. Later, when he's rested, he'll send a message to Ellen asking her to back off, to remind her that he's a married man. He won't leave Peggy. She is his wife. They have their troubles, for sure, but they've been through too much to give it all up. Sheryl tried that one on him when he used to visit her, but his answer was always the same - definitely not. That was the main reason he stopped going to see her; her insistence he end his relationship with Peggy. There were times when it'd seemed appealing. Oh God, so often he has come close to packing his case and walking out of the door never to return, but for all her faults - for all *his* faults, they still have a future together. He wants to make a go of things and not give it up as a bad job. Not when they've come this far.

He thinks of Ellen and her curves and the way she struts into his office smelling so good and then he thinks of Peggy's agoraphobia and her many foibles, especially her aversion to sex, and wishes his basic, primal urges could be ripped from his body, tucked away somewhere like a detachable limb. Damn his libido and his wife's deteriorating mental health and desperation for a child. Damn Ellen and her smooth skin and full pouting mouth. Damn it all.

Alec stalks over to the mini bar and stares in at its contents. Miniature bottles of gin and Bacardi and two bottles of cheap beer. That'll do for starters. The meeting doesn't start until nine in the morning. Plenty of time to sleep in and stagger the short distance down to the conference centre after a hefty cooked breakfast. It's about time life cut him some slack.

He twists the cap off the gin and looks around for a glass, snatching it up off the tea tray, then watches greedily as the clear liquid glugs its way into the tumbler. He deserves this after what he's been through. Tipping his head back he drains it in one gulp and quickly pours himself another. Time to start living a little.

# Peggy

She is finding it hard to breathe. Her vision is blurring, a film of fear obscuring everything, and the room has now started moving like a ship on rough seas. She is being tossed about like loose cargo, her insides sloshing about, ready to present themselves if she doesn't take hold of her senses.

She is aware of her mother standing over her, her dark eyes boring into her back, willing her to look up so she can savour the sensation of having power. She is so good at it. Audrey loves nothing better than to be able to exert her authority, make everyone around her feel useless and inferior. Being dominant is who she is. She's probably been waiting for years for this moment, dreamt of it, been working towards it, had it in her sights since the day Peggy's dad died. Nothing else to keep her occupied in her drab and dreary life.

Peggy looks up and is surprised to see tears in her mother's eyes. A lump rises in her throat and she struggles to swallow it down. Her eyes suddenly feel heavy and the dizziness threatens to engulf her completely. She spreads her arms out on the cool, oak table and places her head down, enjoying the feel of the smooth wood against her burning skin. She can hear her mother speaking but can't seem to summon up the strength to listen to what she is saying - just a torrent of words, meaningless, empty and hollow. She wants to enjoy not hearing anything for as long as she can because she knows it won't last. Peggy knows that everything is about to break into a million tiny little pieces and the shattering sound will be heard far and wide, piercing the stillness, ruining the peace and tranquillity and, when that happens, there will be no going back. When the words all start to come together, clear and chilling, Peggy will have reached the point of no return.

Audrey's voice continues to drone on. Peggy closes her ears. All she wants is a few more minutes. Just a little more time to remember how everything is before it all comes to a grinding, earth shattering halt. A hand strokes her back, slim fingers run through her hair, freeing up the knots and tangles. They continue down, over her head, soft and soothing, more caresses than she can ever recall receiving as a child. More than she is worthy of.

'Peggy love, you need to lift your head up. This is really important. It might help you feel better to tell me everything. Get it off your chest, you know?'

She doesn't know. Not at all. But like a small child, she complies with the request and stares up at her mother, her eyes glassy with unshed tears. She is too tired to weep. So exhausted by it all, by the burden of keeping it from everyone, by the burden of keeping it from herself. It's gone on for too long now. Time to come clean. Time to step out of the crushing darkness and back into the light. But it's so difficult, so exhausting. So final.

She puts her head back down and closes her eyes.

# Audrey

This is it. And not before time either. Peggy is upset, she can see that, but keeping it all bottled up isn't going to solve anything. You can tell just by looking at her that this whole sorry business is making her ill. Her arms and legs are stick thin, her face tiny and childlike; a person in miniature. She looks positively malnourished, her clothes hanging off her like loose rags. A walking skeleton. Audrey watches as she rests her head back down on the table and closes her eyes.

'Come on, now. This behaviour isn't helping anyone, is it?'

Audrey reaches out a hand and strokes her daughter's hair, sweeping it out of her face before gently placing a hand under her chin and lifting her head up off the table. Peggy doesn't resist, her body instead succumbing to Audrey's light touch. For once there is no animosity from her, no struggle or conflict, which is just as well. Audrey's scars from the fire were superficial but her skin is still healing. She too, feels sapped of her strength. Fighting with her daughter is beyond her.

'Come on, Peggy, you may as well talk about it. This is making you ill; take a look at yourself! You're a bag of bones.'

'I'm fine, Mother. Stop exaggerating,' Peggy croaks, her eyes suddenly dark and defensive.

Audrey lets out a short, trembling sigh. Never changed. Even after all these years. Why does her daughter insist on making everything so bloody difficult? Stubborn as a mule.

'Well any idiot can see that you're anything but fine, so why don't you stop lying to me and to yourself and tell me why Sheryl's sister was here?' Audrey taps her long, slender fingers on the wood, the vibrations travelling up her arms and into her neck making her head buzz and quiver.

'I don't know why she was here,' Peggy's voice is slurred, her words one long stream of connected sounds as she turns her head away from Audrey and stares at the wall.

This is silly now. It's all too much, this denial and pretence. Audrey strides around the side of the table, gets down on her haunches and places her face just centimetres away from Peggy's. She *will* make her daughter talk, whether she wants to or not. Such an obstinate creature. Always was, probably always will be. If she hasn't learnt to yield to the will of others by now then she never will.

'Right,' Audrey hisses, tiny flecks of spittle landing on Peggy's cheek as she speaks, 'if you won't tell me why she was here then I will tell you. We spoke in the hallway, Rachel and I, so I already know what information she has,' Audrey leans in even closer, a fire starting up in her belly, 'but I would rather hear it from you before I go to the police ...'

Peggy's head snaps up, her eyes bulging in horror, 'You wouldn't, Mother!'

'Try me!' Audrey yells. She is fast losing her temper. Why in God's name is Peggy protecting him? What kind of a hold does that man have over her daughter?

She waits, her fury tangible as she stands up and stares up at the clock on the wall. It feels like forever while she waits for her daughter to speak. Twice Peggy opens her mouth to say something and twice she shakes her head and closes it again. Audrey presses her lips together. Enough is enough.

'Okay, have it your way, and don't ever say I didn't give you a chance to save him, to give me his side of the story.' She heads into the hallway and comes back carrying her coat and bag.

'What are you doing?' Peggy snaps out of her trance-like state and turns to meet her mother's gaze, their eyes locking together in a hard stare.

'I'm calling a taxi and then I'm going to the police station to tell them everything I know about your husband's affair with Sheryl. He is somehow connected to her and she came to visit him before she disappeared.'

'NO!' Peggy's voice rings through the kitchen, a clear, sharp sound, full of fear and intent.

Audrey shoves her arms into her coat, punching her way through the fabric, her temper in full flow, 'Yes! I am fed up of being ignored and your refusal to see any wrong in him, to talk about his affair with that poor woman. I mean, Jesus Christ, Peggy, she is missing!' Her voice is trill, almost a screech, 'Can you not see how serious this is? I honestly thought you were better than this! Your husband has something to do with her disappearance and you don't seem to care.'

Peggy stands up now, her eyes blazing, and faces her mother.

'Oh, don't give me that look!' Audrey snorts derisively, 'Rachel already told me everything I need to know when we were in the hallway and you were in here going into a complete meltdown. Sheryl got dropped off here prior to going missing, telling the taxi driver she was coming to sort out some relationship issues. Don't try and act as if Alec is innocent in all of this because I now know he's as guilty as sin.'

'He is NOT guilty!' Peggy sways as she faces her mother, 'He's got absolutely nothing to do with Sheryl's disappearance and he is definitely NOT having an affair with her!'

Audrey steps forward, her face so close to Peggy's they are almost touching, 'How do you know?' Her fingers reach out, pale and accusatory as she grabs Peggy by the shoulder, shaking her hard. 'You don't know that for sure, do you, Peggy? You have no idea what your husband has been up to, do you? No idea at all!'

'I DO know what he's been up to and I can tell you he definitely hasn't been having an affair with Sheryl.' Large tears begin to roll down Peggy's face, glassy goblets, dripping off her face.

'How do you know that, Peggy? How the hell can you be sure? That's not what Sheryl told the taxi driver, is it? She said she was coming here to sort out her relationship issues. And I SAW them together Peggy. Sitting together chatting, giggling like teenagers! How can you be so sure he wasn't having an affair with her?' Audrey's nostrils are wide, her eyes blazing.

'BECAUSE IT WAS ME!' Peggy screams, her arms in the air, her fingers tearing wildly at her hair, 'IT WAS ALL ME!'

The words hit Audrey like a slap in the face. Her breath catches in her chest, a bubble of fear and shock sending her brain into a state of confusion.

'What was you?' Audrey enunciates, the words buzzing in her ears. Everything begins to blur and she feels as if she needs to sit down. The tiled floor rises and falls under her feet as Audrey staggers helplessly. She straightens up but her head continues to swim. Gripping onto the edge of the table for support, her fingers suddenly feel cold and clumsy.

'The affair,' Peggy murmurs as she slumps awkwardly into her chair, her hands covering her face.

She sniffs loudly and Audrey can see Peggy's fingers shaking as she begins to paw at her right eye. Audrey winces. She wants to stop her, to tell her to not say it and to leave her eye alone but the words stick in her throat; hard, angry rocks blocking her windpipe, depriving her of oxygen.

'It was me having an affair with Sheryl,' Peggy says, her voice a mere whisper, 'It was me she came to see. Nothing to do with Alec …'

'I don't understand.' Audrey averts her gaze away from Peggy. This can't be happening. Her daughter is still lying to cover for him. She has to be. None of this is making any sense. It's all lies. A dreadful web of deceit concocted by Peggy to cover for him.

'Sheryl and me, we were lovers. I was the one having a relationship with her, not Alec.'

'But I saw them together!' Audrey feels a rage take hold, an inner core of heat and anger. This isn't happening. She won't allow it to happen. It's Alec who is responsible for all of this. Not her daughter. Not Peggy …

'You don't get it, do you, Mother?' Peggy shakes her head despondently and Audrey is shocked to see she is actually smiling, her face contorted into a grimace, 'You actually have no fucking idea, do you? Not a bloody clue. Yes, Sheryl and Alec did used to meet up to chat and have coffee. She was his *therapist* for God's sake! He used to visit her in town, go to a cafe or to her office where they would talk about his issues and how he should manage his temper.'

Audrey feels her legs buckle once more and clings tighter to the table to steady herself.

'Therapist?'

Peggy rolls her eyes and stares at her mother in exasperation. 'What, so just because a man and a woman spend some time in each other's company, it means they're sleeping together? You didn't for one minute consider the fact there could another reason for their meet ups? He was seeing Sheryl for his anger issues but stopped a while back. Said it was going nowhere and he was going to do it on his own. The whole thing made him feel uncomfortable, made him feel like a failure. He can't even bear to walk past her office any more.'

Audrey is unable to speak. She needs a drink. Badly. After the fire, she promised herself there would be no more alcohol but now ...

She shakes the thought from her head, does her best to ignore the craving, to keep at bay the desperate, clawing urge to down a glass of whiskey. She can almost taste it - that deep, earthy flavour - and feel the comforting kick as it hits her stomach.

'Where is she?' Audrey manages to murmur, hoping the scenario she has got in her head is the correct one. He will have found them together and done something. He will have been upset - naturally; outraged even, and lost his temper. Peggy has told her he has problems controlling himself. He's a violent man, a wicked man. He will have gone over the top, done something terrible, something final.

'I - I can't talk about it.' Any remaining colour drains from Peggy's face. Her scars remain a vicious shade of scarlet as she pulls at her hair, twiddling long, dark strands with trembling fingers.

'You don't have any choice, Peggy,' Audrey says, her voice monotone and functional. It's just a matter of time now, that's all. 'Rachel has already told me she's informed the police so the sooner you tell me what he did, the better. Time to stop covering for him now, sweetheart. The worst is over.'

Peggy's laugh fills the entire room, bouncing off the walls and ceiling, her teeth bared in a grimace. Audrey feels her skin crawl at the very sight of her, this woman before her that she hardly recognises. She watches Peggy's skeletal features morph into something she can barely bring herself to look at, someone she no longer knows.

'Over?' Peggy barks, 'You really think this *thing* is almost over? Jesus, Mother, you are so fucking naive. This *thing* is only just beginning. This is just the start of it. You have *absolutely* no idea.'

'The start of what?' Audrey closes her eyes. She doesn't want to think about what is coming next. Everything is spiralling out of her control. She wants to reach out, grab it, put it all back where she can guard it and manage it, be in command of the situation, not be a passive bystander and watch as her daughter's life disintegrates before her very eyes, an implosion on a grand and unprecedented scale.

'Oh Mum, come on, please stop this!'

'What? Audrey cries, every nerve and fibre in her body screaming out for alcohol, 'Stop what?'

'The blindness, Mum. You know *exactly* what I mean. Alec didn't do anything to Sheryl. He didn't even know she was missing for God's sake! How could he have done anything to her? It was me that did it! Can't you fucking well see that? It was me ... it was me!' Peggy's sobs ricochet around the room as she collapses onto the floor in a mangled, bony heap. 'Oh God, Mum, it was me! I killed her! I killed Sheryl. What the hell am I going to do Mum? What the hell am I going to do ...?'

# Peggy

In a perverse sort of way, it's a relief. She has no idea how long she could have gone on for, living that lie. It has been the undoing of her, keeping it all together, trying to live a normal life. And now it's all coming apart, untangling and falling to pieces and there's absolutely nothing she can do about it. There's nothing she wants to do about it, truth be told. It's gone on for too long now. It needs to come to an end.

The floor feels cool and welcoming beneath her burning skin. Her bones ache and her head is on fire. No more than she deserves after what she did. Her mother's voice wafts about somewhere over her head. She tries to listen, to take it all in but her brain has frozen. She is trapped in time, in this moment. A hell of her own making. She moves slightly, uncoiling herself, stretching her aching limbs before they lock into a position of permanent pain. Her mother's words continue to drift over her, dream-like, an unnatural gathering of syllables. She pictures them like a river; a snaking entity, a jumble of sounds all struggling to fit into a coherent order, fluid and swirling above her head until at last they come together; they flit into her brain and she is finally able to make sense of them. They come across loud and clear, a booming reminder of her predicament; her mother's voice, shouting, telling her to get up, to sit up, to sort herself out. Like a dutiful child, she obeys and feels Audrey's long arms looping around her body, hoisting her up into a chair. She slumps, ragdoll-like, all her energy gone, no fight left in her. Perhaps she is having a breakdown, her madness on show for all the world to see. No more hiding away, no more fear, no more dread at being found out.

'You need to listen to me, Peggy,' Audrey's face looms into view, her breath warm and smelling slightly of coffee and toothpaste, 'you have to pull yourself together. We have to sort this out before Rachel goes to the police and they come here. Because they will. In no time at all there will be a police officer knocking at that door wanting to know what happened when Sheryl came here to see you and if they find you like this, helpless, guilt written all over you, then they will throw the bloody book at you!'

Peggy feels Audrey's temper building, her frustration at Peggy's inability to do anything tight and hard as a drum.

'They have a witness now, Peggy. You HAVE to do something!'

Peggy looks up at her mother, the woman she has actively avoided for the past twenty years, the same woman who is now about to help absolve Peggy of the most heinous crime ever, 'What, though? What am I going to do Mum? Oh my God, I've killed somebody! What the hell am I going to do?' Peggy starts again, tearing at her hair, clawing at her scarred face, sobbing until she has no breath left.

The slap takes her breath away, sends her eyeballs rolling up into her head with the sheer force as Audrey's hand connects with her face. 'Pull yourself together! This is no time for hysteria, Peggy! Tell me what happened. I need to know everything so I can help you.'

She can barely breathe. Everything is coming tumbling down just as she knew it would; her life is a flimsy pack of cards collapsing around her. Nothing left to live for.

'She came here to see me,' Peggy says, her voice raspy, her throat sore and tender. Each word feels like an attack on her vocal chords. 'Alec was at work. I had tried to break it off with her but she wouldn't listen. I—'

'How did it start? This *affair?*' Audrey's voice is laced with incredulity.

Peggy shakes her head miserably, 'We started off as friends. Sheryl was a counsellor and I opened up to her about some problems Alec and I were having with our marriage ...'

Audrey tuts loudly, disapproval written all over her face, disappointment etched into every pore, 'Oh for God's sake. What a cliché, Peggy! What a bloody stupid cliché this all is ...'

'It's true!' Peggy cries at her, tears rolling thick and fast, a stream of fear and dread, her tone defensive.

'You're going to tell me that one thing led to another now, aren't you?'

'Yes! Because it did!' Peggy is shrieking, her voice a rattle as her pitch increases in volume. 'Alec and I have tried for years to have children but I've had miscarriage after miscarriage. I got depressed, found it difficult to leave the house, became fixated on these fucking things!' she yells, pointing at the mesh of scars covering her eye, 'and Sheryl was there for me. She listened to me. But then it all started to go wrong. She became obsessive, refusing to take no for an answer, telling me I should leave Alec and be with her ...'

'And?' Audrey says sharply, her expression hawk-like as she watches Peggy.

'And she came here that day,' Peggy whispers, 'determined that she was coming in. Alec was out, fortunately. It may well have turned out very differently if he'd been here.'

'But he wasn't, was he? So, what happened, Peggy? What happened to Sheryl that day? What did you do to her?' Audrey stares up at the clock and back at her daughter, sending her heart jiggling around her chest. Peggy thinks of Rachel and the taxi driver and the police and pictures them arriving at Chamber Cottage, at her home, an official, angry mass of officers like a swarm of killer insects, slapping her in handcuffs and arresting her, and before she can do anything, she is violently sick, vomit spewing out of her, spreading on the table, dripping onto the floor, covering her clothes, a thick trail of bile oozing over everything; warm and sticky, a pool of guilt for all to see.

'Oh Peggy!' Audrey cries as she stares down at the mess, 'For heaven's sake, girl! You need to stop this right now!'

In an instant, she moves away and Peggy watches silently as her mother sails around the room, purposeful and determined.

She arrives back wearing rubber gloves, armed with a bucket and mop and a handful of towels and clothes. Peggy feels her arms being yanked upwards and her clothes hoisted over her head. Her trousers are pulled down and she feels her legs being guided into something soft. She looks down and sees that she is wearing a pair of joggers. A sweatshirt is pulled on over her head as Peggy stands, pliant and malleable, no energy left. Nothing in reserve. She watches her mother as she mops it all up, the contents of Peggy's stomach, the acidic tell-tale signs of the terrible atrocity she has committed. Even her own body wants to reject her.

The smell remains despite Audrey using every detergent she can get her hands on and scrubbing until everywhere gleams. It refuses to leave. Just like the stain on the step. *All blemishes are residual guilt,* thinks Peggy as she remembers the blood on the concrete, how it kept reappearing, a reminder of what she did. A reminder that she is a cold-blooded murderer.

Audrey flops down in the chair, her brow beaded with sweat, 'Right, once I've put everything away, you're going to explain it all to me, how it happened, what you did and of course the most important thing,' she says, her breath a series of small, hot gasps as turns to face Peggy.

'Which is what?' Peggy cries, her rapidly shrivelling sanity barely able to take any more prodding.

Audrey darts a look Peggy's way, veiled and mildly threatening. Peggy feels herself shrink under her mother's gaze as she listens to her words, 'You know what I'm talking about, Peggy. Please don't try to be coy. I need to know where you've put her body ...'

# Alec

Dinner is a blur, quite literally. After draining the mini bar in his room, Alec continues to drink downstairs. Propped up on a barstool, he talks to the waiter about his journey down, the troubles of working in a school and the joys of living so close to the North Sea with its fabulous views and unwelcoming weather. Only as the barman moves away and stands idly at the other end of the bar, drying glasses all too slowly, does Alec slow down and think that perhaps he should really get something to eat to soak up the copious amounts of alcohol he has consumed on an empty stomach.

Stumbling through to the dining room, he finds a seat and orders the first thing on the menu, chomping through it noisily when it arrives, a plate of tasteless food, no more than fuel to fill the gnawing hole in his belly where the beer and red wine are currently sloshing around; a gallon of alcohol making him giddy and reckless.

He stares around. The place is empty. Everyone else from the other schools will be stopping at the hotel over the road. He prefers it here. It's quieter; gives him time to think, to relax and prepare himself for the conference in the morning.

Alec wipes his mouth and pushes his chair back from the table. An adequate meal. Nothing too fancy, which is just as well, given the amount he's had to drink. Anything different would have made him feel queasy; too many culinary delights would have pushed him over the edge. He stares over at the bar. Inviting, but he's already had far too much to drink. He looks around. A couple in the corner are sitting close together, their hands cupped together, their eyes locked in a romantic gaze. He feels a pang of guilt and a small stab of jealousy as they continue to stare at one another, oblivious to the world around them. He remembers a time when he and Peggy used to do that, spend long evenings whispering sweet nothings to one another with the promise of hot, rampant sex afterwards. Now all they seem to do is argue and bicker; their lives one long round of work commitments, financial woes, and marriage problems. He would give anything to go back to those days, to a time when nothing mattered but one another. Even being saddled with debt didn't feel so cumbersome and worrying when you had love and a raging libido to keep you going.

He stands up and staggers over to the stairs before deciding he's had too much to drink to even attempt them and makes his way over to the lift instead. His fingers jab at the button, clumsy and exhausted. He needs to sleep; the drive has just about done him in.

An image of Audrey fills his head as he waits for lift doors to open. Funny how things have turned out, isn't it? Her living with them after so long apart. Got to be a good thing, really, her and Peggy getting back together after all these years. A fresh start. A way forward out of all the shit they've been through. All that rubbish in the past. He can see that Audrey is a strange one - she dances to her own tune. And dominant too. But so what? That's not always a bad thing. The world would grind to a halt if it was full of shrinking violets. Nothing would get done.

The lift doors open, the whooshing sound jolting him out of his thoughts. He steps inside, thinking that Peggy needs to get over it all and move on and stop being so difficult and unyielding about everything. When he gets back they will all talk about it. He'll get her to start being more positive. He'll do his bit as well. He'll start being more supportive, they'll go out places together. All it needs is a bit more effort, a touch more thoughtfulness and everything will be just fine. Audrey stepping back into their lives may well prove to be the catalyst for getting their lives back on track. She might just be the tonic they all so desperately need.

Alec steps out of the lift and unlocks the door to his room, suddenly grateful for the bed that seems to beckon him the minute he steps inside. He stares at his watch. He should really give Peggy a call. She hasn't answered his message. Kicking his shoes off, he flings himself sideways onto the duvet, a tangle of drunken arms and legs as he lands in an indecorous heap on the mattress. He just needs five minutes to let his food settle then he'll ring her. That's all he needs. Just a little time to rest after all the food and drink.

The room begins to spin as Alec closes his eyes. Too much wine. He doesn't know why he does it. It always has the same effect on him. Stupid, really. He closes his eyes to stop the spinning and before he can stop it, the arms of darkness drag him away.

\*\*\*

When he wakes, it's pitch black outside and the noises of the city have slowed down, become a dull thump in the distance. Fatigue swamping him, he climbs under the bedsheets fully clothed and falls back into a deep, deep sleep.

When the call wakes him he sits up, dishevelled and disorientated. Rubbing at his eyes, he snatches up his phone and barks into it, still dog tired, his voice gravelly from the drink, wishing he hadn't had that last glass of merlot as the voice down the phone tells him things that his addled brain is in no state to comprehend. He's still asleep. He has to be. This isn't real. Things like this don't happen to people like him. He tries to stand up but the room tilts violently, so much so that he feels nauseous. He flops back down on the bed and listens to the voice on the other end, refusing to believe what he is hearing.

# Audrey

The wind is starting to whip up outside. Audrey listens as it claws at the windows, its icy fingers scratching at the glass. Peggy sits opposite her, head dipped, her hair a tight mass of black curls. Audrey waits. Easier to let her cry. Get it out of her system, but at some point, they need to do something. Time is against them. Rachel didn't make any threats but any fool could see she meant business.

'Lift your head up, Peggy. You need to talk to me. The longer you leave it, the greater the chances are of the police calling round. You have to tell me what went on.'

Peggy's eyes are baggy with despair as she slowly raises her head and stares at her mother. Audrey has to stop herself from letting out a gasp. Her daughter suddenly looks a hundred years old, as if all the life has been sucked out of her. Her skin is grey, her body emaciated from the strain of keeping such a dark secret from everyone. Audrey wants to cry, to shriek at how unfair this all is. She has her daughter back after so long and is now about to lose her again. All this time she was so sure it was Alec. She was desperate for it to be him, would have given anything to see him burn, and now everything has been turned on its head. Her world has been inverted and she needs to work out what she should do to limit the damage. Peggy is in no fit state to deal with any of this. It's down to her to do it. And she will. Whatever it takes, Audrey will do it. What Peggy has done is obviously a terrible thing, but now it is her job, as Peggy's mother, to help and protect her. For so many years she let her daughter down. She has a lot of time to make up for, so the sooner she starts, the better.

'She tried to get in the house,' Peggy whispers, 'and I tried to stop her. I had to. She would have stayed, told Alec. She even threatened to ruin my career. She would stop at nothing to get what she wanted.' More tears fall as Peggy stares at her mother. Audrey has to bite her lip to stop herself from crying. Her own daughter, sitting here, describing to her how she killed somebody. This is outrageous. Worse than anything Audrey has ever encountered. Worse than Peter dying, worse than almost losing her life in that blasted fire.

'And?' Audrey asks tentatively, her skin hot with the horror and shame of it all.

'We got into a tussle. She was demanding to come in. I just knew if I let her in, I wouldn't be able to get her out again. She was always so determined with everything she did. Oh God!' Peggy dips her head again and covers her face with her hands, 'I didn't mean for it to happen! I tried to push her away, get her away from me so I could close the door, but she fell and hit her head on the step. The blood ...'

Another shriek escapes as Peggy's body begins to rock backwards and forwards. 'There was so much blood coming out of her head. I didn't know what to do! I just panicked.'

'So ... what exactly *did* you do?' Audrey stares again at the clock, acutely aware of each passing second, aware of the pressing need to do something about this whole ghastly situation.

'I ... I dragged her round the back of the house. I couldn't see her breathing or anything. No movement. She was dead, I'm sure of it, and I was terrified so I—'

'You're SURE of it?' Audrey shouts, her pulse racing, galloping around her chest and rattling in her neck, 'Jesus, Peggy! Please tell me you tried to help her? To call an ambulance or clean her up or ANY bloody thing?'

'STOP IT! Just stop it, please!' Peggy tears at her hair again, great, long strands of it coming away in her fingers.

'Peggy! Calm down and tell me what you did.' Audrey's voice fills the room, authoritative and booming. It stops Peggy in her tracks.

She stares at her mother, bleary eyed, mouth gaping open before speaking slowly, enunciating each word as if they are poison she is trying to spit out, 'I dragged her body round the back of the house and put it in the tunnel.'

Audrey feels herself swoon as she leans back and takes a deep, rasping breath. 'Tunnel? Peggy, what the *hell* are you talking about? What tunnel?'

'There's a tunnel under the house,' she replies quietly, staring at her mother.

Audrey watches in silence, notices how the light has gone from her daughter's eyes. Nothing but darkness. She's said it now; there's no going back.

'It runs from the back garden through to the cellar under the cottage. We never use it. It was the only thing I could think of ...' Peggy doubles over, her body deflated, defeated. Audrey wants to straighten her out, to shake her back to life. They have to do something. Not tomorrow or even in an hour. They have to act now, get that lady out of there; drag her rotting body out and dispose of it.

An idea charges into her head, stampeding over every rational thought, pushing logic and emotions aside. It's possible. They could do it. It's the only way she can see of them getting out of this mess they're in. Because it is them, in it together. She won't leave Peggy on her own with this. Not again. They've had too long apart. There's no way she will go through another twenty years without her daughter at her side. Beatrice will never come back home now. She can see that. Her life is in America. She is settled and happy. But Peggy is here. They can get things back on track - make a go of it again. Despite all this *nonsense* that is happening, Audrey can see beyond it. She can visualise a life with her youngest daughter at her side, their rifts finally healed. She has had a lot of time to think about it and no way is she about to let this chance pass her by. She will do this and she will be Peggy's saviour. They'll be united by guilt. But that's fine. She can handle that. Time will heal that particular wound and she will be around to help Peggy through it. Her daughter always was vulnerable - an overly sensitive soul. Audrey is stronger than that. She will have enough strength for the both of them.

'Show me where it is,' Audrey says coolly, 'this tunnel you mentioned. Lead me to it and then I will tell you exactly what we are going to do.'

\*\*\*

'Why is it here? I mean what is the purpose of it?' Audrey stands behind Peggy, her eyes darting everywhere. She hunches down, partly to look at the doors concealed by the shrubbery and partly to escape the biting wind that feels as if it contains shards of ice. She stares around at the surrounding grassland and moss-covered stones. Nobody around to watch them. Peggy is fortunate in that respect. What would she have done if she had lived in the suburbs, closed in and overlooked on every side? She would have had to let Sheryl in, suffer the consequences of her visit. But here they are, high up on a cliff with a body to dispose of and all because of one split second decision.

Peggy sniffs hard and rubs at her eyes as she bends down and pulls the weeds and undergrowth apart. Audrey watches her hands, sees how they tremble and wonders if she will actually be able to go through with this.

'We don't know for certain. Possibly a hiding place for smuggler's goods hundreds of years ago. Rumour has it some of the coastguards were corrupt, helping the smugglers by stashing the contraband.' Peggy stops abruptly, her breathing shallow and erratic.

Audrey watches as she stands up and brushes the dirt from her hands, rubbing them on the old fleece she put on her after the bout of sickness. She really needs Peggy to hold it together now, to be the strongest she can be. She has to do it if she wants to get out of the mess they are in. The police will find the body in no time at all. The sniffer dogs can seek out a cadaver in a matter of minutes.

'Okay, Peggy, I need you to look at me and listen really, really carefully. We have to move quickly and we can't afford to make any mistakes. Do you hear me?' Audrey takes both of Peggy's arms and stares at her closely, not wanting to register the haunted look in her eyes or her gaunt, grey features. Time is of the essence here.

Peggy nods mutely, her jaw hanging loosely as she watches her mother silently. A small line of saliva runs down out of her mouth, bubbles of spit clinging to her quivering chin. Audrey reaches forward and gently wipes it away with her outstretched finger.

'Right, I realise you don't want to see this but I'm going to have to open these doors and get her out of here. I want you to go back inside and get a large sheet, something big enough to cover her up with.'

Peggy's eyes widen in horror and she begins to moan, slow and quietly at first, building in crescendo and strength as it suddenly dawns on her what her mother is going to do. Without thinking, Audrey clamps her hand over Peggy's mouth, a tight vice of silence.

'Stop it Peggy! You have to calm down; do you hear me?'

Audrey sees the terror in her eyes and feels Peggy's head shake as she nods. Great blobs of tears roll down her face, sliding over the side of Audrey's hand as her fingers stay clasped over Peggy's trembling, slack mouth. She looks around quickly and drags Peggy down onto the cold, damp grass.

'I'm going to explain what we're going to do, okay?'

Peggy's head rocks back and forth, her eyes darting around her head like tiny, black marbles.

'Once you've got a blanket or something to put her in, we're going to put her in the car. Are you with me so far?' Audrey is speaking slowly, desperate for her intentions to be crystal clear in Peggy's head. They can't afford to make any mistakes.

'Wh ... where are we going?' Peggy asks, her words a whisper, a battle to be heard against the raging wind behind them.

'I know a place,' Audrey says softly, wanting to soothe Peggy, to get her to think straight, 'I'll be with you in the car. You just need to drive and I'll do the rest.'

'Is it far?' Peggy asks, her eyes pleading, 'I can't drive too far. I just can't!' she cries, her entire body convulsing with fear.

'No, it's not far at all,' Audrey replies, 'You know where the local recycling and waste centre is, on the outskirts of town?'

Peggy's eyes widen, 'NO! We can't just dump her body there! Please, no, Mum! I'm begging you ...'

'Peggy, shhh! Please listen to me. We're not just going to dump her body at the local rubbish tip for goodness sake. There's a place I know,' Audrey looks around furtively, forgetting their current isolated location, and huddles closer to Peggy, 'they have a place there. I know this because my friend - my companion John, works there and he's told me about it.'

Peggy's eyes are veiled in fear. Audrey touches her hand and is shocked at how cold she is.

'They have a place, a kind of bunker, I suppose. It's where people go to dispose of anything that contains asbestos. John has told me time and time again how none of the people who work there will ever go near the place. Whenever anyone comes in claiming they have something to put in there, the staff direct them over and leave them to it. It's then locked up with a bloody huge padlock to make sure nobody can get in.'

Peggy begins to shake her head and Audrey grabs her shoulders, suddenly angry, 'Do you have a better suggestion, Peggy? Do you? Because try as I might, I can't think of any other way out of this mess we're in!'

Audrey stops, fatigued by it all. The only way she will get Peggy to do this is if she is removed from the situation. Audrey will have to locate the corpse, drag it out - a horrific task for sure but a necessary one - and get everything ready for Peggy to bring the car round. That's all she wants her to do. Just drive.

'Right,' she says sharply, her temper and energy waning by the second, 'you go inside, get a large blanket, a few of them if possible, while I do what I have to do. Okay?'

She watches Peggy stagger to her feet and lets out a sudden, sharp shriek.

'The messages on the phone!'

Peggy bends over and clutches her stomach as if wounded.

'What happened to the phone, Peggy? What else did you do?'

'I - I found it after I moved her. It must have fallen out of her pocket!'

Audrey gasps. What was she thinking? Her frail, helpless daughter adding lie upon lie until she was so steeped in duplicity and immorality that there was no way out.

'Find it and bring it down with you!' Audrey shouts.

Peggy nods limply and staggers to her feet before Audrey's hand pushes at the small of her back and propels her inside.

# Peggy

This isn't possible - any of it. It's a nightmare. It has to be. Peggy floats through to the kitchen, her legs numb, her mind verging on hysteria. She stops and stares around. Why is she here? She can't remember. Everything is so messed up in her head right now. She gasps for air and tries to put everything in order in her brain. Something big - a sheet or a blanket. And the phone. Oh God, the phone ... Catapulted into action, Peggy darts upstairs and rummages in every cupboard and drawer, pulling items out, watching as they come toppling and crashing to the floor. Piles of things everywhere, jewellery, clothes, bags; they sit at her feet, strewn around the room; items that used to mean so much to her which she no longer cares about. Nothing matters anymore.

Yanking a drawer open, she pulls out an old purse. With shaking hands, she unzips the inside pocket and grabs Sheryl's phone, the battery long-since dead. After sending a few desperate messages, she couldn't bring herself to look at it anymore, to be reminded of what she had done, so she'd stuffed it away with the intent of destroying it when her courage allowed. She tucks it in her pocket and stands up.

Sheets and towels. Her head buzzes. She can't remember where the sheets and towels and bed linen are kept. Why can't she remember? This is ludicrous. Chamber Cottage is her house for God's sake and she can't even think where anything is stored anymore. She is going mad, she feels sure of it. Her sanity is slowly slipping away, bit by bit, the working parts of her brain ebbing away from her like the tide that sits two hundred feet below her, crashing into the rocks before departing and disappearing from view. Peggy brings her hands up and slaps the side of her face over and over. *Think! For God's sake, woman - just think!*

She slumps down on the side of the bed and looks around trying to control her breathing, hoping that logic will return and not desert her completely when she needs it most. She just needs to calm down, dampen the fire that is raging in her mind and start thinking straight. She dips her head between her knees and takes a few seconds to think.

It suddenly hits her. Jumping up, she dashes into the bathroom and pulls open the doors of the large cupboard in the corner. Alec is always telling her she should sort it out, that there is too much in there. A stack of sheets tumbles down on top of her, along with a mountain of towels. She stands - a tower of white linen draped over her - and wonders where to start. She needs the largest ones she can find. Dragging a mass of cotton fabric around the floor, Peggy scoops up a pile of bed sheets, holding them tight to her chest, her arms locked over them, and heads downstairs. She stumbles on the last few steps, the white material caught under her feet. Managing to tug it free whilst remaining upright, Peggy practically throws herself into the living room, a vision of fabric and fear as she sees her mother standing there, her face frozen with horror, her presence ethereal and ghost-like. Pulling the phone from her pocket and throwing it as if it is burning hot, it hits the floor with a thump and spins around, the dull vibrations another reminder of her what she has done.

'What?' Peggy cries, sensing thing are about to get a whole lot worse. Something has happened.

'Are you sure you got it right, Peggy? You're absolutely sure you put her body in there?'

Peggy nods, too numb and terrified to speak. Her stomach goes into a spasm and the floor begins to spin.

'You must have got it wrong, love, because there's nothing there. No body, no Sheryl. She's gone ...'

# Audrey

For such a tiny creature, Peggy feels inordinately heavy and cumbersome as Audrey hauls her up off the floor and lays her down on the sofa, the sheets bunched up and tangled under her body.

'Come on, Peggy! You need to wake up, sweetheart. Talk to me. Tell me what's going on.'

A low moan emanates from Peggy's chest, rumbling up through her throat and her slightly parted lips. Audrey taps her face gently and drags her upright into a sitting position, Peggy's head lolling as she moves.

'Where did you put her, Peggy? Did you actually do this?' Audrey wants to scream. Has she made this up? Were her first suspicions that Alec was involved not unfounded after all? 'Peggy, you need to wake up and explain this. Are you making this up and covering for Alec?'

Audrey starts to feel a deep resonating hum begin to take hold in her head. She is so tired. Her body is aching, her brain too weary to think straight anymore. A ball of fury starts to build in her chest, growing and burning until she can no longer hold it in. It explodes into the room, an orb of angry, accusatory flames, white hot and unforgiving,

'ARE YOU COVERING UP FOR YOUR HUSBAND?'

'No!' Peggy suddenly kicks into action, her head shaking uncontrollably, tears and snot streaming.

'Then where the HELL is the body, Peggy! Where has it gone?'

Audrey slumps on the floor and rests her head against Peggy's legs, her pulse a deep ticking in her neck, strong, regular, a sign that this is real.

'There's another door,' Peggy says weakly. She sniffs and wipes her face with her sleeve. 'You can get to it from the hatch on the kitchen floor under the rug. We had mice and rats a while back and …'

'Another door?' Audrey screeches, 'Jesus Christ, Peggy, it's a dead body we're talking about here and not …' she stops, her breath rattling about in her chest. Surely not? Audrey can hardly bring herself to think about it.

'Peggy, please tell me she was dead when you put her in there? Please, *please* tell me you checked for a pulse?'

Her daughter's silence says it all. With a source of strength she didn't know she possessed, Audrey jumps to her feet and drags Peggy up with her, the urge to shake the very life out of her so strong and overwhelming, she has to grit her teeth to overcome it.

'SHOW ME!' Audrey screams at her, too far gone to keep any kind of decorum. She feels her mouth begin to contort as she rages at her daughter, the tiny creature in front of her who is sobbing uncontrollably, 'Show me EXACTLY where this other door is right now!'

Peggy lurches forward and hobbles into the kitchen, staring at the raffia rug sitting in the centre of the tiled floor, 'Under there,' she squeaks.

Audrey bends down and pulls it aside, dust scattering and swirling in the thin shafts of light filtering in from the window. She stares up at Peggy and then down again at the handle before yanking it open and peering down into the darkness below.

'There's a light,' Peggy whispers, 'if you go down the ladders, there's a switch on the wall at the bottom.'

'Show me,' Audrey barks as she glares at her. She cannot believe this is happening. Only a couple of hours ago she was planning how she could rekindle their relationship and now - well, now they are doing the unthinkable, something Audrey never once dreamt she would have to do. She has seen plenty of dead bodies in her time as a nurse, but never under such dire and extreme circumstances. Never like this.

Audrey steps aside as Peggy makes her shaky descent down to the dark basement. She hears a squawk and watches as the place is flooded with light. Peering down she sees Peggy almost bent double, her hands covering her mouth as she begins to sob. Audrey clambers onto the top rung and makes her way down. She lands at the bottom with a clatter, her legs weak with fear and dread.

'Where is it, this door to the tunnel?' Audrey's voice is husky. She is finding it hard to breathe.

Peggy points to a large wooden unit against the wall, 'There,' she replies, 'it's behind that chest of drawers.'

Stalking over, she pushes the large unit aside and takes a deep breath. Behind it is a large steel door. She turns and stares at Peggy, 'Have you or Alec ever opened this before?'

Peggy shakes her head and widens her eyes, 'The lady who sold us the house showed us it but it always scared me down here so we put that set of drawers up against it. I was concerned it was a way in for burglars or intruders ...'

'Or a way *out* for a dying, suffocating woman?'

'STOP IT!' Peggy starts up again, a river of tears dripping off her chin, running down her neck, soaking into her clothes.

Audrey can't stop it. She is furious with her daughter. Exasperated, swamped with pity, exhausted; filled with every emotion it is possible to feel. But right now, their priority is opening that door and getting that poor woman out of there.

'Turn and face the other way, Peggy,' she says.

Peggy stands unmoving, a slobbering, heaving mess of snot and despair. Audrey closes her eyes for a second and lets out a deep, quivering groan, then stares at her long and hard.

'For Christ's sake, Peggy, JUST DO IT!'

With a shriek of terror, Peggy turns away. Audrey can see her legs trembling and shaking through the fabric of her trousers and is torn between wanting to hug her and wanting to slap her. She steps forward and places her fingers around the cold metal handle on the door. With a mighty tug, it gives way, creaking ajar and sending Audrey reeling backwards, almost colliding with Peggy. It takes her breath away as it hits her. She knows what it is instantly; the stench of rotting flesh is like no other. She is down here. That poor, poor creature was put in here still alive. And Audrey's daughter was responsible. She put her in there to die.

'Get the sheets,' Audrey says, as she straightens up and tries to set her brain into motion. Peggy is going to have to help with the grisly bit now. They don't have the time for sensitivities or protecting Peggy from any of it. This is her doing. She is part of it. Audrey simply cannot do this alone. It's too big an undertaking. She is tired, not thinking properly. She needs help. 'In fact,' she adds quickly, 'before you do that, you'll need to bring the car round to the house. Get it as close as you can to the door. Reverse up as close as you can. I'll come with you and direct you. You need to be close but with enough room so we can still open the boot. Do you understand?'

Peggy nods like a frightened child; bleary eyed and submissive. Audrey pushes her ahead and they both climb the ladder back up into the kitchen where the air is clear and she can breathe properly without the omnipresent stench of death filling her lungs.

Audrey hands Peggy the car keys and holds her tightly by both arms as she stares hard into her eyes. 'Now remember what I said, yes? Slowly reverse the car up to the door. I'll guide you in and let you know when you need to stop so we can open the boot. Understand?'

Again, Peggy nods, docile and silent. Audrey pushes her towards the door and watches as her daughter stumbles over to the car, unlocks it and slides into the seat. She looks like a small child behind the wheel; tiny and frightened, her expression a mask of horror. Audrey's breath comes out in shallow, desperate gasps as she watches the car begin to move. They can do this. All Peggy has to do is drive a bit closer, haul the body into the car and get away from here before the police arrive. This thing is nearing closure. She can feel it. Soon it will all be behind them, a thing of the past, an occurrence they will never speak of again. Their very own terrible, dark secret.

The sound of the engine alarms Audrey as Peggy begins to drive the car closer to the house. Her speed is erratic and Audrey feels a tic take hold in her jaw as she watches. The car judders as Peggy gets closer, the wheels screeching and crunching on the gravel. She should have done this. Peggy is too much of a state to concentrate properly. She is a wreck. Audrey should have known better than to let her do it. What was she thinking?

Audrey steps forward and raises her hand, indicating for Peggy to stop, but she takes no notice, moving forward, the engine screaming under the strain. Peggy is close enough now for Audrey to see her face. She is crying still, her body shaking as she grips the steering wheel. Audrey stands in front of the car and holds up her hand, but Peggy swerves around close to the edge, taking Audrey's breath away. What the hell is she doing? Audrey breathes hard, her nostrils flaring as she inhales the freezing air. She has to gain control of this situation right now. Peggy isn't capable of this task. She should have known. Spinning around, Audrey watches as the car begins to reverse up to her, wheels still screeching. She lets out a sigh, then widens her eyes and swallows hard as Peggy drives away once more. *What is she doing, for heaven's sake?*

The space behind the house is limited but there's enough room for her to turn around and come back. Audrey bites her lip as she watches Peggy slowly edge the car around back towards the door. She moves forward, her legs weak from exhaustion and fear and tries to guide her round, indicating that she is close to the edge. Their eyes lock for a fraction of a second and Audrey feels a needle of ice trail its way up her spine as she watches Peggy's hands rest on the wheel.

'Swing back round! You need to reverse up!' Audrey mouths the words at her but Peggy doesn't respond. She sits mutely, her hands resting on the wheel, her eyes glazed and uncomprehending.

'I said move back round!' Audrey half-shrieks it this time, panic beginning to grip her as she watches Peggy's bland features morph into something unrecognisable, something she can't bring herself to look at.

The small car suddenly splutters into life as if remembering it has to move. It jolts forward and stops momentarily, the engine revving hard. Audrey breathes a deep sigh of relief.

'Right, now just move back round a bit more and then you can start to reverse up to the door.'

Audrey watches as Peggy's eyes darken. She tenses. Just a few more minutes. That's all it will take. Just a few minutes to manoeuvre the car round and then her bit is over and done with. Audrey will take over and do the rest. Peggy just has to hold it together for a little while longer and—

It all happens so quickly and Audrey is unable to do anything to stop it. Heart hammering and thrashing in her chest, she stands helpless as Peggy stares over at her, then begins to edge the car closer and closer, still in first gear. Audrey clenches her fists together, her nails digging into her palms, watching and waiting. What is she doing? She needs to swing the car round and reverse up to the step.

The engine roars, smoke billowing out from under the wheels, the acrid tang of burning rubber filling the cold air, seeping into Audrey's nostrils, making her feel sick. The car lurches forward again and stops.

Audrey runs forward and shrieks at the dead expression on Peggy's face as she sits waiting. 'Too close! Move back. You're too close to the edge! You need to turn around and bring the car up to the door. Just do it. Do it now!'

Continuing to press her foot down on the pedal, Peggy appears to take no notice, her eyes dark and unresponsive. She edges forward some more, the vehicle perilously close to the sheer drop below. Audrey almost throws herself at the passenger door, wildly gesticulating for Peggy to reverse. For a second, the car grinds to a halt and Peggy seems to snap out of the trance she is in, a look of horror evident on her face. Then Audrey feels herself slipping to one side, pushed away by the momentum as the car begins to move once more, gaining in speed, the engine shrieking as it slowly but surely edges towards the tiny wooden fence that scales the perimeter of the cliff edge - an ancient, decaying piece of wood; the only thing between Peggy and certain death. The car stops once more and Audrey almost cries, bringing the heels of her hands to her eyes to stem the flow of tears. She watches as Peggy begins to reverse back into the tiny space behind the cottage. She turns the vehicle around and slowly starts to reverse back around the corner. *Finally!* Then she stops again, the car engine howling under the strain, the wheels kicking up tiny sprays of moss and gravel.

Clambering back up, Audrey runs forward, terrified by the look on Peggy's tiny, elf-like face. She turns and stares at her mother and mouths something, her small teeth perfectly white as she speaks. Audrey widens her eyes. She can't hear her. She needs to find out what her daughter is saying. She needs help. Audrey steps forward. She will spread-eagle herself over the bonnet if she has to. But before she can do anything at all, the car starts to reverse once more. It continues on, the wheels turning the wrong way.

'Your right lock!' Audrey screams, 'You need to put your right lock on. You're going the wrong way!'

Audrey steps forward again, her legs wobbling as she tries to grab the driver's side door handle. It's locked. She hammers on the window, her fists pummelling the glass and bouncing off soundlessly. What is Peggy thinking? They are so close to sorting this thing out. All she has to do is turn the steering wheel around and back the car up. But before Audrey can do anything, the old fence begins to crumple and disintegrate, splintering into a thousand tiny fragments as it is hit by the sheer force of Peggy's vehicle. Audrey watches, fear gripping her as the fence slowly disappears under its wheels. It's too late. She knows it. Too late to do anything except stand by and watch as her daughter disappears over the edge of the cliff.

# Audrey

The rain splatters against the windows and bounces off the skylights; a horribly grey day to match the ambience in the room. It's full of people, a blur of grey faces, most of whom she doesn't recognise. Heads dipped, they all avoid her gaze, murmuring to one another how dreadful it is, how unthinkable this whole situation is. She knows none of them; a sea of alien expressions, dark and condemnatory. Apart, that is, from a couple who are deeply familiar to her. Audrey stares ahead and can see her in the distance, head down, holding hands with a tall, good-looking man. They both have a Californian tan, incongruous against the mass of pale, washed out faces surrounding them. She tried to speak to her earlier but Beatrice ducked away, slid into the crowd and disappeared. No more than a perfectly groomed head, bobbing in and out of the gathering of people outside the crematorium. Since then she has done her best to divert her eyes every time Audrey looks her way. She has burnt her bridges now with her only remaining child but then she knew that when she made her decision. It didn't take her long to work out what she was going to do. It was the only option left open to her and one that anybody in her position would have done, she feels certain of that.

'You okay there, love?'

Audrey nods and stares ahead, too proud to answer. She has been quite helpful has this lady; this Lorna who is half her age. As helpful as one can be in a situation as peculiar and surreal as the one finds herself in. Still - it was Audrey's choice; all her doing, and there's no going back now. It's all too far down the line to unsay what has been said. She has no regrets.

The service is brief. Insulting, really. How can you possibly encapsulate a person's life in half an hour; sum up all of their deeds and actions, all of their achievements in such a short space of time? Tears prick the back of Audrey's eyes. She blinks them away. She won't cry. She will not let them see her cry, all of these people, all of these voyeurs, sitting here watching her, waiting for her to crack. It won't happen. She will do all her crying in private, away from the prying eyes of the public. Away from the snapping shutters of the press. Keep what little shred of dignity she has left, intact.

Alec passes her on the way and rapidly diverts his gaze to the pew behind her, his eyes flickering as he accidentally catches her eye then quickly looks away. Just as she expected. She has lived for many years without speaking to him so having no further contact will be of no great loss to her. She watches as Beatrice and the tall man sidle over to him and become engaged in deep conversation. About her probably; about how they always knew this would happen and how she has always been slightly deranged. Well, let them. None of it matters anymore. People can think whatever they like about her. Call her a freak, a psychopath, the mother from hell. The papers are already doing it anyway. Lorna has tried to protect her from the bulk of it, but she has eyes and ears. She knows exactly what's going on in the world around her. Despite what everybody thinks, she isn't completely mad. She has a purpose, a plan, and intends to see it through. She cannot live the rest of her life thinking that all of this happened for nothing.

The crowds slowly filter out past her as she and Lorna wait till the end to stand up.

'You ready?' Lorna asks, her lashes fluttering as she speaks. She has lovely skin, this young lady, and beautiful, azure eyes that twinkle in the sunlight.

'As I'll ever be,' Audrey replies softly as they stand up and edge their way out of their seats and into the aisle.

The press will be outside. She was told there wasn't any way to stop them attending. Alec and the police appealed to them for some privacy but, at the end of the day, this is a public place and funerals don't come with invitations. She hopes there won't be as many here as there were at Sheryl's funeral but you never can tell with these things, can you? She saw snippets of that particular event on the television and it made her want to weep. Swarms of reporters, snapping away, screaming a stream of endless questions at the grieving family as her coffin was being carried into the church. The audacity of these people knows no bounds. They live to prey on the vulnerable; feeding off their misery. All in the name of news. News indeed. Audrey exhales deeply. It's no more than gutter gossip dressed up as a human interest story. They disgust her, these people, with their probing questions and foul mouths, hollering things at her as she dives in and out of the car. Pond life is what they are. Lorna has told her to ignore them, save her energy for what she is about to go through, but it's so difficult when lies are being spread around about you - splashed all over the newspapers, bandied about on the television. Writers putting things down in print, claiming they have the story of your life sussed, when in actual fact they couldn't be any further from the truth. But she supposes that's to be expected, considering the situation she's in and what she has told them. One of the newspapers even printed a story about a local lady who reckoned her mother witnessed it all, the whole attack and subsequent burial of Sheryl's body. The story was made even more implausible and ludicrous by the fact that the same lady is now in a care home with advanced dementia, barely able to sit up in bed, let alone remember the details of a crime scene.

'Over here!' A voice screams at her as she and Lorna try to make their way past the crowds gathering outside. Cameras are held high as Audrey appears in the small courtyard, her head dipped.

'Look away. Don't give them any eye contact,' Lorna hisses at her as they file past, their arms locked together, 'Keep walking. The car is just over there.'

Audrey complies, her eyes fixed firmly on the ground, her heart thrashing around her chest in a wild, uncontrollable frenzy.

She needs to get used to this. This is her life from here on in. This is the life she has chosen for herself.

The car door swings open and Audrey and Lorna bend down and practically throw themselves headlong inside, leaving the swarms of reporters and a handful of the angry, chanting mob behind them. They sit side by side, Audrey panting for breath as the driver starts up the engine and they head out of the car park, leaving them all in the distance, the crowds of people, all baying for her blood.

'Well done Audrey. You handled that really well,' Lorna says as she twists about in her seat adjusting her black skirt with her free hand.

Audrey nods gratefully and stares down at her right hand that's attached to the police officer sitting next to her. A wee slip of a girl, handcuffed to an older lady - a woman old enough to be her grandmother. But this is her choice. Audrey has to keep telling herself that. It's still new to her and she will take some time to adjust to it all. She is going to have to alter her way of thinking, change her behaviour, adapt her outlook. She is now going to have to think carefully about every single word that comes out of her mouth. Because it's not easy this lying business. Not half as easy as everyone thinks it is. The idea came to her after Peggy's accident. A sudden dawning, a route out of it all. There was no way she would let her daughter take the blame for what was, after all, a dreadful accident. No way at all. Audrey knew what that would entail, what the aftermath of such a confession would be. There would be a barrage of questions, forensics to answer to, an inquest into the whole sorry affair. Her daughter's life paraded all over the front pages of every newspaper far and wide. Death doesn't stop these people. If anything, it fuels their interest. They would sully her good name, splash her beautiful face all over the internet, turn her into a demon.

So, Audrey stepped in, did what any decent mother would do and took responsibility for it, told them that she was the one who killed Sheryl. After all, she may as well spend the rest of her life in prison for all she has left going for her. The only difference between the life she had and the one she now faces, is the bars in a prison cell. Her life is worthless. No family, no friends, nothing to live for. Prison will be her penance for all she has done - ruining her daughter's gorgeous face, subjecting her to a life where she was forced to hide away, to retreat into her own well of misery.

She stares out of the window, concentrating on getting her story straight. Everything she tells them is put under the microscope, her every word scrutinised, shaken up, stirred about and thrown back at her. She has to stay alert, be ready for their reverse psychology, their need to catch her out. She hoped they would simply take her word for it, be glad the perpetrator of such a horrific deed had at last owned up, but it would appear it's not quite as simple as that. The questions the police fire at her are endless, day in and day out,

*'Where was Peggy when it happened?'*

*'How did you know about the tunnel?'*

*'Was your daughter involved?'*

She told them it all in as much detail she could - that she had gone to visit her daughter and caught her arguing on the doorstep with this woman who simply wouldn't leave Peggy alone. She was being abusive, trying to rekindle a friendship that Peggy had ended. Audrey had taken her daughter inside, told her to ignore the woman and Peggy had gone for a lie down to calm her nerves. While she was asleep, Audrey had tried to reason with Sheryl, tell her to leave but she was having none of it and had tried to get inside the house, pushing and shoving Audrey around with force. Audrey had pushed back and Sheryl had fallen and banged her head on the step, smacking it against the corner of the concrete.

*'Why didn't you just call an ambulance? How did you know about the tunnel under the house?'*

Endless questions. In the end, she chose to ignore a lot of them. Especially the one about Peggy and why her car went over the cliff. Did she think it was suicide or an accident? That was one of the questions she could answer truthfully. She had no idea. She hoped it was a gross error of judgement, a slip of her foot on the pedal, but Peggy's mental health was well known throughout their social circle. The rumour mill didn't take long to get going, to spew out its venom. The truth is, none of them will ever know.

She thinks of Alec and what he will do now. That sad little boy from the council estate, who she spent so long hating, now despises her in return. What goes around comes around.

The car pulls up outside the huge gates; elongated, spiky claws that tear at the cloudless sky. Audrey uses her free hand to straighten her clothes out and smooth her hair back into place. This is her home now. She needs to make a good impression. Appearances are still important.

'Ready?' Lorna asks, her smile bright enough to light up an entire room.

'As I'll ever be,' Audrey replies as they step out of the car and head inside.

# Acknowledgements

As always, I am eternally grateful to the people who helped this book get into print. Thank you to my brilliant husband Richard for his never-ending patience and countless cups of tea, as well as some fairly unique ideas when my muse decided to up and leave me. I am blessed with the most supportive family and friends, who are always ready with kind words and a ready ear.

A huge thank you to my editor Emma Mitchell who never fails to spot the cracks and holes in my stories and is there ready to plug them with her amazing suggestions and ideas. I cannot thank Fred Freeman and Betsy Reavley enough. They believed in me when others didn't and gave me the chance to fulfil my lifelong dream of becoming a published author. You guys are the best. I would also like to extend my gratitude to the team at Bloodhound Books - Alexina Golding, Sumaira Wilson and Sarah Hardy - you folks are dynamite and always there when needed!

A final thank you to all my children and grandchildren. You all mean the world to me - I just don't tell you often enough xx